Erasing the Past

Geri Dreiling

Copyright © by Geri Dreiling 2010

All Rights Reserved.

This edition published 2018

Cover design by Enrique Serrano Valle

Subjects: BISAC: **FICTION** / Romance / Science Fiction. |

FICTION / Romance / Suspense. | **FICTION.** / Fantasy / Romantic.|

First Edition: July 2010

ISBN-13: 978-1-7907-1601-2

This is a work of fiction. The novel's story and characters are fictitious. However, certain institutions and landmarks, such as Forest Park, the St. Louis Art Museum, and the St. Louis Symphony, are real. They're also lovely places. If you happen to be in St. Louis, I hope you get a chance to visit them.

To Enrique

CONTENTS

Prologue	1
Chapter One	3
Chapter Two	8
Chapter Three	10
Chapter Four	14
Chapter Five	17
Chapter Six	22
Chapter Seven	25
Chapter Eight	28
Chapter Nine	30
Chapter Ten	33
Chapter Eleven	37
Chapter Twelve	39
Chapter Thirteen	41
Chapter Fourteen	46
Chapter Fifteen	48
Chapter Sixteen	51
Chapter Seventeen	55
Chapter Eighteen	57
Chapter Nineteen	60

Chapter Twenty	62
Chapter Twenty-One	66
Chapter Twenty-Two	68
Chapter Twenty-Three	70
Chapter Twenty-Four	72
Chapter Twenty-Five	74
Chapter Twenty-Six	77
Chapter Twenty-Seven	79
Chapter Twenty-Eight	81
Chapter Twenty-Nine	83
Chapter Thirty	85
Chapter Thirty-One	89
Chapter Thirty-Two	91
Chapter Thirty-Three	93
Chapter Thirty-Four	96
Chapter Thirty-Five	98
Chapter Thirty-Six	99
Chapter Thirty-Seven	101
Chapter Thirty-Eight	104
Chapter Thirty-Nine	107
Chapter Forty	109
Chapter Forty-One	111
Chapter Forty-Two	115

Chapter Forty-Three	117
Chapter Forty-Four	120
Chapter Forty-Five	122
Chapter Forty-Six	125
Chapter Forty-Seven	127
Chapter Forty-Eight	129
Chapter Forty-Nine	132
Chapter Fifty	134
Chapter Fifty-One	138
Chapter Fifty-Two	142
Chapter Fifty-Three	148
Chapter Fifty-Four	151
Chapter Fifty-Five	155
Chapter Fifty-Six	157
Chapter Fifty-Seven	160
Chapter Fifty-Eight	162
Chapter Fifty-Nine	167
Chapter Sixty	170
Chapter Sixty-One	174
Chapter Sixty-Two	180
Chapter Sixty-Three	185
Chapter Sixty-Four	189
Chapter Sixty-Five	191

Chapter Sixty-Six	193
Chapter Sixty-Seven	196
Chapter Sixty-Eight	198
About the Author	201

Geri Dreiling

PROLOGUE

AUGUST 2008

People searching for a way to release pent-up energy were drawn to Forest Park in early summer. Cyclists painted with thin coats of black spandex whooshed past rollerbladers with padded elbows and knees. Helmets were splashed with the same red and yellow hues as the zinnias scattered throughout the park. Young lovers holding hands strolled down sidewalk paths, whispering secrets and dreams, each disclosure punctuated with a passionate kiss.

Everyone seemed to relish the fact that they were alive—except for one man.

That man, his back stooped by the weight of a lifetime of lies, shuffled to a bench with a magnificent view of the Grand Basin. The location—situated at the foot of a lush, green hill crowned at the top by the imperial, timelessly styled St. Louis Art Museum—was a favorite haunt for many of the Forest Park visitors. Like the end of a ladle, the Grand Basin held a pool of water in which geysers served as the exclamation points for the marriage of natural and man-made beauty. Ringed by railings of white marble and planters as big as baby carriages, the Grand Basin paid homage to the once-mighty gardens and baths of Rome, now long since crumbled.

Much like the old man. In his good hand, his right hand, he clutched the Sunday edition of the St. Louis Post-Dispatch, a notebook, and an easy-to-grip fat black pen. His left arm, the useless one, was frozen to his side, his empty fingers curved into a permanent claw.

He lowered the body that had betrayed him onto the bench. Or maybe he had betrayed his body, just as he had betrayed others. He placed the notebook and pen carefully to the right, close enough so he could easily reach them but not so near that he'd knock them off. If they fell to the ground, he'd have to endure the humiliation of trying to pick them up.

He opened the newspaper. A photograph of two people in the gossip column caught his attention. Unable to control himself, the broken man began to sob.

"Sir, are you okay?" a gentle young voice asked.

He looked up, drinking in the vision of a freshly scrubbed face; a woman in her late twenties. His trained eyes noted that the glow of youth was the only makeup she wore.

The empty man, his eyes clouded by tears and time, mumbled:

"I am alone. Alone in my regret. Alone in my grief. Alone with my pain. It wasn't always this way. Once upon a time, I was happy. Once upon a time, we were happy. But that's all changed. My future has vanished, and the present laid waste; all because the past was erased."

CHAPTER ONE

APRIL 2008

Kate Holly pulled the wand out of a mascara tube, scraping the bristles against the mouth of the cigarette-thin container to strip away some of the extra tar. She leaned forward, her face so close to the mirror she could've kissed it. Her eyesight—like the rest of her body—was failing her. At fifty-eight, Kate had long since passed the period where her body underwent transformative change and growth. She'd already reached life's peak, a moment as brief as the summit reached by a child seated on a swing. Now, no amount of makeup could stop her gravitational descent. No matter how hard she tried, eyeshadow, lipstick, and blush couldn't erase the telltale signs of a decaying body.

"What's on tap for today?" she asked her husband, whose face was also reflected in the mirror.

He lifted his hand in the air, a not-to-be-argued-with command for silence, afraid that if he answered her question, he'd lose the nugget of information he was trying to record in his notebook, information he believed could still make or break his fading career.

"Honestly, Joe, you've been scribbling in those notebooks for thirty-seven, almost thirty-eight, years. My morning routine never changes. I don't know what is so important about this morning that prevents you from talking to me," Kate said. Her flat Midwestern accent didn't betray any hint of agitation, but her eyes were shifting from blue to gray. Like a mood ring, Kate's eye color signaled her emotional state. When she was happy or relaxed, they were as turquoise as a piece of Native American jewelry. Get her angry or upset, and they turned misty gray. Right now, the shade hovered somewhere in between. No matter; Joe had work to do.

That work included studying Kate's morning routine, an endeavor spanning more than three decades. Every morning, as she got ready, Joe took notes. At the outset of their marriage, the only place he could find in their pint-sized apartment bathroom was a closed toilet seat. Years later, when they were well off enough to afford a custom-built home, Joe requested a master bathroom large enough to accommodate a comfy sitting chair with armrests tall enough to serve as a makeshift desk for his notepad.

His fascination with Kate's makeup routine began in 1970, on the first morning they spent together as husband and wife. A recent chemistry graduate, Joe had just joined the research and development department of a cosmetics company. Chemical reactions, he knew. Women were a mystery. How he had ever been able to land Kate, he hadn't a clue. And he could never quite shake the nagging feeling that he would wake up and discover that it was all a dream; that nothing about it was ever real.

Joe had also feared losing his job. So, understanding the beauty needs of women went from self-preservation to obsession. Boosting a woman's confidence and helping her improve the face bestowed—or inflicted—upon her at birth consumed him. Studying Kate meant Joe could better do his job. And, Joe discovered, it allowed him to uncover the mystery of Kate.

Joe continued writing as Kate tossed her makeup into a tan canvas tote. The more he scribbled, the harder the plastic cases clanked against one another inside the bag, a gift he had to force his wife to accept. If Joe had not taken matters into his own hands, Kate would still be using the same hard-sided, blue vinyl piece of luggage she had carted around after they were married. The thing was built like a fortress and as attractive as a tackle box, and Joe never understood why she clung to it for so long. Even though the hinges on the gold clasps threatened to pull away and the vinyl covering on the handle had worn off, exposing the metal underneath, it took him ten years of badgering before she let go.

Joe finished jotting down his final observation, put the cap back on his pen, and, with as much care as an artist might use when storing a prized paintbrush, placed the notebook on a nearby shelf built to hold his work. Kate now had his complete attention. Even though time had extracted its toll from his wife—the price tag that came with that not-so-free gift of life—she'd fought the good fight. Her twice-a-week weightlifting sessions kept her arms tight. There was no forearm Jell-O jiggle when she waved. Three days each week, she jogged. Fast food had not passed her lips in twenty years. He admired her discipline. With that same focused determination, Kate made—and kept—six-week appointments with her beautician. Her frosty blonde streaks were painted on at every visit. Even though crow's-feet had left their mark around her eyes, furrows were etched deeply into her forehead, and brown spots sprouted like mushrooms on the back of her slender hands, she was still gorgeous. Kate had aged well, and Joe found her as desirable as he did on the day they first met.

Disciplined in his work and single-minded in his pursuit of Kate, Joe had always been lackadaisical about his appearance. Compared to her, he was an old weathered farmhouse, battered by wind and rain, paint peeling, shingles missing, and porch steps creaking. Hair sprouted out of his ears and nose. His eyebrows seemed to be getting wirier and denser while the hair on his head vanished. Although he had never been a large, muscular man, his body was now downright squishy. Unlike Kate and her bag of makeup tricks, Joe turned to tailors who created expensive hand-crafted suits and Brooks Brothers sport coats to hide the rolls of fat that spilled over his leather belt. No matter, he told himself. Women judged men by their wallets, not whether fat made their pockets bulge.

"Joe," Kate said, "I need to speak to you." She took a deep breath then added, "It's important."

"Yes?" he responded, his eyebrow arching.

Unable to match his cool demeanor, Kate blurted out, "I've been thinking about plastic surgery."

Joe squared his shoulders, pursed his lips disapprovingly, then said, "Plastic surgery? For who?"

Kate cleared her throat before summoning her last ounce of courage. "Me."

Joe shook his head side-to-side but said nothing, trying to find the right words that would convey succinctly and forcefully his thoughts on the matter. "It is out of the question," Joe said. He turned away from Kate and walked out of the room. The conversation was over.

"Joe, I'm talking to you!" Kate said as she followed her husband. Her insistence made Joe all the more determined to leave the house without any further discussion. "I really want to discuss this with you."

Joe reached the kitchen, and in the few seconds it took for him to pick up his briefcase, Kate had wedged herself in between her husband and the door leading into the garage.

Seeing the path to a hasty exit blocked and unwilling to use the front entrance as a way out, Joe spoke. "Kate, if I filled up this kitchen with fiftyish women, you'd be head-and-shoulders more beautiful than anyone else in the room. What more could a woman ask for? Plastic surgery is for fools. Speaking strictly from a scientific point of view, the risks you take by going under the knife outweigh the benefits. I will not allow you to die in the name of vanity."

Kate's eyes turned tornado gray. "This? Coming from a man who has devoted his entire life to a woman's vanity? A man whose whole career is based on the message that women aren't beautiful enough, desirable enough, or young enough without the help of a miracle powder or magic cream?"

"What I do is much different. No one gets hurt. No one dies on a table in search of the fountain of youth. I offer women the opportunity to feel better about themselves; more confident in their looks. I don't ask them to go into surgery so they'll come out a youthful-looking corpse."

"Joe," Kate said, trying to soften her tone, "this is what I want. I want my looks back, and with them, my confidence. I'm not talking about changing my looks, only tightening them up. Undoing the damage caused by gravity and time that makeup won't fix."

Joe snorted. "Tightening up your looks? You'll end up looking like a has-been Hollywood actress with eyes so wide open she always looks like she's just been the victim of a surprise paparazzi attack. Is that what you want?"

"No, that isn't what I want," Kate said. "What I want is to be seen again. You don't know what it's like to walk through life as a woman approaching sixty. I'm invisible. At work, people don't hear me when I speak. In public, I feel like I'm a child. I stand at a counter, but I'm the last one waited on for service. In a crowd, I get bumped into and stepped on. I can remember a time when I stood out from the crowd. Now, I don't just blend into the crowd, I've been trampled by it."

Shaking his head, Joe said, "Look, Kate, if you're old, then at sixty, I'm ancient. Don't you think I've experienced the same thing? You want to talk about being viewed as past your prime, come to my office where the top executive is young enough to be our son. I'm a relic going the way of the television armoire in the age of the flat-screen."

"I understand work hasn't been easy," Kate said. "But it's not the same. When we go out to eat, I see young women looking at you. They see the luxury watch on your wrist, your tailored suits and shined shoes. They see money and security, two aphrodisiacs that erase your wrinkles and allow them to ignore your protruding gut. Those same women see me as someone who can easily be pushed out of the picture—if they see me at all."

"Kate, I'll never push you away. If you're feeling insecure about us, you needn't. I'm never leaving you," Joe vowed. "This whole plastic surgery issue is nonsense."

Joe couldn't escape the sense of doom that seemed to hang over their conversation. Using his shoulder, Joe nudged Kate away from the doorway.

"Don't you dare leave!" Kate shouted.

Joe swung open the door of his Mercedes and climbed in.

"I mean it!" Kate shouted.

The slam of the car door echoed through the tidy garage. Joe turned on the radio, trying to tune out Kate's anger with classical music. His chest tightened as he pushed the ignition button. Joe felt pressure in his jaw. He revved the engine. His hands were cold and clammy on the steering wheel.

He gripped the gearshift to put the car into reverse, eager to make his escape.

CHAPTER TWO

SEPTEMBER 1968

September 18 started out like every day before it that semester. Joe Holly, a junior attending Washington University in St. Louis, woke at 5 a.m., crammed in a couple of hours of studying, choked down two pieces of dry toast, and drank two cups of electric perk coffee. Then he showered, smoked one cigarette, and walked to campus.

But this was no ordinary Wednesday.

As Joe crossed the Quad, his mind preoccupied with experiments that needed to be completed and lab reports that needed to be written, the faces that passed him blurred into a hazy wall. It took a laugh—innocent, melodic, and hearty—to shake him out of his reverie. It was a feminine laugh, one of pure joy, but not a flirty, fake giggle meant to attract the opposite sex. Rather, it was the sound of true happiness. Like the music made by the Sirens of Greek mythology, Joe was instantly drawn to it.

In the river of students, he was downstream from the sound. Instead of remaining on the sidewalk, Joe jumped onto the grass and jog-walked past the congestion while cradling a stack of books in his arms. His ears, guided by the enchanting voice, helped his eyes find a girl with hair that had been kissed by the sun. Long and straight, it cascaded down her back. As she walked, her mane waved to and fro, a pendulum brushing against the top of a well-formed derriere tucked nicely into a pair of low-rise bell-bottom jeans. For a few moments, Joe froze, staring as the girl walked. The longer he lingered, the more intense his desire became to catch a glimpse of her face.

Again, he pushed ahead of the crowd. Then he stopped, air knocked from his lungs. His chest ached as though he had been violently shoved by a pair of invisible, outstretched hands.

High cheekbones, almond-shaped eyes, long lashes, a delicate nose, and a graceful neck were put together in perfect proportions. Her breasts, like her behind, were round and firm. She was flawless.

Joe noticed her companion, a guy he'd seen around campus for a few years. Joe didn't like him one bit. He was one of those guys who forced their views on others—not because they were smarter, but because they talked louder. He was handsome, so his boorish behavior was often mistaken for confidence. He was exactly the type of man Joe loathed.

Was this beautiful girl with him?

Joe followed her even though the pursuit took him in the opposite direction that he needed to go. "Where's she going?" he muttered to himself. If his hunch was right, she was probably headed to one of those useless liberal arts "ology" buildings; psychology, sociology, anthropology. Degrees that Joe believed had little practical significance but allowed a woman to say she possessed one before retiring to a lifetime of baby-making housewife drudgery.

She stopped in front of the business school and heaved open the wooden door of the gray stone building. Her golden hair shimmered before the dark interior hallway closed in around her.

After the angel slipped into the business school, Joe found an empty bench with a view of the doors that had swallowed her up. He sank down on the seat as an endorphin rush washed over him, a tingling sensation that began at the spot where his neck and head met, then moved down his neck and flowed into his arms. He remained in a catatonic stupor until the good feelings subsided.

So, this is love at first sight, he thought. The girl with the sweet-sounding laugh was a drug and Joe was instantly hooked. The question that rattled around inside his head wasn't whether he should pursue her. The only question was how he would go about doing it.

CHAPTER THREE

Sunlight bounced off the glass and steel walls of Galatea Cosmetics, nestled up against Highway 270 in St. Louis. For commuters driving to work, the reflection caused a moment of terrifying blindness. For Joe, the glare seemed unusually bright that morning; it didn't just shine in his eyes, it seemed to surround his whole body.

Galatea's headquarters resembled all the others that sprang up in the outer suburbs of St. Louis, or any other U.S. city for that matter. Plop it down in Kansas City, Atlanta, Chicago, Minneapolis, or Phoenix and the ubiquitous architecture would blend—a model McOffice.

And it was so unlike Galatea's original headquarters. That building had been made from brick; hewn from the red clay found in the St. Louis earth, baked in St. Louis ovens, and assembled by the sons and grandsons of Italian immigrants. Galatea's first home boasted ornate designs and carvings over arched windows and above doorways. To Joe, it was the perfect architectural marriage of God and man, fashioned with materials harvested from the earth and refined through ingenuity, creativity, and sweat; a warm building of skilled craftsmen who took pride in their work. Its replacement? A cold, mass-produced impostor.

The model for the new headquarters had been unveiled three years ago, soon after Huff Pennington, at age thirty-nine, took the helm as the chief executive officer. The boy chief unveiled the prototype in a company-wide meeting, whisking the white drop cloth off with a dramatic flourish. Joe even hated the drop cloth because it had been emblazoned with the company's new emblem. The original emblem was a drawing of Galatea, a mythical woman sculpted with the beauty of a goddess. One of Huff's first moves was to strip the goddess from Galatea's logo. In its place, an oversized, yellow "G" inside a blue circle. Underneath, in block letters, the words "Galatea Cosmetiques." The change had not gone down well with

Joe, even when Huff had insisted, "We're an international company. We want to embrace the twenty-first century, not stay stuck in the twentieth."

And so it was with the new headquarters. "Take a look at Galatea's future!" Huff shouted as he removed the white covering from the model showing what the new headquarters would look like. The employees gathered around and applauded. At first, Joe thought it was a kiss-ass move, but as he looked around at the young faces of his colleagues, he realized that his company had changed.

Modernization and globalization seemed to threaten Joe and his carefully constructed, hard-earned way of life. Rumors that Huff was toying with the idea of moving the research and development lab to India had intensified recently. As long as Stan Markowsky remained the chairman of the board, and as long as Stan remained involved in the daily operations, the dramatic move might be thwarted.

Stan, only a few years older than Joe, had come of age alongside Joe at Galatea. The son of Galatea's founder, Stan was the only person who felt more passionately about the company than Joe. But even that seemed to be changing.

Stan was sixty-five, but it wasn't age that had drained Stan of his enthusiasm for the business. Instead, it was Barbara's death. For decades, Joe and Kate had met up with Stan and Barbara for drinks or dinner. But after her death two years ago, Stan didn't seem interested in maintaining the friendship. Joe had been hurt by the drift in their relationship, but Kate was more forgiving. "How can we not be a reminder of what he has lost? I know if the roles were reversed, and you had died, I would find it very difficult to go out to dinner with Stan and Barbara. The worst part would be driving home alone. Joe, just be patient," Kate advised.

Joe tried to be understanding. Then, six months after Barbara's death, about the time he thought Stan had worked through some of his grief, Stan walked into Joe's office, sat down in the chair across from Joe's desk, and made a stunning announcement.

"I'm giving up the role of CEO," Stan admitted. "I wanted you to hear it from me first."

Joe leaned forward, as if he hadn't heard Stan correctly, and asked, "Did you say you're stepping down as CEO?"

Stan nodded. "Yes. I just informed the board of directors. The news will be officially announced at the end of the day today. Then we're going to launch a search for someone new, someone younger, an outsider, to bring the company into the new millennium."

Joe slumped back in his chair. "Why? We're doing so well."

"Joe, I've had a lot of quiet time to reflect on my life since Barbara died. I missed watching my children grow up. I missed baseball games, basketball practices, Christmas plays, and field trips. But I always had Barbara. She was my eyes and ears. She always briefed me on the children and briefed the children about my business conquests. She was my memory of our children's childhood. When she died, I lost not only her but also all the memories a parent has of their offspring when they were young, the funny anecdotes, the late-night feedings, the arguments over curfews and car keys. I always thought that we'd get old together and as we watched our grandkids grow, she could entertain the grandkids with the stories of their own parents' exploits, foibles—and victories. Lord knows I couldn't do it. That period of our lives is a blur of balance sheets and shareholder meetings. Barbara was the bridge that covered the wide expanse of our married life. Cancer blew that bridge to bits. I made a vow to her as she lay dying that I'd be there for our grandkids, memorize every one of their moments, the first steps, the first birthday parties, the high school proms. When I die and return to her side," he said, his voice wavering, "I promised her I'd tell her everything and spare no detail."

He paused for a moment. "You know what she said?" Stan cleared his throat one more time. "She said 'Good, I'm counting on you.' Then she died."

Stan took a deep breath and then added, "By handing over the day-to-day duties, I'm keeping my promise to Barbara."

Yet letting go of Galatea was easier said than done. The company was still his baby as much as one of the flesh-and-blood beings he'd created with Barbara. Just as most parents never completely cut the cord, Stan couldn't make a clean break of his ties. He remained chairman of the board and kept abreast of long-term R&D projects—Joe's area. And though Stan had developed a deeper appreciation for the fleeting things that make living worthwhile, he was no fool. Money still made the world go 'round, and a healthy trust fund would secure the financial position of his children and his grandchildren.

But while Stan remained somewhat connected to the company, Joe believed he had a valuable ally. Yet the fact he had to rely on Stan's protection only stoked Joe's resentment. After all, his work had made the company hundreds of millions of dollars over the course of a thirty-five-year career. Smudge-proof eyeliner was his first hit, inspired by the memory of Kate's face the morning after their wedding. He came up with twelve-hour eyeshadow after he noticed that when Kate came home from a long day at work, her eyeshadow had faded, save for a line of powder that had clumped up in the crease of her lid. There was kissable lipstick, a product he'd invented after too many kisses had been rebuffed by Kate because she claimed he would smear her painted lips. Joe took his passion for one woman and turned it into useful products for millions of other women.

Only the market had changed; at least, that's what Huff and his team of MBAs argued. Now, it was all about Retin-A, antioxidants, collagen, and

Botox. Every product needed an "age-defying" label slapped onto the packaging before it would be approved for distribution. What upset Joe the most was that the makeup did not live up to the marketing department's hype. The company had gone from exaggeration to outright deception. They were betraying the trust of the millions of Kates that Joe envisioned when he thought of their customers. To Joe, it was not only bad business, but it was also unethical.

But, Joe was discovering, even an ethical man, when cornered, can make unsavory exceptions.

CHAPTER FOUR

SEPTEMBER 1968

For two days, Joe could think of nothing but the girl. He reasoned that because she was headed to the business school on a Wednesday, the course that lured her to the building must be offered Monday, Wednesday, and Friday. That's why he stood, two days later, searching a crowd of students for her. Hoping to take the edge off as he waited, Joe broke his one-cigarette-a-day rule. With trembling fingers, he raised a Winston to his lips then struck a match from the pack he had tucked in between the box and gold foil. The tip of the match sparked to life. Holding it to the end of his cigarette, Joe took a deep drag, shook the match between his fingers to extinguish the flame, and exhaled. As the smoke cleared, his dream girl appeared.

He'd braced himself for disappointment. Joe had convinced himself that his mind had most likely deceived him; his imagination had exaggerated her appeal. She'd been appearing in his dreams, both day and night. He'd placed this girl on a pedestal, and the chemist-in-training secretly hoped that the second encounter would let him reevaluate his opinion. Disappointment would free him from his growing obsession.

Before Wednesday, his life had been simple and straightforward. A girl was a complication that had not been accounted for in his life's timetable. Instead, his logical world was ordered first by achieving high grades, then obtaining a highly sought-after job, achieving financial security, and then, around age thirty, looking for a wife. He'd marry a younger woman, perhaps a secretary in his company or a lab assistant. She'd cater to his needs, produce a couple of kids, and take care of them while he earned a living. Once he had achieved the "family man" moniker, his chances of ascending into the executive rank would multiply. It was the perfect roadmap to success. It was all so very sensible. Chasing a bewitching vision across campus was not part of that pragmatic roadmap for success.

Joe had positioned himself so that he was walking toward her rather than coming up from behind. She drew near, the sunlight surrounding her hair and creating a shimmery halo that framed her perfect face.

"Kate!" Joe heard someone yell. Joe felt the brisk shove of a male hand moving him out of the way, which also grazed the cigarette he'd been holding at his side.

"Ow!"

"Geez, I'm really sorry." Joe mouthed the words out loud, even if he didn't mean them.

The aggressor was the jerk he had seen a few days before with Kate, bleach-blond bangs, bronze tan, and chiseled jaw.

"Chrissake. I think it's going to blister."

"Are you okay?" Joe heard a girl ask. He knew before even looking up—it was her.

"Yeah, I'm fine." Then motioning toward Joe, he added, "This klutz burned me with his cigarette."

"Well, it looked to me like you were the one who ran into him," she said. "If you weren't always late and rushing around, you might've noticed the cigarette."

She smiled at Joe. "Don't mind Harry."

"It's okay, I shouldn't be smoking in such a crowded space," Joe said. He didn't mean a word of it, but it was a way to engage the woman in conversation.

"I'm Joe Holly," he said, reaching out his hand to her.

"I'm Kate Taylor," she said with a smile.

"And you've already met Harry Bennett," she added, trying to compensate for the rudeness of her friend.

"C'mon, Kate, we're gonna be late for econ," Harry said.

Kate turned red, embarrassed by Harry's refusal to acknowledge Joe.

"Economics?" Joe asked, unable to conceal his surprise.

"Believe it or not, some girls are attracted to courses like economics," she teased. "I'm taking Econ One right now, and it is far and away my favorite course. I can't wait for Econ Two next semester."

Harry snorted. "Ugh, that class is a drag. You can count me out of the next round of economics."

Kate smiled and shrugged. "Well, I like it."

"I took the class a year ago. I thought it was fascinating," Joe said. He was honest about taking the class—but he lied about his enthusiasm for it.

Kate nodded vigorously and was about to say more when Harry draped his arm around her shoulder and began steering her toward the business school. "Kate, we're going to be late."

Kate let herself be hustled away, but she looked back briefly and shouted, "It was nice meeting you, Joe."

With a deep, quick thrust, the knife of jealousy plunged deep into Joe's gut.

But some good had come of the day. His destiny had a name: Kate. And he'd met his rival, Harry. Information was power. The more he learned about Kate, the more powerful he would become.

CHAPTER FIVE

Joe was in his office only long enough to scan his emails before heading out for a teeth-whitening appointment. Huff's secretary had sent him an electronic missive. He was to appear before the CEO at 1 p.m. Joe briefly considered canceling his dental appointment but decided it was probably even more important to have his smile brightened before meeting with his youthful boss.

The teeth whitening had been Kate's idea. "Joe, you work at a cosmetics company for goodness' sake. It's no wonder, with your yellowing teeth, people think you are an old man."

Kate had made the comment after Joe had launched into another tirade about the young, cocky suits who had been hired after Huff was named CEO. At her insistence, he began trying to brighten his smile to reverse the marks left by coffee, red wine, and even the cigarettes he'd given up in his early thirties.

Unfortunately, when he walked into the full waiting room, he could tell the dentist was already behind schedule. Irritated at the wait, as well as having to endure the unavoidable smell of anesthesia and the sounds of suction machines, Joe rifled through the magazines piled on an end table before he settled on a pop-science periodical. He began thumbing through it when an article on the marula tree caught his eye.

The tree grew in southern African countries such as Zaire, Ethiopia, Kenya, Angola, Mozambique, Zimbabwe, Botswana, and Madagascar. Places that, for Joe, conjured up images of bloody civil wars, child soldiers, sorrowful eyes, and evil dictators in military uniforms. But these were also the places where beautiful and useful things still managed to find a foothold and grow. The marula tree was one such wonder.

Every part of the marula was useful, the article claimed; so useful that, in some countries, it was against the law to cut one down. Humans and animals feasted on the fruit from the tree. About the size of a plum, it was plump and yellow and contained four times the vitamin C of a South African orange. The fruit could be mashed into juice or fermented into an alcoholic drink. Tribeswomen used the bark to treat diarrhea and rubbed the inner bark of the tree on the skin to reduce the pain, itching, and swelling that accompanies a nasty bug bite. In some countries, where the economies had been decimated by war and medical supplies had been pillaged for sale on the black market, Western doctors, armed with advice from local healers, turned to the marula's leaves as dressing for burns. Much to their surprise, the leaves not only soothed burned skin, but it also repaired it in a way that the doctors had never witnessed in the West. The discovery, the article pointed out, had been ignored by the Western world's established medical community.

Just as Joe finished the article, his name was called. Not knowing precisely why, he couldn't bring himself to put the magazine down. Instead, he rolled it into a cylinder and twisted it in his hands, ignoring the quizzical look from the hygienist who was holding the door open that would lead him back to his waiting dental chair. He stopped abruptly in his tracks just before he reached her.

"That's it!" he shouted, startling the hygienist.

"Are you all right?" she asked.

"I'm fantastic!" Joe answered as he hurried toward the exit.

"Sir, your appointment?"

"Later," Joe said. "I'll reschedule later."

Rachel James peered down the neck of a microscope, disappearing into a world invisible to the naked eye. Pulling her away for even a simple conversation was next to impossible. Ever since that day in high school so many decades earlier, when she was finally able to get her hands on what was considered a good-quality microscope, Rachel knew that science was her calling, her vocation, her religion.

"Rachel!" Joe shouted. He'd been standing next to her, trying to get her attention for a few minutes, growing impatient with Rachel's absentminded "hmmm?" replies.

"What?" Rachel said, looking up and breaking her connection to the tiny visions below her.

"Read this!" he said, thrusting the crumpled magazine he had stolen from the dentist's office into her hands.

"Jesus, Joe. Can't you see I'm busy?" she asked, turning the magazine over in her hands, frowning when she saw the publication's title.

Rachel had been Joe's assistant for almost as long as Kate had been

Joe's wife. In fact, he'd known Rachel even longer than he'd known Kate. When Joe was first hired by Galatea, they were colleagues who rode the bench together. Before that, they were classmates, chemistry majors at Wash U. Rachel graduated a year ahead of Joe and started at Galatea before he did. She'd won a few more honors in school, but he had both the people skills and the zeal for the product that Rachel lacked. Over the years, he leapfrogged in front of her up the corporate ladder. In the beginning, the arrangement might've bugged her, but, Joe believed, Rachel realized her contempt for vanity and disregard for fashion meant she would never be the face of research and development at Galatea. But he vowed that while he headed the department, he'd make sure Rachel was protected.

When they first began working together, the only adornment on Rachel's makeup-free face was a pair of black cat-eye glasses with fake diamonds embedded in the frame. In the mid-1970s, she updated her eyewear, favoring large round frames with earpieces that dipped down at the cheek. She'd kept that same style up to the present day, only replacing the lenses occasionally. The latest reincarnation included bifocal lenses.

Her hair color evolved over the years, going from inky black to a dry, ashy black streaked with silver. Her hairstyle remained constant—a tight ponytail fastened at the base of her skull. Unfortunately, the silver hair was the stubborn sort, refusing to remain bound by a rubber fastener. Instead, it looked as though she'd been shot by arrows of white wire, the tips embedded into her scalp.

"What on earth could possibly be so important about this rag?" Rachel sniffed with the superiority of a scientist who only gleans information from peer-reviewed journals written in tortured English.

"Page fifty-six. Read the article."

Rachel opened the front cover then one-by-one she turned each page until she reached fifty-six. It had been starred in the upper corner, just as she knew it would be. Rachel bent her head down and began digesting the information while Joe paced the room, his dress shoes tapping against the floor with each impatient step. When she was finished, Rachel looked up at Joe with a blank expression on her face. It wasn't the one he expected.

"So? There's an all-purpose tree in Africa. That's why you interrupted me?"

"Come on, Rachel. Connect the dots."

"You're going to have to spell it out for me because I'm not seeing any of the magic dots to which you are referring."

Joe took a deep breath and began pacing again, too excited by his thoughts to stand still. "Huff is always urging us to 'think outside the box; get creative; embrace the future,' right?"

Rachel snorted. "Well, that's what all of the inspirational posters on the walls say."

"And haven't we also been lectured by the clueless young wonders up in the executive suite that we need to stop thinking of ourselves as a cosmetics company that supplies paint for faces? Instead," he said in the most sarcastic tone he could conjure, "we're a health and vitality company that provides products for an improved way of life. Well, don't you think a burn gel is a health and vitality product? There's no doubt that it would improve the quality of a person's life."

Rachel interrupted, "Whoa. Back up. How did you make the leap from a tree to a burn gel? And what in the world does a burn gel have to do with a cosmetics company?"

"The marula leaves! They're used to dress burns, and they repair skin. Repair! Let's figure out what is in those leaves, extract the compound, make a synthetic version for a burn cream that repairs skin," Joe said.

She chewed on her bottom lip for a moment, trying to fill in the logical leaps he had skipped. "You mean sort of like the cream on the market right now that erases the scars that can be left by cuts and incisions?"

"Yes, yes! The lines between cosmetic cover-ups and medical solutions are blurring. Why not take one more step into that murky abyss?"

"But how would we get the leaves, and would we run into any problems with the FDA?" Rachel asked. "That is, assuming we were able to get the stuff shipped out of Africa. The countries you mentioned aren't the most stable."

"My guess is that the leaves aren't regulated," Joe informed her. "My plan is to get our hands on a big sample, analyze the compounds, and then make synthetic copies of the active ingredients, which would free us of any supply concerns."

"Even if I was interested in the project—not saying that I am—but I still don't see how this will improve Galatea's bottom line," Rachel said.

"Here's how I see it. We should model our product after Retin-A. It was originally approved by the FDA for acne use but was quickly adapted after its ability to reduce the appearance of wrinkles was recognized. While it might have been expensive to obtain FDA approval, the cachet that comes with being perceived by the public as a potent product that requires medical oversight meant that even over-the-counter creams using weak concentrations of Retin-A's active ingredients commanded top-dollar pricing."

Joe continued, rehearsing the speech he would make that very afternoon to Huff. "We should develop the burn gel product, obtain FDA approval for use in hospitals and trauma centers. If it actually does what I say it will—repair burned skin—it will cause a big stir. We then start marketing it to dermatologists and also begin testing it for off-label uses such as fading sun spots and repairing sun-damaged skin."

Rachel chewed on the bottom corner of her lip some more. "I thought you were opposed to Galatea masquerading as a pharmaceutical company, that it was no better than selling alcohol-filled cough syrup to teetotaler old ladies living in cow towns."

"This is different," Joe insisted. "I'm talking about a product that delivers on its promise. Think about it. Modern medicine hasn't been able to mimic real skin. Modern medicine hasn't yet been about to return God-given beauty once it has been licked by heat and flames. The best that's been done is harvesting skin from an undamaged part of the body and grafting it on the burned skin. It doesn't look natural. It leaves the impression that someone is wearing a mask, less disfiguring than burned skin, but still somehow unnatural."

Rachel's face softened. She wasn't smiling—but then again, she rarely smiled. Her brow was no longer furrowed, and her lips were no longer pursed.

"You might be on to something."

CHAPTER SIX

JANUARY 1969

By the time Kate walked into Econ II for the spring semester, she and Joe had become friendly acquaintances. After his initial run-in with Harry, Joe conceived of a plan to cross her path once every week or two, taking care to ensure the meetings were never at the same time, in the same location, or in any place where Harry might appear. Harry would catch on to Joe's game quickly. Men were hardwired to detect the scent of a rival.

Joe followed Kate for several days, learning her routine and studying her habits without being caught. Their first "on-purpose" chance encounter occurred ten days after the incident with Harry. Joe walked past the table in the library where Kate was studying. He stopped in his tracks, turned around, and said, "Kate, right?"

Kate, whose head had been bent over her book, lifted it. She smiled, recognizing Joe but unable to recall where or how they'd met.

He grinned. "Joe, the guy with the cigarette who burned your boyfriend."

Kate's face brightened. "Yes! Of course. Hi. How are you?"

"I'm doing well," Joe said. "I just thought I'd say hello. I've got to run to class. I'm a lab assistant for a freshman chemistry class, a pleasure seeing you again."

Friendly, nice, trustworthy, and easygoing was how Joe hoped Kate would think of him. In time, those warm feelings could be fanned into something more. Most men shuddered when they were tagged with the "nice guy" label; women wanted bad boys.

Yet Kate seemed different. Adopting the persona of a cad would have set off alarm bells and caused her to put up a defensive wall designed to keep him out, Joe sensed. After all, Harry, a true jerk in Joe's book, seemed careful to hide the full extent of his nature when Kate was around. But Harry couldn't keep up the pretense as a good guy forever. In fact, he was already slipping. Eventually, Harry would do something stupid, Joe told himself.

As the fall semester stretched from September to finals in December, and Joe continued running across Kate on campus, he decided to gamble on an Economics II course. Kate loved Econ I and admired her professor. Joe hoped she'd decide to sign up for his Econ II class.

When she entered the lecture room for Econ II in January, Joe was waiting.

"Hi, Kate," he said, waving to get her attention.

"Hi, Joe," Kate said with a smile. "What are you doing here? Aren't you a science major?"

"You're right. Chemistry," he answered. "I'll more than likely wind up working in the research and development department for a company. My career advisor, a cranky old man with hair growing out of his ears and nose, recommended I take basic business courses before I graduate, you know, enhance my marketability."

Joe scrunched up his face to deliver his best imitation of the counselor, and in a voice turned gravelly with age and cigarettes said: "'Companies need scientists who understand the reality of the business climate.'"

Kate giggled, oblivious to the power her laugh had over Joe.

Joe struggled to continue. "To tell you the truth, business courses aren't part of my natural academic strength. Give me a flask and some chemicals, and I'm happy as can be, tackling a chemistry equation is a real gas. But mention LIFO, FIFO, or the equilibrium point between supply and demand and I just can't seem to wrap my brain around it," he said.

"Harry says the same thing," confessed Kate. "He's majoring in business but only because his parents forced him to choose it or engineering. Engineering freaked him out—and he can't understand how I could pursue this course of study when my parents have left the choice of a major up to me."

Kate squared her shoulders and lowered her voice to imitate her boyfriend. "'Honestly, Kate, why don't you study anthropology? Margaret Mead and all that cool stuff. You won't use your education once you're married anyway.'"

"Ouch." Joe winced. "Who says you aren't going to use it?"

"Harry believes a woman must pick kids or career. I want kids, but I also want a career," Kate confessed.

"Why choose? I believe a woman can have both," Joe replied.

"Really? That's so refreshing," Kate said. "With that sort of attitude, you must have a girlfriend."

"Naw," Joe admitted. "I dated a fellow chemistry student briefly. I just haven't found the right combination of beauty and brains, as well as a genuinely nice personality. If you're looking for someone to share your life with, why not aim high?"

Kate's face brightened, and she flashed Joe an enthusiastic grin. "My sentiments exactly."

"Here, why don't you sit down," Joe offered, gesturing to the seat next to him. She hesitated, then dropped her books on the elongated desk, pulled out a chair, and sat down.

"Why thank you," Kate said. "This should be a great class."

CHAPTER SEVEN

A small sip of pinot noir was all that remained in Kate's glass by the time Joe arrived at the restaurant for dinner. After his meeting with Huff, he'd called his wife. "Let's eat out tonight," he suggested, coming up with a trendy place that Huff had mentioned.

"Joe, I've got a lot of work to do. I'd rather stay at the office late," Kate protested.

Still angry with her husband's plastic surgery veto, she was in no mood to make small talk over dinner. And it was true. She was swamped.

King Industries, Kate's employer, made electric motors that were supplied to manufacturing companies who incorporated them into their own products, from small hand tools and washing machines to motors for tool and die makers. She'd started out as a secretary in quality control and had worked her way up over the years to the post of internal quality control manager.

Like Joe, the world had changed as Kate aged through it. She'd watched as Title VII and the Pregnancy Discrimination Act had been passed. She'd seen the benefits—and the limits—of the equal opportunity promise. At first, she believed discrimination would be eradicated. An even playing field was what she imagined. But as she'd aged, Kate still couldn't escape discrimination, only now it was more subtle. First, she experienced bias because she was a woman. Then she was treated differently because she was a married woman. Then, there was bias because she was an older woman. Discrimination had become like Wi-Fi: She couldn't see it, but somehow her career was often connected to it.

She'd experienced other changes too. When Kate started in the corporate office, the products were made in St. Louis. In the late 1970s and early 1980s, the union plants were shuttered, and the work was moved to Tennessee and other right-to-work states like Mississippi and Alabama.

Then in the 1990s, those plants went silent, and operations mushroomed in Matamoros, Mexico.

In search of cheaper labor still, King Industries now subcontracted work to Chinese companies. For employees who wanted to keep their jobs, the choice was simple: adapt or die. Kate adapted and found a niche in quality control, in charge of a department that checked the shipped parts to make sure they were not substandard. A recent shipment from overseas had been flagged as full of problems. Kate was tasked with fixing them—fast. A dinner date didn't fit well into her plans, but she'd finally acquiesced.

"You're late," Kate said as Joe pulled a chair out to be seated at the white-clothed table.

"Judging from your empty wineglass, I think you found something to occupy your time," Joe retorted.

The waiter materialized before Kate could respond.

"Gin and tonic," Joe said before the waiter had a chance to speak.

Kate's left eyebrow arched upward. "Gin and tonic? Either something very good —or very bad—has happened."

Despite the upscale nature of the restaurant, Joe loosened his tie. "I would say tonight goes into the positive category."

Kate leaned forward in her seat, waiting for him to continue.

"What are the specials?" Joe asked.

Kate rolled her eyes. "Come on, Joe. Don't tease me. What's going on?"

The waiter reappeared, chunks of ice clinking against the glass as he set the drink down in front of Joe.

Kate turned to the waiter. "Can you give us a few minutes before we order? And can I have another glass of wine?"

Kate waited as Joe lifted the glass to his lips, taking a long sip of the slightly bitter drink that he only drank when he was feeling very up or very low.

"Well?" Kate said as she ran her fingers along the stem of her glass.

Joe cleared his throat. "I came up with a groundbreaking research idea today, and I think Huff is going to sign off on it."

Joe laid out the concept for Kate. "I even suggested we name it the Phoenix Project after the eternal, mythical bird that ignites and resurrects from its ashes."

"Oh, Joe, that's fantastic," Kate said, raising her glass. "A toast: To the Phoenix Project."

Joe laughed and leaned forward, clinking his glass against hers.

Hoping to capitalize on his good humor, Kate said, "Now, I have some good news."

Joe smiled and reached for her hand. "Yes, my dear, what is your good news?"

She paused for a moment, her upper teeth tugging at the corner of her bottom lip. "I had a consultation with a plastic surgeon."

Joe suddenly felt cold. He was no longer smiling.

"We never agreed to that," Joe said as he shivered.

Kate sat back in her chair and spoke as calmly as possible. "Joe, honey, it was just a consultation. It isn't like I've signed up for anything or money has changed hands."

"Let me be clear," Joe said as he polished off his drink. "I am against plastic surgery. I am opposed to you getting plastic surgery. I won't allow it."

"But Joe, can't we please discuss this?"

"Can I take your order now?" the waiter interrupted as he placed Kate's second glass of wine in front of her.

Joe pushed his chair back, pulled the napkin off his lap, and laid it across the empty plate before him. "No thank you. I'm done."

CHAPTER EIGHT

FEBRUARY 1969

Spending one hour, three times a week next to Kate more than made up for the beating Joe's GPA might suffer because of Econ II.

Being Kate's friend was easy. In addition to her dazzling beauty, Kate's mind was sharp; no subject off limits. Politics, religion, current affairs, and Wall Street were all fair game when the pair sat down together before class. Though the two seemed to be on opposite sides of almost every issue, Joe cherished their spirited debate. Kate opposed the Vietnam War while Joe supported the fight against the spread of communism. Kate loved President John F. Kennedy, Camelot, and the Peace Corps. A Nixon supporter, Joe believed that finally there was an administration in power that would put the country back on course.

Through their before-class conversations, Joe pieced together the story of Harry and Kate. They were hometown honeys, Harry a year older. The two began dating when Kate was a junior in high school and he was a senior. He played football, she was a cheerleader, an all-American couple that everyone at home figured would get married, settle down, and raise a family.

When Harry went away to college, they vowed to remain boyfriend and girlfriend. During her senior year in high school, when she should've been dating, she stuck with Harry. He would come back home to attend the occasional high school dance. If he couldn't return, Harry refused to allow her to invite even his most trusted friends to serve as a stand-in. The rule was that she could not go without him. And so, she stayed home.

To Kate, it wasn't a sacrifice. On more than one occasion in economics, Kate mentioned how much she loved Harry and how hard it must've been for him to resist the temptation to date one of the many pretty coeds who walked the campus.

On Mondays, the two would summarize their weekends. Joe regaled Kate with stories about experiments gone haywire and clueless freshmen who turned in terrible lab reports. He didn't confess that in between grading papers and working hard to set himself apart from his peers, he fantasized about her.

Kate's stories revolved around study sessions, parties, protest rallies, and Harry. Joe soon realized he could tell when Kate's weekend had gone badly. She telegraphed it in the way she said Harry's name.

Joe's happiest Mondays were Kate's most miserable; Harry's name uttered with a quiver, her gaze firmly fixed on her notebook.

From these Mondays, Joe concluded Harry enjoyed wounding Kate, perhaps to see how far he could push her. Though Kate was kind and forgiving, Joe was certain that one day, Harry would go too far. That's when Kate would need a friend, and Joe would be that person.

But Kate's happiest Mondays were the worst for Joe. Early in the semester, Kate summed up her weekend with a dreamy smile. "Harry and I spent most of the weekend alone."

"You were studying?" Joe asked hopefully.

Kate blushed. "Joe, if two people truly love each other, if your souls are already joined, do you think it is wrong to fully manifest your feelings physically?"

The hand of jealousy squeezed Joe's throat, its firm fingers crushing his windpipe.

"No, I don't think," Joe stammered, "I don't think there's anything wrong with it, so long as they're married."

"Oh," Kate said, "I didn't realize you were so old-fashioned."

"I don't consider myself old-fashioned," Joe said. "I just think that a woman has more to lose than a man. A man who really loves a woman, who truly has a deep spiritual, soulful connection, would do nothing to hurt her. Forcing her to run the risk of being an unwed mother is not a gesture of love in my book. And let's face it, there are plenty of young women who wind up pregnant, and the man walked away. Or worse, forces her to seek an abortion in some rundown clinic."

Kate chewed on her pen. "Say the man vows to always love her and be there for her. Not in a million years would he do something like that, then is it wrong?"

"Like I said, if he truly loved her, he would propose marriage first and consummate it second," Joe replied before gathering up his books. "I don't feel so good. Will you take notes for me?" he asked. Before she could answer, Joe had disappeared from the classroom.

CHAPTER NINE

It wasn't the décor of Huff's office that Joe studied while he waited for his boss to arrive—it was Huff's hard-to-ignore executive assistant, Sue Schmidt. Clad in a clingy, black wraparound dress, her surgically enhanced breasts overflowing the low-cut V-neck, Sue wobbled around the office on three-inch stilettos, a silver-and-diamond anklet circling her spray-on tan leg.

A good-looking woman, in that slutty sort of way, and just the type Huff liked to collect; Sue was a stark contrast to Huff's wife, Lauren, a dark-haired beauty with a Princeton pedigree.

Early in her life, Sue, a farm girl from southern Illinois, concluded her body and not her brains was her most marketable asset. The day after she graduated from high school, she fled to Chicago, landed a job as a receptionist for a large insurance company, and set her sights on marrying well. While she waited to find a rich husband, she used her paychecks for extreme beauty interventions such as fake boobs and Botox—considering the expense part of her unconventional retirement fund.

But after a very public affair with a married, upper-level executive, Sue found herself on the receiving end of the company's firing squad. The executive, too valuable to lose, kept his position. Sue, an expendable underling, was given a check for $10,000 before an armed security guard escorted her off the premises.

Humiliated, Sue fled to St. Louis and found Huff, knowing she was repeating the same mistakes she made in Chicago, but unable to stop herself from doing so.

"Joe," Huff said as he breezed into the room and gave the researcher a slap on the back. "Congratulations! The Phoenix Project has been given the green light. The number crunchers are putting together a budget for you even as we speak."

Joe could hardly contain his glee. "Really? They liked the project?"

"This is just what we're looking for as a cosmetics company for the new millennium. You've got the full backing of management. And I've got even better news for you, Joe. You're heading up the project."

The odds that the Phoenix Project would succeed were slim—Huff knew it. Yet he pushed upper management to bankroll it anyway—with the proviso that Joe would lead the effort. If the project achieved its goal, Galatea stood to make a killing not only in the immediate future but for years to come. If it failed, Joe, Huff's long-standing detractor, and an obstructionist, would be forced out of the company, making room for the young talent Huff wanted to hire. The prospect of purging the lab of its aging workforce was so appealing that Huff found himself rooting for the project to be a bust.

Joe grinned. "Wonderful! This is going to be an excellent addition to the Galatea line. Naturally, Rachel will be second-in-command. We've got to get our hands on the marula leaves. I imagine it will take several months."

"Well, Joe, you better acquire your magical ingredient faster than that. The project has a six-month window."

"Six months!" Joe exclaimed. "For a project of this scope and complexity, two years is considered the fast track, there's no way we can meet that sort of deadline."

"Six months," Huff countered, concealing a sadistic delight in imposing the near impossible timetable. "I am confident I'll be pleased with the end results."

When Joe announced the six-month time frame to Rachel, she nearly dropped a test tube.

"Do you realize all of the bureaucratic checkpoints we'll have to make it through to get our hands on those marula leaves?" Rachel asked. "Does Huff think we can simply run up to Walmart and pick up a bundle in the produce aisle?"

Rachel was right. A sacred and spiritual tree, many of the countries where it could be found had designated it as a protected natural treasure. Although it had gone unspoken, Joe and Rachel understood that to get a large quantity of the leaves, they might have to resort to bribing tribal leaders who controlled the precious ingredient and then find a way to smuggle it out of the country.

Joe ushered Rachel into his office and shut the door behind him.

"Look, I know this is an impossible timetable," Joe began. "Do you think you—do you think you could, you know, call in some favors, get us some help?"

Rachel interrupted. "Oh no. Please, Joe. Don't ask me. It could get a lot of folks in trouble."

Joe said, "If this project fails, the ax will fall on my head. With me gone, the rest of my staff will soon follow."

Rachel shifted her weight from one foot to the other, weighing the costs and benefits of the request Joe had made without ever formally making it. She knew he wouldn't ask aloud either. It was a way of protecting himself, retaining plausible deniability—in case things went badly.

CHAPTER TEN

FEBRUARY 1969

Joe dreaded going to class on Monday, February 17. Valentine's Day had been the previous Friday, and no doubt Kate would be in one of her smitten, dreamy states.

He expected to see her lost in the clouds when he walked into the lecture hall. Instead, her seat was empty. Minutes passed. Class started. And still, no Kate. Fifteen minutes into the professor's lecture, Kate crept into the room, her shoulders rounded and her chin a bit lower than usual. It looked as if she was trying to get over a punch in the gut or a couple of cracked ribs.

"What's the matter?" Joe whispered, alarmed by her crumpled posture.

"Nothing," Kate answered, opening her textbook with a forced determination.

Joe continued looking at her profile, hoping to catch her attention. But her gaze refused to meet his. Even so, she could not hide the water that pooled around her eyes, the moisture she flicked away with a finger and then concealed by resting her hand against her temple.

The remaining forty-five minutes of class were the longest. As the minute hand on the wall clock inched toward the end of the lesson, the tension mounted. As if sensing the coming questions, Kate gathered her books and fled the room moments before the class officially ended.

Shocked by Kate's erratic behavior, Joe hesitated before scooping up his things and taking off after her.

"Kate! Wait," Joe shouted.

His urgent calls caught the attention of not only Kate but everyone else around her. Kate kept walking, so Joe called out even louder.

Hoping to stop the public spectacle, Kate halted in her tracks. But she would not turn and look at him.

"Look, Kate, I don't know what is going on, but something's not right. I care about you. Won't you please tell me what is wrong?"

Kate circled her arms tightly around her books and refused to meet his gaze.

"Kate," Joe whispered, stepping forward and gently pulling her to him in an embrace.

"Joe," she said before her voice started to crack.

"Come with me," Joe said.

He took her across campus, toward the Ratskeller, a dingy basement pub for students. It was dark and because it was an early Monday afternoon, empty. The bartender was clearly more interested in his school books than in waiting on his customers.

Joe found a booth in the very back of the bar. "Wait here, I'll go up to the bar and get us a couple of beers."

Kate slid across the wooden bench without a word. When he returned with two beer mugs, Kate protested. "I've got to go to class."

"Listen to me," Joe said, unwilling to take no for an answer, "today you are missing your classes. I know that's not something you do, but I can assure you that your grades aren't going to suffer. Besides, the professors test from the book not the lectures anyway. Now, tell me, what is going on."

She slumped back in her chair, twisting a napkin with her fingers.

"Harry and I went to a party last Friday night; one of those huge fraternity gatherings. Just about everyone was there: Greeks and non-Greeks, athletes, ROTC guys, anti-war protesters. Everyone. In fact, it was such an eclectic mix, I thought I might even see you," Kate said as a weak smile passed across her lips.

"I didn't want to go," she continued, "it was Harry's idea. I hoped we'd spend a quiet, romantic Valentine's Day together."

Kate lapsed into silence before looping her fingers through the beer stein's handle, raising the mug to her lips, and gulping down several swallows, draining a third of it before returning it to the table.

"Harry was standing next to me. He'd just brought me a beer from the keg when I noticed a girl walking our way. I didn't recognize her. But when Harry saw her, he grabbed my arm and told me it was time to leave.

"Well, I suggested we stay a bit longer. He gripped my arm even tighter and then pushed me to the front door. He'd never acted that way before. It scared me, and so I told him to stop."

She paused again, running her fingers through her hair.

"He's never tried to use his physical size and strength to control me."

Kate continued, "The girl who had been walking toward us slapped

Harry across the face and screamed, 'You bastard!' The room got quiet. Attention was riveted on Harry, this girl—and me."

Kate ran her fingers through her hair again. "The girl was furious. She turned to me and asked, 'Are you with him—this, this monster?'"

Joe clenched his beer handle tightly. "What did you say?"

"Well, I told her that of course I was with Harry, that I was his girlfriend," Kate answered. "And do you know what she said next, Joe?"

Joe shook his head.

"She practically screamed, 'So you're the one who nearly killed my best friend.'"

"What?" Joe asked in disbelief. "What was she talking about?"

"I didn't know, and then Harry was trying to pull me away, claiming I shouldn't listen to drunk women. But I yanked my arm back as hard as I could, surprising him. The girl, she was shouting even more hysterically."

Kate's voice trailed off.

"Joe, Harry got a girl pregnant last year. He refused to marry her. Confused, not knowing what to do, she went for an abortion. Joe, the girl almost died."

Kate picked up her beer, willing herself to drink fast to numb the pain.

"What happened next?" Joe asked.

Kate grabbed a new napkin and started twisting the paper.

"At first, Harry called her a liar and denied everything. Then someone in the crowd said he was the liar and an asshole."

Kate finished her drink. She was silent but clearly still agitated. There was more to the story. Joe went to the bar for two more beers. Kate didn't protest.

Joe sat back down and set the beer in front of the distraught young woman. Her hands began to shake.

Kate took a drink, then continued. "I couldn't take the humiliation, the public betrayal. I fled the party and took off running across campus without Harry. All I could think about was getting back to my dorm room and locking myself inside.

"But when I got there, Harry was waiting for me. I tried to keep him out of my room, but he demanded I hear him out.

"You know what he told me?" Kate said. "He admitted the affair. And he admitted that he forced the poor girl to have an abortion. You know why he had her do it? He told me it was because he loved me."

Kate continued. "I started to cry and told him to get out. The one thing I cannot have is a man who lies to me. Not as a boyfriend, not as a husband."

Kate fell silent. Joe waited, forcing himself to sit in his chair rather than go find Harry and punch him.

"Harry grabbed me and forced his mouth on top of mine. I was crying, pushing at his chest and telling him to get off. I could hear my shirt ripping. His hands were running up my skirt. He said, 'I got one girl pregnant, I can get you pregnant right now. If I get you pregnant, you'll never be able to show your face at home unless you marry me.'"

Joe gripped the table, his body awash in fury. It took a touch from Kate's hand to bring him back to the conversation.

"I shouted for him to stop. But he wouldn't. I was crying and begging for him to stop, but he kept going," Kate said. "I was half-naked, and he was almost naked when my roommate walked into the room."

"So, he didn't...?" Joe said, unable to finish the sentence.

Kate shook her head.

"The campus police and the dean of students were summoned. They told me that rape and attempted rape don't occur on college campuses. If I reported it to the police, the school would not back my version of the events. They had a different solution in mind. They called his parents and told them to come get him right then and there. He was expelled. I was offered a scholarship and told to get on with my life."

"So Harry's gone?" Joe asked.

"Yes, Harry's gone, and I will never see him again."

"And are you okay?" Joe asked. "Of course you're not okay."

Kate answered, "Promise me you won't do anything crazy."

"Why do you think I'd do something reckless?" Joe asked.

"Your clenched teeth, tight jaw muscles, closed fists, and the way you keep rocking back and forth in your chair," Kate observed. "Look, I don't need you to fight my battles or to take care of me. What I need is a friend."

Joe sighed, leaned forward across the table, and grasped her hands. "You already have that, Kate. You can count on me."

CHAPTER ELEVEN

Rachel James had something Joe didn't—connections to a group of discreet people with clandestine power; relationships forged while Rachel was a senior in college.

She'd won a prestigious fellowship with a St. Louis pharmaceutical company. The work focused mainly on a joint project between the company and the US Army. Early on, the project heads concluded Rachel possessed superior abilities, and, as a result, they gave her a level of responsibility unusual for someone who didn't even have a degree. Rachel assumed it would also produce a job offer; after all, every prior fellowship recipient had received one, and there was no question that Rachel had outperformed them all.

When none was given, Rachel demanded to know the reason why. And she learned another hard lesson taught in fields dominated by men: It was decided the offer would go to waste. Even though she was the most qualified, she'd likely quit after a few years to get married and start a family. Better to hire the second-best candidate who would stay than bring the best one in only to have her quit after they'd invested so much time training her.

Fortunately, the other young researchers recognized the injustice—only they had no power to change the outcome. But they remained close to her throughout their careers. And when she was in a jam and needed something special, she could count on the researchers with top-secret clearance to get it. No questions asked.

When the marula leaves arrived at the lab within two weeks of the project's start, Joe knew Rachel had prevailed upon her contacts. But Galatea's top brass, including Huff, believed Joe cajoled contacts in Africa and customs officials into supplying the leaves on an expedited delivery basis.

Once they arrived, Joe set Rachel in charge of unlocking the chemical compounds of the marula. Her dedication to any task was dogged and unflagging, her ability to analyze compounds unparalleled. Rachel didn't disappoint. Only a few short weeks later, Rachel had unlocked the chemical makeup and set to work making synthetic replicas of the active compound.

Joe concentrated on procuring cadaver skin. Some of the skin came from burn victims, people who had died in car crashes, house fires, natural gas mishaps, and meth lab explosions. Some of the other samples were from normal skin taken from the bodies of the elderly. The skin went into petri dishes bathed in the new material.

He also tried to keep anxious executives who wanted to visit the lab, and constant progress updates, at bay. Only five weeks into the Phoenix Project, Joe already found himself fielding requests for results.

At that point, he reported in an executive meeting that the active ingredients of marula had been identified, analyzed, and synthetically replicated. A prototype had been whipped together. Although they referred to it as a gel, the cloudy, sticky mass had the consistency of raw egg whites. Once it was ready for the mass market, it would be reformulated with artificial dyes and thickeners to enhance its appeal.

The skin had spent one week immersed in the petri dish. Each day, Joe posted the same question in the morning when he walked into the lab. Each day, Rachel peered through the neck of a microscope, examined the flesh in the dish, and announced: "No change."

CHAPTER TWELVE

MARCH 1969

When Dean Andrew Landry heard the rap of knuckles against his office door, he answered reflexively, "Come on in." Landry had been the dean of students for twenty years at Wash U., and he was accustomed to having students drop by to complain, pontificate, or just pull up a chair and shoot the breeze. Landry loved his job and, by and large, the students adored him.

Joe had never met the man, but he needed his help.

Landry stood up from behind his desk and stretched out his hand. Joe grasped it firmly, giving it a confident shake.

"Dean, I'm here today because I'd like to talk about a good friend of mine, Kate Taylor. I'd like you to help her land a summer research assistant job with one of the professors in the business school."

Landry, used to brash young men strutting in with demands, wasn't surprised by the bold request. "Well," Landry answered, "it is usually the professor who picks his summer assistant. The positions are extremely competitive. What year is your friend?"

Joe cleared his throat. "Sir, she's a freshman. But she has all A's."

Landry's brow furrowed. "Hmmm. It is almost unheard of for a freshman to be offered such a position. I don't think there's much I can do to help. If she needs a job, perhaps I could find something else for her on campus, something a little less prestigious, the bookstore perhaps. Why don't you have her stop by?"

"That isn't an option, Dean. Kate doesn't know I'm here. This is my idea, and she must be offered a research assistant job. Anything less won't do."

Landry clasped his hands together on top of his desk. "Why don't you explain?"

"If she doesn't get the job, then she'll have to go home this summer," Joe answered. "She'll have to go home to that monster you kicked out of school."

Landry leaned forward. "Which monster would that be?"

"Harry Bennett, the student who got one girl pregnant. Harry Bennett, the student who then tried to rape his girlfriend, Kate. My Kate, the one we are talking about now," Joe said. Looking Landry in the eyes, Joe added, "If you send Kate home, Harry will be there. Waiting. To save his reputation, he'll pressure her to get back together with him. His parents and her parents will also probably try to convince her to do the same, maybe even get married. The problem gets swept under the rug and paves the way for him to reapply for admission."

Landry sat back in his chair and sighed. "Tell you what, I'll make a few calls and see what I can do."

"Thank you, Dean. I appreciate it," Joe said as he rose to leave.

Before he got to the door, Landry said, "Mr. Holly, I presume you already have a research assistant post for the summer and will be staying on campus?"

Joe nodded.

"I see," Landry said.

CHAPTER THIRTEEN

"So, are you going to talk to me or shall we ride in silence?" Kate asked Joe.

Six weeks had passed since the Phoenix Project had first been given the go-ahead. Joe had spent the bulk of his weekends at work and in the lab. The long, frustrating, and futile day had left him tense. The fact that he now had to attend a cocktail party at Huff's house had turned his mood downright dark.

"Sorry," Joe said in an attempt to restore some civility. "Nothing is going right. The burned tissue hasn't shown any signs of change."

The tissue sample had been marinating in the synthetic marula goo for about two weeks. Joe spent that Saturday reexamining the marula as well as the synthetic compound, looking for ways to further artificially enhance the plant's active ingredients.

"By the way," Joe said, loosening his tight grip on the steering wheel, "you look stunning."

Kate added, "For an older woman."

They had not discussed plastic surgery since the night Joe stormed out of the restaurant, creating a mini-scene and leaving Kate to settle the check. She had not given up but now was not the time to revisit the issue.

Joe guided his Mercedes into the grand circle driveway of Huff's Chesterfield manse. When Huff told his wife, Lauren, that they were leaving Chicago and moving to St. Louis, she'd pitched a fit. But with her background and breeding, it didn't take her long to ingratiate herself into St. Louis society. She'd gotten their three kids into the most exclusive private school in St. Louis. She used her volunteer time at the school to network with other well-heeled mothers and squeezed her way on to a few charity boards. It was impossible to pick up The Ladue News or St. Louis Magazine without seeing Lauren and Huff's pictures on the see-and-be-seen pages.

Joe handed the valet his car keys and guided Kate toward the front door. "Okay, let's get this over with," he whispered in her ear.

Kate led the way into the home. "Lauren, so nice to see you again," Kate said.

Lauren leaned forward and air kissed Kate on the cheek. "I'm so glad you could make it. I was worried that Joe would be holed up in his lab and you'd be forced to spend the night at home alone."

"He did spend the day in the lab, and you're right, I had to pull him away," Kate replied. "He's so dedicated to his latest project. He thinks of nothing else. How are the kids?"

"Wonderful." Lauren beamed. "Thank you for asking."

Joe admired the way Kate could deftly point out his hard work and then seamlessly change the subject, even if that subject was children, a particularly difficult area for Kate. Despite years of trying, they had been unable to have any of their own, much to Kate's sorrow.

Kate spotted Rachel James in a corner and headed toward her.

Kate and Rachel had always gotten along. Kate's natural warmth could melt even the most severe feminist.

"Watch this," Rachel whispered to Kate. "Sue Schmidt just entered the building."

"You're terrible, Rachel," Kate said even as she giggled with anticipation.

Wearing a tomato-red dress with spaghetti straps that looked like they might snap under the weight of her breasts, Sue had taken special care in choosing just the right outfit for her first visit to her lover's home.

"Such a lovely home," Sue told Lauren with a mixture of envy and wistfulness.

"Thank you," a tight-lipped Lauren replied. "You know, very few women can wear that sort of dress without looking cheap."

Sue grimaced. But Lauren was the wife of the boss. "Thank you."

When Joe snickered at the backhanded nature of the compliment, Kate shot him a look that warned him to keep quiet. Kate leaned forward into their circle of three.

"I almost feel sorry for Sue," Kate said. "She's out of her league and doesn't realize it. Huff will never leave Lauren and Sue will never receive what she craves. What happens to a woman like that when she reaches my age?"

The question hung in the air, and Joe cleared his throat, a warning to Kate and Rachel that the subject should be dropped. "Huff. Good to see you."

"Rachel, Joe, thank you for coming," Huff said. Unable to recall Kate's name, he acknowledged her by nodding his head and smiling. "It is always nice to meet up with your colleagues in a more relaxed social setting. Wouldn't you agree, Rachel?"

Rachel gave her glasses a slight nudge, pushing them up higher on the bridge of her nose, and nodded her head up in agreement.

"So, how's the Phoenix Project coming?" Huff asked.

"Coming along, coming along," Joe answered, trying hard to fight the urge to wipe the moisture collecting on his brow. "Still a little early in the project but we've been able to break down the active ingredients and mix up a gel. I'm really excited."

Huff smiled and replied, "You know what excites me, Joe?"

"What?" Joe asked as he crossed his arms in front of his chest and balanced a mineral water in his hand.

"Results!" Huff said loudly, punctuating his statement with a slap on Joe's back.

A new voice chimed in. "Research and development projects are like marriages, wouldn't you say? You don't just say 'I do' and from then on, everything is caviar and crème brûlée. It takes time, trial and error, and above all, patience and perseverance."

"It's great to see you, Stan," Joe said with a mixture of glee and relief.

"Stan," Huff said stiffly as he extended his arm for a handshake. The two men had an uneasy relationship. Because Stan owned the biggest chunk of the company and controlled the board of directors, he could have Huff kicked out on a whim, and given the fact that the two men didn't particularly like each other Huff often wondered why he still even had a job. But Huff ran a tight ship, tighter than Stan had when he was at the helm. Huff's flair for management, number crunching, and keeping a firm grip on the budget meant that he not only maintained Stan's status as a rich man but had elevated him to a super-rich one.

"Hello, Rachel," Stan said. He looked briefly at Kate. "Mrs. Holly, so good to see you."

Kate opened her mouth to reply, but Stan had already turned his attention back to Huff. "Huff, I was wondering if I might have a moment to speak with you privately."

"Certainly, my den is just around the corner. We can talk in there."

Stan nodded to Joe, Rachel, and Kate. "Please excuse me."

Kate's lips came together and formed a tight frown.

"I told you Huff was an asshole," Joe said quietly to Kate.

"He's not the one I'm mad at," Kate replied. "Everyone knows Huff is arrogant and egotistical. It is Stan who I could throttle."

"Why?" Joe asked.

"You mean you didn't notice?" she said incredulously. "What is the one thing that he has always said to me that has gotten under your skin?"

Joe stood there stumped—until Rachel chimed in. "He didn't say,

'Hello, Kate, you look as lovely as ever.'"

Joe shot Rachel a dirty look.

"I can't help it if I have a great memory," Rachel laughed.

"To be fair, Kate, times have changed," Rachel added. "Men shy away from commenting on women's appearances. They're afraid of offending feminists, or worse, if it is in the workplace, they might get sued."

"I'm not an employee," Kate argued. "I never objected in the past."

"Can we talk about something else?" Joe interjected. "This is a ridiculous conversation."

Kate turned to Rachel. "I tried to explain to Joe that it isn't about the beauty that drives my desire for plastic surgery, but the feeling that I've been pushed into a corner by some unseen hand."

"Welcome to my world," Rachel said. "I've been at this company for decades, never married, never left to have children, and I'm still not considered management material. If it weren't for Joe, I'd probably still be the very lowest assistant in the lab instead of second-in-command. I eventually had to make peace with it or drive myself crazy."

"I think you're both being ridiculous," Joe said. "Kate, I love you. You're my wife, the woman I chose to share my life with. That should count for something. Rachel, you are an invaluable part of the research team. Without your help, Galatea would not be one-tenth of the company it is today. I know how valuable your contributions have been, shouldn't that be enough?"

"C'mon, Joe. Is it enough for you if I appreciate the work you do in the lab or that Kate appreciates your brilliance?" Rachel asked. "You crave attention, approval, and acclaim just as much as the rest of us. If Kate thinks that through plastic surgery, she'll get her need to be noticed met, then I think you should go out of your way to help her get it done."

Joe was stunned. "How can you of all people say that? You hate vanity and mock the women who fork out a small fortune every year for our products."

"I may mock the women who do that, but I would never take away their ability to choose it," Rachel answered. "I am a feminist, the sort who believes feminism was all about giving women choices. I choose not to wear makeup, Kate likes makeup. To me, a feminist is someone who believes that women are free to make up their own minds. Whether a woman keeps her maiden name or changes it, whether a mother goes to work or stays home, whether a woman chooses to have an abortion, keep the baby, or put it up for adoption, or even whether a woman has a face-lift or not, the point is that it was up to her to decide. If it is something Kate wants—and she's willing to live with the risks associated with her choice—so be it."

"Aaarggh," Joe said, putting his hand to his forehead. "You two are ganging up on me. I don't want to talk about this anymore. I know what is best for Kate."

Joe regretted the words in an instant. Rachel's face contorted into what Joe thought for a moment was contempt. Kate blinked her eyelids several times before they narrowed into a gray glare.

"I'm going to get a drink," Kate announced.

As she walked across the room toward the bar, she crossed paths with Sue. Stan took a step back to watch Sue's ass jiggle from side-to-side. As he did so, he bumped into Kate. "Oh, I'm sorry, dear, I didn't see you."

CHAPTER FOURTEEN

MARCH 1969

"I need your help," Kate said to Joe as soon as class finished. A beautiful woman asking for aid was bound to grab any man's attention, and Joe was no exception.

"With what?" he asked, trying not to sound overeager.

"My parents."

Apart from a superficial discussion about their hometowns, the two friends had not talked much about family. The college campus existed in a bubble consisting of classes, parties, gossip, romance, and tests—making it easy to forget the outside world existed.

"Of course I'll help you," Joe said.

Kate flashed a smile, not one of her big, light-up-the-room grins, but instead, a restrained curve of her lips, betraying her gratitude and tension. "Don't you want me to tell you what I need before you agree? What if I was up to no good?"

Joe scoffed. "Kate, you're as wholesome as Doris Day. I'm not worried."

Kate playfully slapped Joe's arm as they strolled through campus. "Doris Day! Thanks a lot! I've always fancied myself more like Lara in Doctor Zhivago."

Summoning up the best movie imitation Joe could muster, he joked, "What happens to a girl like that when a man like you is finished with her?"

But as soon as the line passed over his lips, Joe regretted it. It reminded them both of Harry and the woman he'd gotten pregnant.

"Listen, I'm hoping you will help me rehearse a speech. I need to call my parents to tell them our economics professor offered me a summer research assistant job."

"Wow!" Joe said. "Congratulations! A research assistant. You're the first freshman I've ever met who has been offered the position."

Kate nodded. "I know."

"So why don't you seem more excited?" he asked.

"Believe me, I almost fainted when I got the offer. But then there's the complication of my parents." Kate paused. "And Harry."

Joe stopped. "What do you mean, 'And Harry'?"

Kate gestured to the bench and sat down. "After Harry was expelled, he went home. His parents told everyone, including my parents, that Harry got sick and the university had recommended that he take a semester off to recuperate."

"Your parents know that's a lie," Joe said.

Kate fidgeted. "Not exactly. I was so ashamed, I just couldn't bring myself to tell them. Now he's been dropping by my house, hinting to my parents that he's going to propose to me this summer.

"And he's been writing me. He tells he loves me and he'll never hurt me again. Then, in the same letter, he'll write that if he gets drafted by the Army because he's not in school, it is my fault. If he dies, his blood is on my hands."

Joe shook his head. "Unbelievable. After everything he's done to you!"

"That's why I need your help. I'm afraid that when I call my parents, they're going to insist I come home for the summer. I'm not sure if I'm strong enough to hold my ground," Kate said.

"Sure, I'll do whatever I can to help you. We should rehearse your phone call. It's just—" Joe started before he caught himself.

"What?"

"The job offer is an honor and will be a real boost to your career. I wonder if we'd even be having this conversation if you were a man," Joe said.

Kate laughed. "Of course we wouldn't. Perhaps you're the one who is naïve."

Now beaming, she popped up from the bench, amazed at Joe's ability to change her outlook. At long last, she'd found an ally.

CHAPTER FIFTEEN

Joe hated cell phones in the lab, Kate knew. He worried the radio waves would impact the molecular research. So, when she wanted to avoid direct confrontation, it was his cell phone she called. This time she called to tell him she was going out for drinks after work with her staff.

It had been almost a week since the cocktail party and Kate was still mad at Joe's refusal to even discuss plastic surgery. But another issue began haunting her. She'd lost her autonomy but didn't know how or when it happened. Like shoreline beaten back under the continuous assault of waves, her independence had been whittled away during her lifetime with Joe. There were so few ways left for her to assert herself. Screaming or tears never worked; Joe was immune to the standard tools of female warfare. The silent treatment wasn't an option. She'd tried it, but he retaliated with such fury, she never tried using silence as a weapon again.

After a week, Kate concluded her will was no match for his. But on the question of plastic surgery—more importantly, his refusal to discuss it—she wasn't ready to give in, not yet.

And Joe sensed Kate's distance—he also heard it in her voice when he played his cell phone message before leaving for the day. It was time to bring her back in line. He dialed her number.

"Good morning, King Industries," a perky recorded message said. Joe punched in Kate's five-digit extension. If his wife was at her desk, she would pick up by the third ring.

"Kate Holly," he heard her say in a competent work voice.

"Who are you going out with tonight?" Joe asked.

The line was quiet for a moment. "As I said in my message," Kate stammered, "I'm joining some people in my department."

"Like who?"

Kate sighed and recited a litany of names.

"Where will you be going?"

"I don't know, we haven't decided. The weather is gorgeous, so probably somewhere with an outdoor patio."

"Why don't I join you?"

Kate paused. "This is a work gathering. All we'll talk about is quality assurance and how frustrated we are with King Industries, two topics you can't stand."

"That's not true," Joe snapped.

"You start tapping your foot and drumming your fingers whenever you meet up with us," Kate said. "Besides, don't you have to work late on the Phoenix Project?"

"How long do you plan to be out?" Joe asked.

"Not long, an hour," Kate answered, "two at the most."

Neither spoke.

Joe gritted his teeth. "Kate, when are you going to give up this silly quest for plastic surgery? You're making a fool of yourself."

"I've wanted to discuss this issue for a week. Unfortunately, I can't right now. I've got a transcontinental conference call scheduled to start in five minutes. Goodbye, Joe, I'll see you later tonight."

The line went dead. Before he could redial the number, Joe's office door swung open. "I've been knocking on your door for quite some time, and you haven't answered," Rachel said.

"I was on the phone with Kate."

"Forget about Kate," Rachel said. "I need you to come to the lab, now."

Rachel turned on the heels of her sensible shoes and headed out the door. Joe followed her back into the lab.

"For heaven's sake, Rachel, what's so damn important? We've been working for weeks and we've come up with nothing but a big fat zero."

She motioned to an empty space on the research bench. "Sit. Humor me," she commanded before picking up a petri dish and sliding it under the microscope.

"Here is a control sample of the burned skin, what do you see?"

"Destroyed skin cells."

Rachel removed the petri dish and replaced it with the burned skin that had been treated by marula.

"What do you see?"

"Destroyed skin cells."

Joe started to his feet, but Rachel put her hand on one of his shoulders, forcing him to remain seated.

"I'm not done."

She then slid the control sample of normal, aged skin.

"What do you see?"

"Some normal cells, some dead cells; some collagen and elastin have become disconnected," Joe said. "The usual stuff you expect to see in aging skin."

Rachel replaced the sample. "Now tell me what you see."

Joe peered down the neck of the microscope. "Very healthy skin. Collagen and elastin are tight. The cells aren't sluggish. Very healthy. Is this a sample taken from a young person for one of our other studies?"

Rachel shook her head. "No. This is the same aged skin I just showed you. Only it was treated with marula. Do you realize what this means?"

Joe squinted at Rachel and shoved his hands in his pockets. "Let me see those samples again."

Without a word, Rachel presented the skin samples for Joe to review. Several minutes elapsed before Joe finished his examination and looked at Rachel, his face awash in amazement.

Rachel spoke, giving voice to what they were both thinking. "If the damage to the skin has faded, that means we're repairing the skin, that we're undoing the ravages of time."

Joe stood up and grabbed her by the shoulders. "You're right. You're so right, Rachel. The damage hasn't just faded. In fact, some of the smaller wrinkles have been erased. Really erased, not like we claim on all our ads. The wrinkles are gone. We've erased the past!"

CHAPTER SIXTEEN

JUNE 1969

Even professors didn't work much during the summer, a bonus for research assistants. For Kate and Joe, the summer settled into a pleasant routine. The workday started at nine in the morning when they would check in with their professors, or, if the professor was a no-show, the professor's secretary. Expectations for the research assistants were explained on the first day of work. Usually it involved only a few hours in the library or lab before calling it a day.

Kate's professor assigned her the job of fact-checking the chapters of his textbook before it was shipped off to the publisher for final editing.

Joe's assignments were meatier, his responsibilities greater. He was working on experiments. It was part of a larger study on synthetic compounds and chemicals. No one quite yet understood the purpose of the substances, but Joe's professor was convinced that some savvy industrialist or military scientist would figure it out. "Combine science, greed, power, and creativity, and you're bound to come up with something astounding," Joe's professor often said.

But for Joe, it wasn't the heady atmosphere of the lab that put a bounce in his step each morning. It was the magical hour of three in the afternoon, the image of a stunning Kate wearing nothing but a black and white polka-dot bikini, that propelled him through the day.

Joe and Kate each finished their work between one and two. Then they'd meet up at the dorm pool. Joe still couldn't believe his good fortune.

"Can I help you?" Joe asked one afternoon in mid-June as an already-bronzed Kate struggled to rub baby lotion on her back.

"Absolutely!" Kate said as she rolled over onto her belly.

Joe picked up the bottle; if his trembling hands dropped it, there was always the grease to blame.

A few other students lounged around the pool. Joe realized he wasn't the only man who found Kate's body dazzling.

"You're awfully quiet. Tough day at the lab?" she asked as Joe's hands neared the clasp on her back that kept her bikini top fastened.

"Yeah, right. Professors have a cushy job, ideal hours and student slaves who are eager to do their bidding. The only real stress is making tenure."

Kate sat up, moving with the languid grace of a dancer, and said, "Another bonus is that you work teacher's hours but with a lot more prestige and pay."

Kate adjusted the towel beneath her. "Don't you think the job would become a little tedious?"

Joe put the oil down and rinsed his hands in the pool. Unless he wanted to end up the color of a radish and feel as though his flesh were being ripped from his body, he stayed as far away from the stuff as possible.

"Maybe. It would be torture to spend every afternoon for the next two and a half months at the pool."

Kate laughed. "I thought you didn't pay too much attention to the fairer sex. I thought it was all test tubes and beakers with you."

Maybe his persona of indifference had been working too well, Joe thought to himself. "I also love art. There's nothing better for the soul than a visit to the St. Louis Art Museum or St. Louis Symphony."

"I've never been to either," Kate said. "I've heard wonderful things, but during school, my free time was pretty much devoted to studying." Her voice trailed off. Joe knew that Harry had consumed any remaining moments.

Kate continued, "Why don't we go to the art museum?"

"Sure, um," Joe responded, struggling to remain calm, "um, how about two thirty tomorrow afternoon? It's in Forest Park, just five minutes from here."

Kate flashed a dazzling grin, pulled her sunglasses down, and peered at Joe over the top of the rims. "It's a date," she declared.

For the next twenty-four hours, Joe obsessed over Kate's declaration of a date. What did she mean? Had she used the word simply as a casual throwaway line between friends? Or was she hinting at something more? By the time he picked Kate up the next day for their art museum rendezvous in Forest Park, he'd convinced himself she had meant nothing.

In 1904, St. Louis hosted the World's Fair in Forest Park, which is even larger than Central Park. Several grand buildings were constructed for the event. When it was over, the St. Louis Art Museum moved from its original downtown location into a new home, one with an impressive, nearly white, stone edifice modeled after the Beaux-Arts style that was popular with the nineteenth-century industrial barons. Even though it was now about sixty-five years old, the elegant structure had aged beautifully; art within art.

Kate was quiet when they walked through the front doors, but her eyes absorbed everything. After a few moments, she turned to Joe and proclaimed in a hushed tone, "I love this place."

Joe laughed. "We haven't even seen any of the art yet."

She smiled and shrugged her shoulders. "I know. But have you ever walked into a place and the atmosphere, the personality," she struggled to find right words, "the very essence of the place rushes into your chest and fills up your soul, and you feel like you're going to burst?"

Joe nodded. "Yes, I think I know what you mean," though he didn't confess he felt that way about a person rather than this place.

Kate continued, "When we walked in, something just grabbed me and gave me goosebumps. Perhaps the artists poured so much of their own creative souls into these works that their paintings still radiate their aura." Kate giggled. "I'm so embarrassed, you must think I'm dropping acid."

"Naw," Joe said. "From a scientific standpoint, we're still discovering so much about radiation and invisible waves and energy. The whole science of quantum physics would probably have a lot to say about your theory."

"There you go, science stuff again," Kate teased. "C'mon, show me the art."

For their first stop, Joe picked the section of the museum with paintings done by masters from the Middle Age.

"Look closely at these artworks," Joe said. "If you look carefully, you can see the artist's brush strokes."

Kate squinted her eyes and leaned forward. "My god, you're right."

"My favorite thing to do is find the brush strokes in the painting, or in the case of someone like Van Gogh, globs of paint with fingerprint marks in them," Joe admitted. "Remnants, physical manifestations of living people—the artist becomes a person. Perhaps those same brush strokes also exude that creative spirit that moved you when we walked in."

"Mmmhmm, I like that," Kate said. "This is unbelievable. Works painted three hundred, four hundred, and even five hundred years ago, yet, look how deep that cloak's red is or how the Virgin Mary's robe is still a brilliant blue."

"The museum goes through a lot of time and expense to preserve the paintings. They must remain in a temperature-controlled environment, carefully shielded from direct sunlight and oily fingers, handled only by gloved professionals."

"Hmmm," Kate answered. "The lengths that people will go through to save art."

"Ah—I would describe it differently. I would say that it isn't just the art, but the beauty. The art is preserved so that successive generations can admire and appreciate the beauty."

Kate asked, "Would you say the same about some of the modern art pieces with all of the crushed glass and distorted faces?"

"No. That stuff isn't beautiful," Joe answered. "To me, it isn't worth preserving."

"Well, I guess beauty is in the eye of the beholder," Kate said with a grin.

When they finally emerged from the art museum, neither was ready to go back to the four walls of a dingy dorm room.

"Why don't we walk?" Kate suggested.

They headed toward the reflecting pool at the bottom of Art Hill, the warm evening air stroking their skin with the soft touch of a lover. Side by side they wandered, a comfortable silence setting in as they watched a mother duck and her babies paddle across the water in a winding trajectory.

Kate grasped Joe's hand, weaving her fingers in between his. Startled, he looked at her, but she continued to gaze at the spectacle in the pond, though her face seemed flushed, almost beaming. Joe pressed his fingers softly into the flesh of her hand. She returned the squeeze.

He thought to himself, This is true happiness.

CHAPTER SEVENTEEN

When Kate walked through the front door of their home, she expected to find Joe waiting. And he would be furious. Facing his anger took all the fun out of the evening, so she didn't stay out late.

Yet the house was empty and dark. She changed into her white flannel nightgown and crawled into bed, reaching for the remote control. Much later, when Joe walked into the room, the television was still on, but Kate had nodded off.

"Kate, wake up," Joe said, nudging his wife in the shoulder.

Without opening her eyes, Kate mumbled, "Where have you been?"

"Working," Joe answered.

"I tried calling your cell phone, you didn't answer," Kate said.

"Yeah, I know. I turned all the ringers off, then I lost track of time."

Kate opened her eyes and wearily sat up. Something wasn't right. "What happened?"

Joe grabbed the remote, turned off the television, and sat down on the bed.

"Something incredibly intriguing and wonderful!"

Kate perked up. "Go on. The burn gel? Is it working?"

"No, it isn't working, at least not on the burned skin. But it is doing something to my control sample. This is hard to believe, I barely believe it myself, but the gel seems to actually reverse the aging process on the control sample."

"Yeah right," Kate scoffed. "There are a million creams and gels and lotions on the market that falsely claim to reverse the aging process. You read the fine print, and the label states the cream reduces the appearance of wrinkles. The reality is they simply plump up the skin around the wrinkles to create the illusion that the wrinkles disappeared."

"Kate, I'm talking about something different. Instead of a fountain, I may have discovered a gel of youth. The skin damage is wiped from the skin. On the cellular level, the cells are functioning like they do in a young person, not an older person. Sunspots? Gone. Wrinkles? Gone. Saggy skin? Gone," Joe said. "It's as though the skin had undergone a facelift procedure in which the doctor cuts old flabby skin away and tightens what remains, stretching it like you stretch our loose bed sheets across the mattress to make them firm. Only this doesn't require a scalpel, lasers, or anesthesia. Rather than the freakish results doctors obtain when they try to replicate Mother Nature, we're giving the body a jolt to repair itself. With a plastic surgeon, the face you get is something not quite your own; with our gel, you rewind the clock to an earlier time in your life!"

Kate stared at Joe in disbelief. "That is too good to be true."

"I've never been more serious in my life."

"Joe, it would be a miracle if you could really rewind time. I would give anything to look like I did in my thirties."

"I know, I know," Joe said. "I want that for you. I want to give you that gift. I think you are so beautiful now. But you were once breathtaking. I'd much rather see the woman I knew from a decade or two ago rather than what some plastic surgeon thinks you might have looked like back then."

"How long do you think it will be before you bring the product to market?" Kate asked.

"It is going to take a while," Joe said. "How would you feel about being our first test subject?"

"Are you serious?" Kate asked. "Do you think they'll agree?"

"It is going to take some doing, but Huff is going to want this product on the shelves as quickly as possible to make the most amount of money in the least amount of time. Using you as a test subject means we won't have to go through the tedious process of recruiting someone. Plus, I'll be able to monitor your progress daily. What could be more convenient?"

Kate wrapped her arms around her husband. "I'm so glad I married a genius."

CHAPTER EIGHTEEN

JUNE 1969

Ike and Tina Turner. Jimi Hendrix. The Rolling Stones. That pretty much summed up Kate's record collection. Not only had her schooling in the arts been overlooked, so too, Joe thought, had her exposure to music.

Despite Joe's outward appearance as a buttoned-down square, he had eclectic musical tastes, some of which Kate thought were downright dangerous. "You did what?" she asked incredulously when Joe admitted that, as a teenager, he would drive across the Mississippi River and sneak into smoke-filled clubs in East St. Louis where both drugs and jazz flowed.

Kate wasn't quite ready for jazz clubs, Joe decided. If he was honest with himself, he also wasn't ready to introduce her to that scene. He didn't think she was yet capable of appreciating the music. Besides, heads turned when she walked into any room. In a club, where sexuality always bubbled close to the surface, jealousy would be a problem Joe would have to control. The symphony would be a safer bet.

"Are you sure I'll like classical music?" she responded when he'd asked her out on the date.

"You liked the art museum, right?" he said, giving her hand a squeeze. They hadn't gotten past the hand-holding stage. Fearful that she would run away if he pushed their relationship along too quickly, he played the physical part of their blossoming relationship safe.

She accepted his symphony invitation, and he fasted—skipping lunch for a week to scrape together enough money to buy tickets for the worst seats in the house.

When the anticipated night arrived, Joe put on his interview suit. Kate borrowed a dress from one of the wealthier coeds who lived on her floor; form-fitting and deep blue as the Mediterranean Sea. The plunging neckline enhanced Kate's tan cleavage. The back of the dress dropped down even further, revealing the slender lines of her smooth back and perfectly formed shoulder blades. With her hair swept up into a chignon, Kate's neck rivaled that of the princesses depicted in the art museum paintings.

When Kate crossed the yellowed linoleum of the dorm lobby's floor, Joe swallowed hard. "Wow!"

Self-conscious, Kate smoothed her bangs with a hand covered by a white glove that didn't stop until it reached her elbow. "Am I overdressed?"

"No, no. You're perfect."

Her beauty made him nervous. On the drive to the Powell Symphony Hall, Joe launched into a history lesson about the venue to calm the pounding waves of attraction washing over him.

"My parents used to go to the St. Louis Theater, as Powell was originally known, when they were kids—to catch vaudeville acts. When I was growing up, I'd take a streetcar down here and spend the day at the movies—Ben Hur, Bridge on the River Kwai. The theater closed in 1966. But then a widow with money decided to invest a bunch of cash into the place, and it was completely renovated. I haven't seen what they've done yet, but I'm anxious to see the results. Not to mention that the music critic for The New York Times declared that the acoustics are extraordinary," Joe said.

"And that's just about the venue. We haven't even talked about the symphony itself," Joe added. "The St. Louis Symphony has been around since 1880. It performed in the Kiel Opera House. But in January of 1968, it moved into the Powell."

The renovation, Joe decided when they entered the movie house of his youth, had been a success. Powell exuded a classic European grace; cream-colored walls and ceilings with red and gold accents. The architects claimed they modeled the foyer after a royal chapel at Versailles. A brilliant chandelier hung from the ceiling, and an enormous stained glass window depicting St. Louis IX on horseback added to the splendor.

"Gosh, I feel like a little girl playing dress-up," Kate said, intimidated by what she saw around her; men in tuxedos and women in evening gowns.

"How about a glass of champagne before we find our seats?" Joe suggested. "I wanted to arrive early so we could fully appreciate the architecture. We may as well go all out and enjoy the experience with champagne in our hands."

"Um, okay. But I feel bad. I'm sure the tickets weren't cheap—and the bite of buying books looms," Kate said, her voice trailing off.

"Well, we are sitting in the cheapest, nosebleed seats. Someday, though, I'll be able to afford the ones on the floor, center stage right in front of the orchestra. For now, the terrace circle balcony is our lot in life," Joe admitted. "I hope that's okay."

"Joe, are you kidding? This is, this is, this is breathtaking. I've never seen anything like it, except maybe the art museum. Another amazing experience, courtesy of you—and I haven't even heard the music yet."

The couple found a small space in the foyer balcony, the perfect spot to people-watch. Joe pretended to watch the symphony's patrons to avoid staring at Kate. It was hard not to look at her. Kate's gloved fingers gingerly raising the thin champagne glass to her mouth, the golden liquid alive with bubbles as if anticipating the moment they would touch her lips—it was a sight more intoxicating than any amount of alcohol. She was as much a work of art as the Powell or Tchaikovsky's Symphony No. 5, which they would soon be settling in to listen to that evening.

"When I grow old, I hope I look like her," Kate whispered to Joe, nodding toward a woman walking underneath the King Louis stained glass window.

The woman had to have been in her early sixties. Her head held high, she was thin, her dark hair peppered with silver and pulled up into a chignon, the soft wrinkles around her lids merrily accenting the hazel green of her eyes.

"Kate, you will be even more striking," Joe said.

Her face flushed. "Aw, Joe, you're way too sweet to me," she said, laying a hand on his forearm.

An usher with a chime passed. The performance was about to begin.

"We should finish our champagne and find our seats," Joe suggested.

Kate took a large sip, unwilling to let the drink go to waste. She knew Joe didn't have a lot of money, and she didn't want to seem ungrateful.

Inside the auditorium, the musicians were finishing their warm-up for the evening's performance, two selections from Mozart and a moody turbulent piece from Tchaikovsky.

"Try closing your eyes and listening to the music," Joe whispered as the music of Tchaikovsky gathered strength, swirled in the great cavern, and settled into the listeners' souls. "It is a whole different experience."

She looked at Joe as if he were crazy, then settled back in her chair, her chin held high as if she were soaking up the sun at the pool but instead absorbed the music for the first part of the program.

Goosebumps rose on her arms. When the sound had gone silent, and it was time for the intermission, Kate opened her eyes; her face was flushed with passion. She turned toward Joe, cupped his jaw with her hand. "Oh, Joe, thank you."

Right there, sitting in the cheap seats, Kate made the first move. She kissed him.

CHAPTER NINETEEN

Rachel slammed her palm down on the conference room table. Joe had expected this sort of reaction.

"You're going to do what?"

Rachel's question bounced off the conference room walls and echoed through the room. Stan and Huff listened but said nothing.

"You heard me," Joe answered. "Kate's going to be our test subject."

The news of the marula gel's potential for wiping away wrinkles had electrified Galatea's executives. The question on the table now was how to proceed. And for the three men in the room, their own agendas played into the decision-making process.

For Stan, the new product would be his company's finest achievement, ensuring the financial security for his children, grandchildren, and beyond.

Dollars dazzled Huff. A wrinkle-erasing product was bound to be a blockbuster. Huff pictured media interviews and magazine covers. Of course, the blockbuster profits would benefit both the company and Huff. His contract with Galatea included generous stock bonuses. If the gel were successful, Huff might just join the ranks of the super-rich.

No longer aimed at helping burn survivors, Joe focused on preserving the harmony in his marriage—and his hold on Kate. With Joe holding the keys to the cabinet containing the fountain of youth, Kate would not stray far.

"What you're proposing is clearly unethical!" Rachel said, "You don't go straight from the lab to a human subject without testing the safety of the gel first. Second, you don't use family members as your guinea pig."

"Joe, Kate understands the risks, correct?" Huff asked.

"Of course. But she's willing to give it a try."

Stan volunteered, "Rachel, don't you think Kate is more than old enough to provide informed consent?"

"Not in this case," Rachel answered. "You're underestimating vanity's sway over reason."

She continued. "Not only is it unethical, but it is also junk science. Kate knows what the gel is designed to do. There's no control group, no placebo, no double-blind study. Joe has now created an expectation in Kate that could taint the results."

"Rachel," Joe responded, "to set up a double-blind study would take time." Hoping to appeal to Huff and Stan's objectives, Joe added, "And delay bringing this product to market."

Stan spoke. "As long as Kate signs an informed consent and release form drafted by our in-house lawyers, I'm okay with Joe's proposal."

Huff nodded in agreement. Turning to Rachel, he asked, "Are you going to remain working on this project or should we bring in someone else to help Joe out?"

Rachel stood up angrily. "I'm going to stay. Someone has to protect Kate because it is clear the three of you aren't going to."

CHAPTER TWENTY

OCTOBER 1969

"Do you really think a woman can balance a career and a family?" Kate asked Joe, her voice husky after drinking too much beer at a Halloween party.

The party was Kate's idea. As a senior, Joe had grown weary of the college scene. Kate, a sophomore, still savored the taste of freedom that came from living away from home. The desire to assert her independence, the need to blow off steam, and the urge to have fun all needed an outlet. If Joe didn't agree to go to the party, he knew Kate would go alone.

Even though he went, stepping too far away was a hazard. He disappeared for a moment to get her a beer from the keg. When he returned, a cluster of football players surrounded her, hanging on her every word. Joe tried not to look too dour as he watched the spectacle. He worked hard to conceal his insecurity. As his jealousy gathered strength, he tried to douse it by drinking.

The longer they stayed, the more they both drank. For Kate, full cups seemed to magically appear. After midnight, Joe was finally able to persuade her to leave.

They walked arm in arm across the dark campus.

"You didn't answer my question," Kate cooed. "Do you think a woman can pursue a career and marriage and kids?"

"Sure," Joe said, draping his arm around her shoulder. She leaned in closer to circle her arm around his waist. A soft night breeze lifted strands of hair and floated them near Joe's face, a trace of Wind Song perfume wafting to his nose. "I bet we're only a few decades away from a woman president."

Looking up at Joe in the moonlight, Kate asked, "But what about you, Joe Holly? Would you allow your wife to have a career?"

He pulled her tighter.

"Me?" he asked. "C'mon, don't I seem like a modern man? If my wife wants both a family and a career, then I want it. The added economic security of a two-income family is another benefit. Besides," Joe said, kissing her on top of the head, "working gives the woman something to do. I don't trust the mailmen and milkmen who would like nothing better than to entertain beautiful, lonely young housewives."

Kate giggled. "Oh, Mr. Postman, do you have a special delivery for me?" she asked in a flirty voice.

Joe laughed. "I need to stop by the lab; make sure the cleaning crew locked up all of the chemicals. We're nearby. You want to come with me?"

As the senior teaching assistant, Joe's duties included securing the lab. The administration was afraid an anti-war activist would try to break into the lab, steal flammable chemicals, then bomb the ROTC building.

"How could I resist such a romantic offer?" Kate asked.

When they got to the lab, Joe reached into his jacket and pulled out a key. He opened the aging door, and once they were inside, he locked it again. Joe disappeared into a back room. Kate, still in the main classroom, fidgeted with test tubes standing at attention in a rack.

When he reemerged, Joe said, "Everything is as it should be. Let's go."

Kate had a mischievous grin on her face. "Don't you want to stay in the lab a little while longer? You could combine two passions, science—and me."

A surge of desire washed over him at the sound of her seductive voice.

Kate stepped toward him, boldly pressing her body into his, and then she kissed him, a deep, full kiss. Joe tried to move back, create some space to separate their bodies, but he only managed to pull Kate along.

Her lips coaxed his mouth open. As her kisses grew more ardent, Joe's hands seemed to take on a life of their own. They'd kissed before, but always, Joe had kept the passion to a manageable level. But Kate's sexuality, the moonlight, the empty, locked room and the alcohol fueled an overpowering desire to possess her.

His hand moved over her chest, his fingers cupping the mounds of her breasts. Kate moaned softly and pressed her pelvis against his hips. Joe's hands wandered to Kate's back then down toward her buttocks and pulled her hips hard into his. She did not pull away.

Emboldened, Joe's fingers found their way underneath her shirt and up toward the back of her bra. Somehow, his fumbling hands managed to unclasp the hooks. She did not protest as he lifted her shirt over her head and slid the straps of her bra from her body.

Her round breasts were creamy and firm. Even in his daily fantasies about her body, he had not been able to conjure up such a lovely vision. When his fingertips brushed her nipples, they hardened instantly, telegraphing a wish to be kissed. When his lips took her hot, swollen flesh into his wet mouth, Kate groaned and arched her back, forcing her breasts further into his mouth.

Joe's hands, no longer under his control, grabbed the hem of her skirt and pulled up. Instead, of asking to stop, Kate instinctively parted her legs. His fingers brushed over the top of her underwear. Kate gasped but did not jerk away. Joe gazed at Kate's face; her eyes were closed as if in a trance. He slid his fingers under the elastic waistband of her panties and slipped them inside her.

"Oh, Joe," Kate cried out, tightening her arms around his neck, her knees weakening so that her body slid down to draw him deeper inside.

Hearing his name seemed to cut through the thick fog of lust and alcohol. Joe jerked away. "No, not like this."

"Don't stop," Kate begged, her hands tugging at the zipper of his pants.

"Kate, we can't do this."

"I want this," Kate said seductively. "I want you. Don't you want me?"

Joe's hands trembled. "Oh my God, Kate, I want you more than anything else in this whole world. But it isn't right. We've been drinking. I could never forgive myself for taking advantage of you."

"But you're not taking advantage of me if it is a mutual feeling," Kate said, pushing her tousled hair from her face. The hurt of rejection was already starting to seep into the face that had only moments before had been filled with passion.

"Here," Joe said, retrieving her bra. She began to put it on self-consciously. He turned away to find her sweater and handed it to her without looking as she re-dressed herself, straightened and smoothed her skirt.

"Are you okay?" Joe asked after she was dressed.

"Yeah, I'm fine," Kate said, refusing to match his stare.

"Kate, if I didn't care about you, I doubt I would have stopped."

Kate turned her back to him. "Come on, take me home."

Joe grabbed her shoulders and forced her to turn back around. "Kate, I love you. I love you more than anyone else, more than anything else. I've loved you for so long now. I love you so much that I want you to be able to give all of yourself to the man you marry. I hope that someday that man will be me."

The words continued to rush out despite Joe's cautious nature. "But if you don't love me, or if you decide I don't measure up—because believe me, you could have any man in the world you want—I don't want to take something right now that, in the future, you'll want to give to someone else. Kate, if I didn't love you, I would have had sex with you tonight, even though I could get you pregnant. I would've risked it. But I couldn't. I wouldn't do that to you. I wouldn't leave you with the chance that I cost you your dreams of a career. Don't you understand? I love you."

As soon as his confession had gushed from his lips, Joe regretted it. Kate said nothing for a few moments. Then tears began to form in the corners of her eyes. "Joe, I love you, too."

CHAPTER TWENTY-ONE

"I'm doing this for Kate, not for you," Rachel said, her teeth clenched. She opened her bottom desk drawer, threw in her beat-up old bag that doubled as a purse, and slammed it shut again. She took her lab coat off a hook in her small office and muttered, "Somebody needs to protect her from you."

"Kate should be here anytime now," Joe announced, ignoring Rachel's black mood. "I'll give you a choice; prepare a sample vial for Kate or oversee the photo shoot. I want to make sure we capture detailed images before she starts using the anti-wrinkle gel so we can carefully track her progress. I need unforgiving pictures of Kate's face. No soft lenses. No muted light. Just Kate—at her most raw and naked."

"I'm so mad right now I can't even be near Kate," Rachel fumed. "I can't believe she let you talk her into this. I'll work on the vial. You handle the photo session."

Kate bounded through the door. "Good morning!" she said.

Joe loved seeing his wife happy and couldn't resist bestowing a quick peck on her cheek. "Ready?"

Kate laughed. "Ready for a makeup-free photo shoot? Hi, Rachel!" Kate called out when she spotted the lab's second-in-command across the room.

Rachel nodded, put her lab glasses on, and turned her back.

"This way," Joe said to Kate, gesturing to the door leading out of the lab.

"What's the matter with Rachel?" Kate asked once they were in the hallway.

"Beats me," he lied as he led her toward the clean room. "Menopause moodiness, I think."

The clean room, a space devoid of furniture and stripped of visual distractions, was used by product evaluators and the photographers. With controlled lighting and no windows, the space removed visual cues that might influence decisions about the color of the latest lipstick or the hue of a new hair color.

"Are you prepared for this, Mrs. Holly?" asked the Galatea photographer who had been waiting for them to arrive.

"I guess so," Kate answered before adding, "I want you to know you are the only person who I'd ever let take a photo of me before I put on my makeup."

The photographer smiled. "You're gorgeous. Now, I need you to use this headband to pull the hair away from your face. Sit right here," he said, motioning to a bland wooden stool sitting in front of a plain white backdrop.

Joe studied Kate as she complied with the photographer's directions. Without her makeup and with her hairline exposed, the silver at her temples was noticeable. The skin around her jowls and the area underneath her chin were beginning to sag. She seemed tired. The unforgiving light and the absence of makeup aged Kate at least ten years, he thought.

The photographer snapped picture after picture, thrusting his lens directly into her face. "Mrs. Holly, look straight ahead. My camera loves you."

The session ended after thirty minutes. "I'm going to download these pictures onto a computer," the photographer announced after viewing the tiny images through his camera screen. "Joe, why don't you review them on the computer to make sure we've got everything we need?"

In the photographer's office, conveniently located adjacent to the clean room, Kate sat down on a guest chair where only the back of the computer's monitor was visible. Joe was relieved because she'd probably have been horrified if she saw the pictures. Every enlarged pore, every brown age spot, each wrinkle, pit, and groove on her face appeared. Joe thought back to the summer of 1969 and felt a pang of guilt over his young man's delight at watching her worship the sun.

Though it seemed like decades since she had truly laughed, the crow's feet around her eyes reminded him of the way she used to giggle—and how it made him feel.

The droop around her eyelids, the downward slopes of the wrinkles surrounding the corners of her mouth, reminded Joe of all the crying. The grief and mourning she endured when she found out Joe could not have children. It had taken years for her to come to terms with their childless lot in life—and his opposition to adoption. It was a loss, he knew, that she never fully came to terms with and the lines etched into her face reminded Joe of the terrible toll it took on their marriage.

The photographer interrupted Joe's reverie. "Do they look okay?"

Joe took off his glasses and nodded. "Yep, these will do nicely."

CHAPTER TWENTY-TWO

MARCH 1970

Once his love had been declared, Joe knew his future had changed. His advisor had recommended pursuing a job on the West Coast—a place experiencing explosive growth. Initially, Joe had been enthusiastic about the idea. But moving to California meant leaving Kate behind. With two years left before she would graduate, Joe might be replaced.

So instead, he chose to focus his search near home. While St. Louis lacked the glamour and energy of the West, there were opportunities in the Gateway City. Once he set his mind and effort into finding one, the offers materialized. By March of his senior year, Mallinckrodt Chemical Works and Galatea Cosmetics had made Joe an offer. For Joe, the Mallinckrodt job was more interesting. But the $5,000 signing bonus Galatea offered him would make it possible to further the plans he'd made for a life with Kate.

"I never imagined you'd be creating foundation and blush for women," Kate admitted when he announced he'd taken the job, without mentioning she was the primary reason for his choice.

He broke the news to her just before they were to meet Kate's parents for dinner. They'd come to town to celebrate Easter with Kate. Kate spent most of the day shopping with her mother. Joe volunteered to take Kate's dad to lunch at the Parkmoor.

With a roof the bright color of fresh squeezed orange juice, the diner was hard to miss. The fifty-year-old eatery served locals and students alike. Coffee, eggs, and sausage for breakfast, a greasy Kingburger topped with slaw, and an angel food cake sundae figured prominently on the menu.

While the two men had always gotten along, Joe felt like Kate's dad had never really taken a shine to him. For Kate's father, Harry was idea of the perfect man: handsome, athletic, and confident, not a scrawny, nerdy chemist fascinated with microscopic detail.

Something about Joe had indeed bothered Kate's father. "He's too accommodating," he told his wife on one occasion. "They never fight—and Kate always gets what she wants. No man can keep that up forever. Something is just not right."

Kate's mom had dismissed his unease. "You mean to tell me you object to Joe because he puts Kate on a pedestal and treats her like a queen?"

Her dad shrugged. "I guess. No female deserves to be on a pedestal—including Kate."

Kate's dad had never voiced his reservations to his daughter. More than likely, Joe was a passing phase. Once she came back home, she'd marry Harry. So, when Kate's father slid into a booth across from Joe, the only thing on his mind was food.

"Mr. Taylor, I've taken a job as an entry-level chemist at Galatea, a company here in St. Louis," Joe said after ordering.

"Pay well?" Kate's dad asked.

Joe nodded. "Yes, the position pays very well. They're even giving me a signing bonus."

"Make sure you save your money. Don't go spending it on fast cars and fancy clothes," Kate's dad advised.

"No, sir. Actually, I'd like to use part of the bonus to buy Kate an engagement ring," Joe admitted.

Kate's father gazed out the panoramic window, absorbing the information, before looking at Joe with a critical eye. "Does Kate know anything about this?"

"No, sir," Joe answered. "I wanted to talk to you first."

Kate's dad picked up a napkin and wiped an invisible crumb off the table. "I've got to be honest. I never saw you two as fitting well together. She's a small-town girl. You're big city. You're a nerd. Sure Kate's smart, but she's out of your league in the looks department. She's the sort of girl who moves back home, gets married, and runs the PTA." He paused. "Well, you can ask her, but there's a good chance she'll turn you down. But if she agrees to your proposal, I'm assuming she'll quit school?"

"No sir," Joe said. "I believe Kate should finish school."

Kate's dad folded his hands together and laid them on the table. "Well, son, I'll give you a choice. Again, assuming Kate says yes, I'll either pay for the wedding or for her schooling. I won't be paying her room and board anymore. And you realize a degree isn't much good to a married woman. It goes to waste once she stays home to raise the kids."

"A degree means a great deal to Kate. You continue paying for school. I'll pay for the wedding and our place to live."

CHAPTER TWENTY-THREE

"A dab is all you need," Joe explained to Kate as he twisted the white lid off a tiny glass jar, revealing a gel tinted the lightest shade of green. Suspended within the goo were tiny bubbles, round pockets of promise. When smoothed on her skin they would reinvigorate her face and turn back the clock to her most beautiful days.

Joe had decided that the first application of his new gel would be made at home. And despite his opposition to plastic surgery, the possibility of knocking a few years from Kate's appearance excited him, even more so once he realized how much she had aged while scrutinizing the "before" photos.

The couple stood together in the master bathroom. Kate faced the mirror mounted on the wall above the basin; Joe, a mere step behind. He was close enough to circle his arm around her waist to set the gel in front of her on the countertop, yet far enough away to study her reflection in the mirror.

As Kate peered into the jar, the corners of her mouth turned upward, her lips forming the shape of a reclining crescent moon. Her sky-blue eyes sparkled with the delight of a little girl slipping on her mother's best pair of red, high-heeled, slingback shoes.

She pushed a piece of frosted and bobbed hair behind a dainty ear, the thick diamond on her left hand catching the light and reflecting it back in the mirror. Despite the sunspots and blue-streaked veins visible beneath the surface of the skin, Joe thought her hands were still lovely.

"Go on, go on," Joe coaxed.

Kate giggled, cautiously placing her index finger in the jar. "Ooohh, this is cold—really cold. My fingertip is tingling," she said.

"Don't worry, that's to be expected. We found we had to keep the gel just above freezing. Otherwise it turns runny and the ingredients separate.

However, the ingredients need to work together at the same time to be most effective. Plus, higher temperatures trigger a small chemical reaction which produces heat. Unfortunately, it isn't only heat escaping, it is marula's active ingredient. Releasing it in the air does nothing. But when we put the cold gel on your face, the theory is that your body warms it up. Instead of releasing into the air, it seeps into your skin, attracted by the warm blood that flows through the vessels just underneath your skin. The tingling is the reaction. The longer you dally and keep the gel stuck to your finger, the younger your fingertip will look, but it also means there will be less to do the job on your face. So, get moving!"

Kate lifted her hand to her forehead, sweeping the gel across her furrowed wrinkles. The gel glimmered on her brow for a moment, creating a slight greenish sheen, before her skin absorbed the concoction. To Joe, it seemed Kate's aging skin thirsted for something cool to drink. Kate's previously pale white brow turned light pink after the marula gel was applied. "A reaction to the heat," Joe wrote in his notes.

"How are you feeling?" he asked Kate as he continued scribbling observations in his notebook.

"Um, I'm okay. I wasn't expecting the gel to feel this warm," Kate answered as she continued rubbing it into her face, concentrating on the crow's feet around her eyes. "Reminds me of menopausal hot flashes."

"Hmm, interesting," Joe said, continuing to write. "You handled that transition well, so, without a doubt, you'll be able to do this. The hot flashes of menopause signified an ending. This heat promises a new beginning."

Kate glanced at her husband in the mirror and smiled.

"Now remember, get the whole face, not just the problem spots," Joe reminded her.

"I thought you told me I didn't have any problem spots," she teased gently.

"Well, you don't. I should've called them the areas you perceive as a problem," he said, trying to backtrack out of the hole he'd stumbled into on accident.

Kate laughed. She was happy.

And so was he.

It wasn't every day that a man got the chance to reinvent his wife.

CHAPTER TWENTY-FOUR

APRIL 1970

Wide swaths of pinkish-purple and white blanketed Forest Park. It was April, and the trees were in full spring bloom. Pale yellow marigolds and blood red tulips had pushed their way up out of the dirt and opened themselves up to life.

Kate couldn't yet appreciate the brilliant colors; the blindfold made it impossible. Joe opened the passenger side car door. "Give me your hand," he said.

She reached out and asked warily: "You're not going to let me run into something or fall down, are you?"

"Kate, I would never let you fall," he promised. "Now, we're going to be walking downhill," he warned.

Kate leaned on Joe to help maintain her balance. "Where are you taking me?"

"You'll see in a few moments," Joe said playfully before stopping her. "I'm going to let go for just a moment. Don't move."

Kate giggled. "I'm at your mercy."

He set down the picnic basket he'd been carrying with his left hand, opened the flip top, and pulled out a dark green blanket which he spread at the foot of Art Hill. The St. Louis Art Museum sat like a crown at the top of the summit; the cool reflecting pool of the Grand Basin lay at the foot.

"Okay, I'm going to help you sit down," he said as he eased her onto the blanket. "Now, stretch out your feet. I'm going to take off your shoes."

Kate giggled. "My shoes? Are you nuts? Are you going to let me take off this blindfold or at least tell me where we are?"

"Just a few more minutes," Joe pleaded as he opened the picnic basket he had carefully packed with fresh strawberries, champagne, and two crystal wineglasses, an impulse purchase from Famous-Barr.

The item most important in the basket, though, sat in a black velvet box.

Without removing the blindfold, Joe began, "Kate, you know I love you more than anything or anyone else in the world, don't you?"

She turned her head toward the sound of his voice. "Yes, Joe. And I love you, too."

He untied the cloth knot and pulled the blindfold off. "Forest Park?" Kate said as she tried to place her surroundings.

"I thought that Forest Park, the place where we had our first date, was fitting," Joe said. Kneeling on one knee, he presented the unopened box to Kate.

"Kate, will you marry me?"

Kate's hand trembled as he placed the small package in her fingers. She opened the container and gasped. Inside, a one-carat, single round diamond with a gold band nestled in pink satin.

Kate exhaled. "Oh my gosh."

Joe was frozen, remaining on his knee.

"Well, what do you think?"

"Oh my goodness," Kate said as tears formed in her eyes. "This ring is beautiful—and huge!"

"You deserve it. Especially if you agree to marry me," Joe said. He had spent his entire signing bonus on the ring. If she said yes, he wanted a symbol that other men wouldn't miss: Kate was engaged—and her fiancé had money.

Kate removed the ring from the container and slipped it on her finger, the rays of the midday sun reflected in the pristine diamond.

"Yes, Joe," Kate exclaimed before wrapping her arms tightly around him. "Of course I'll marry you."

CHAPTER TWENTY-FIVE

For three days, the routine had been the same. Kate applied the gel in the evening while Joe took notes and quizzed her about every aspect of the experience. He wanted a full narrative, urging her to describe the sensations she experienced when her finger dipped into the gel, as she spread it across her face, and thirty minutes after the application.

For three days the answers had been the same. The cool gel tingled on the tip of her finger. As she rubbed it into her face and her skin absorbed the ingredients, the area warmed pleasantly. "When I apply the anti-wrinkle gel, I get an endorphin rush," Kate observed, "a wave of pleasure that begins at the back of my neck and flows throughout my body."

"That's the sensation I experienced the first time I spotted you walking across campus," Joe said, the image still fresh despite the passage of time. "How long does the rush last?"

On the first day, Kate reported the surge lingered for a full ten minutes. The second day, the feel-good wave lasted for twenty minutes, and by the third evening, it stayed around for half an hour.

"Even if this gel doesn't erase wrinkles, women will happily hand over their hard-earned money to experience this well-being," Kate said on the third evening, her expression placid and serene after the thirty minutes had passed.

The trial involved other daily rituals. At noon, Joe called Kate for a status report. Once again, he wanted her to describe any new or unusual sensations as well as any perceived changes in her skin. For three days, her answer had been the same. "No change."

On the fourth day of the experiment, Kate was the one who called at lunchtime.

"Joe," she said, "here's a nugget to enter into your little black lab book."

"What?" he asked. "Is everything okay?"

"I'm fantastic!" she exclaimed. "You see, I went to lunch early today. When I came back into the building after lunch, as I always do, I said hello to the receptionist. Today, she stopped me and asked, 'Kate, did you get your hair cut?' I answered no. In fact, I told her I was overdue. 'You sure you haven't tried a new hair color or style, perhaps?' No, I told her. 'Something's different,' she insisted. I told her nothing was different but asked what made her think such a thought. Guess what she said?" Kate asked.

"What?"

"She said I looked refreshed, like the people who come back from a two-week vacation in the Caribbean. 'Happy and rested'—those are her exact words.

"Joe," Kate announced, "your miracle gel is working—and people are noticing!"

Joe's stomach turned a quick flip before he brought his reaction under control. Kate had kept the experiment secret—it was one of the most important conditions contained in the consent form she signed before the experiment began. There were several reasons for the confidentiality. If people knew what was afoot, they might start looking for results. If there was any noticeable improvement—changes that people noticed—they wanted that to occur spontaneously. If Kate's coworkers were searching for improvements in her skin, differences in her face, they were bound to point them out, whether they were legitimate or not. Second, if the news leaked prematurely, Galatea's stock could skyrocket. If the project failed, stock prices would plummet.

"Well, Kate, I'm glad you reported the information, and I will write it down in the observations portion of my journal, but, well, that doesn't prove anything. You could simply be experiencing a placebo effect. You're expecting results, and so perhaps you're acting more confident, carrying yourself more attractively; trying less to fade into the woodwork because you feel beautiful."

"Don't be ridiculous. The only thing I've done differently is the gel," Kate said firmly.

"Look, Kate, when a couple is in the infatuation stage of a relationship, they beam even when they're not around each other. The hormones released because of the sexual attraction change their appearance. The hormones make both men and women more attractive."

Joe continued, "The only new change in the life of each person is the introduction of the other. The amount and kind of hormones coursing through their bodies alter their outlook on life. You might be experiencing a similar reaction. You're excited about the gel's potential, and your hormones are reacting to your optimism."

"Oh, you're such a wet blanket, such a stick in the mud." Kate pouted.

"Can't you ever let go and just be excited, Joe? For once?"

"Kate, I'm a scientist. I'm paid to be rational and thorough, to set aside my emotions and demand proof. I need more proof than the observation of a harried receptionist."

"Yeah, yeah, yeah," Kate said dismissively. "Well, I thought you should know. I've got to get back to work."

Even if the report was a false alarm, Joe was still pleased. The receptionist's comment rattled around in his head. And thoughts of the Caribbean had him wistfully remembering their honeymoon in Florida.

CHAPTER TWENTY-SIX

DECEMBER 1970

On Saturday, December 26, 1970, a light snowfall blanketed Graham Chapel, a Gothic Revival structure built in the early years of the twentieth century. The soft orange glow of candles warmed the double row of darkly stained wooden pews. Cool limestone and granite walls soared toward the heavens, the vertical lines interrupted by sheets of stained glass.

When they toured Graham Chapel, the stained glass window depicting the dedication of King Solomon's temple instantly captured Kate's imagination.

"*To make undying music in the world.*" Kate read aloud the description in the wood below the magnificent wall of colored glass. "That reminds me of our trip to the symphony. Don't you think this is a fitting place for us to exchange our vows?"

Joe smiled. "Sure," he said. He cared about the ceremony because Kate cared about it. He would have been just as happy going to the courthouse. The ritual didn't mean much to him because he already felt as though they were married.

The only difference between them and a married couple was consummation. Kate hinted she would welcome physical intimacy before their vows. For Joe, it was like opening presents on Christmas Eve instead of Christmas Day. He was a Christmas Day guy. But even he had neared his limits. They were catching a flight on TWA that afternoon for St. Augustine, Florida.

Kate had carefully concealed her wedding gown from Joe, so he was not prepared when she appeared. The simple satin gown, her hair swept up as it had been the night of the symphony, and a handmade veil that sent white tulle cascading down her back complemented and enhanced her beauty. Other gowns might have been more expensive or ornate, but they would have only detracted from her loveliness.

Because of the bargain Joe and Kate's father had struck, her family was not covering most of the wedding expenses. Therefore, the ceremony was planned with a tight budget, financed mostly by Joe's job at Galatea. Kate's mother, unhappy with the arrangement her husband made, defied her husband. She secretly shaved money from the family's grocery allowance and saved up the funds to purchase material for her daughter's gown, then sewed it using a McCall's pattern Kate chose. Kate's veil was fashioned after a Butterick pattern.

The small guest list included immediate family, a few friends, and professors, a best man and a maid of honor, and one of Joe's coworkers whom he had grown close to—the son of Galatea's founder, Stan Markowsky, and his young wife, Barbara.

"Do you take this man to be your lawful wedded husband?" the minister asked Kate.

Joe's knees locked, and his hands began to sweat. He could taste vomit in the back of his throat. *What if she says no?* he thought to himself. He steadied himself, bracing for his happiness to be ripped out from under him with one word, "No."

"I do," he heard Kate answer.

Instead of a cathartic release or a sigh of happiness, Joe's anxiety intensified. Instead of feeling relief, he worried, *For how long?*

CHAPTER TWENTY-SEVEN

On Day Six of the experiment, Kate stripped off her makeup and washed her face. Joe grabbed his digital camera and snapped photos before and after she applied the gel prototype. Although the digital photos would never rival the quality of those taken in the clean room at Galatea, they might still provide some rudimentary progress information.

Since the short trial began, before Kate applied the gel, her face appeared pale and saggy, her jowls dipped below the jawline. After she smothered her face in the concoction, Kate's complexion turned rosy, her gaunt cheeks as bright and full as those of a well-bundled baby on a cold winter's day.

By morning, though, the plump deposits had oozed out of her skin, gravity tugged at her jawline, and her pores expanded.

After Kate went to bed on the sixth night, Joe retreated to his home office.

He turned on his laptop and loaded the new photos into the computer. Then he called up two comparison pictures; one taken at Galatea before the first application and the image he'd shot that night before Kate applied the marula gel.

Joe placed the photos side-by-side on the screen. Kate's crow's feet appeared smaller, some of the deeper lines were less pronounced, and some of the fresher wrinkles had vanished.

He examined her cheeks. They appeared to be a half centimeter plumper. There was a slight rosiness to them as well, not the yellowish tinge from the first picture.

He closed the picture file, turned off the computer, and went to the bedroom, where he found Kate fast asleep. She stirred as he crawled under the covers. "Joe?" she mumbled in a slightly dreamy state.

"Yes, dear, go back to sleep," he said before brushing his lips lightly against her cheek.

CHAPTER TWENTY-EIGHT

DECEMBER 1970

Joe and Kate should have been exhausted by the time they reached the hotel in St. Augustine. They had married earlier in the day, had a brief reception, then headed for Lambert Airport. The 7 p.m. flight on TWA out of St. Louis had been delayed an hour because of the snow. Once they touched down in Jacksonville, they still had to pick up the rental car and drive forty miles.

When they finally reached the door to the honeymoon suite, it was just after midnight. Before Kate could enter, Joe stopped her. "Mrs. Holly, I believe it is customary for the groom to carry his bride across the threshold."

"Oh, Joe, you don't have to do this," Kate laughed as Joe swept her off her feet and walked into the room, setting her down near a silver bucket containing a bottle of chilled champagne.

"Shall I?" Joe asked as he lifted the champagne out of the bucket, causing the ice to shift loudly.

"You handle opening the bottle. I'll slip into something more comfortable," she said with a nervous giggle.

Kate grabbed her suitcase and disappeared into the bathroom.

Joe's hands trembled as he tried to remove the foil from the bottle's neck. He twisted the wire cage around the top, doing his best to remember how James Bond handled the task in the movies. He pushed the cork up with his thumbs, sending it flying across the room. A spout of bubbling alcohol rushed forth. Joe reached for the flutes. Without waiting for Kate, Joe gulped down one glass, hoping to steady his hands.

"Here I come," Kate called out as she opened the bathroom door. She'd freed her hair from the chignon, blonde waves spilling over her shoulders. Her sheer white silk nightgown failed to conceal her pink breasts. He'd only seen them once, the night in the lab when he had stopped things before they went too far.

His stare made Kate's cheeks flush with embarrassment. Her nipples strained against the cloth.

"Shall we toast?" she asked, reaching for the glass Joe held out for her.

"To my beautiful wife," Joe said.

They clinked glasses and drank.

"To a happy life, healthy children, and the chance to grow old together," Kate said.

Kate set her glass down and walked over to the bed. "Shall we?"

Once the light was off, Joe undressed and climbed under the covers. "Are you nervous?" he asked.

"A little," Kate admitted before timidly kissing him.

"Me too," he answered, drawing a sharp breath as Kate's hands touched his bare flesh.

CHAPTER TWENTY-NINE

The last two people Joe wanted to see were Huff and Stan, especially on a day Kate was scheduled for a photo shoot. Seven days had passed since the experiment began. As part of the progress evaluation, Kate would sit again for the camera, capturing her every wrinkle, dent, dimple, and pore.

Joe's amateur photos revealed an improvement, but he didn't trust his eyes or his camera work. Before he shared his suspicions with Rachel, Huff, Stan, even Kate, he wanted to examine the official images and obtain an independent review from the staff.

"Huff, Stan, good morning," Joe said, trying to hide his surprise as they walked into the white room. "What brings you here?"

"Rachel told us Kate would be coming in. We wanted to stop by and gauge for ourselves how the experiment is going."

"Fantastic," Joe lied. "I'm afraid these photo shoots are mundane. Why don't you both go on up to your offices? I'll send the images up as soon as we're done."

Stan pulled out a chair and sat down. "We're here, we might as well stay."

Rachel entered. "Where's Kate?"

"She's waiting in my office," he answered as he frowned at Rachel.

"Want me to go get her?" Rachel asked, ignoring his displeasure.

"No, I'll get her," Joe muttered before slipping out of the room.

When Joe found Kate, she had a Vogue magazine in one hand and a Starbucks coffee in the other. "You ready?" Kate asked as she stood up from the guest chair positioned across from Joe's desk.

He shut the door behind him. "Kate, I don't want you to be alarmed, but Rachel told Stan and Huff about today's photo shoot."

"It will be okay," Kate said as she placed the coffee and magazine on Joe's desk.

"Are you sure?" Joe asked, surprised by her calm indifference. "They're in the lab right now waiting to scrutinize and judge your appearance."

"Hmmm, men waiting to gaze at my face. I can think of worse things, Joe. In fact, a good number of years have passed since my face made people stop and stare. I think I'm going to enjoy this," Kate said, much too lighthearted and amused for Joe's liking.

Joe realized Kate didn't grasp the seriousness of the situation. "If they don't perceive any progress, the project might be scrapped. My career would come to an end."

She stepped lightly over to her husband, kissed his cheek, and said, "Don't worry so much, Joe," before heading to the white room.

"Wait a minute, Kate," Joe whispered, grasping her arm. "At least let me go first."

She stopped and let him pass.

Joe cleared his throat when he entered the white room, an unnecessary act because everyone's eyes were already trained on the door.

"Okay, Kate, why don't you come in?" Joe announced.

Stan, Huff, Rachel, and the photographer turned toward Kate. Joe studied Stan and Huff.

"Good morning, everyone," Kate said, entering the room full of confidence. "All this for me? I'm so flattered," she said, a sly but gracious grin on her face.

Stan and Huff froze. Neither man said a word for several seconds.

Stan was the first to break the spell. He walked over to Kate, took her by the hand, and kissed the back of it. "Breathtaking. You are stunning. I must confess, there was a time when you would walk into one of our company parties you'd make me catch my breath. It has been a long time since a woman has provoked that reaction. Today," he said, and his voice trailed off before recovering, "I never expected one of our products could make such a difference."

He likes it! Joe thought to himself.

Kate blushed, unconsciously adding to her appeal. "I'm lucky to be married to such a brilliant scientist," she said.

As if on cue, Huff remarked, "Joe, I was very skeptical about your so-called miracle cream. I'm not a doubter anymore."

Before heading back up to his executive suite, Huff said, "I never realized how attractive your wife is." He slapped Joe on the back and added, "You're a lucky man."

CHAPTER THIRTY

DECEMBER 1970

Inexperience combined with exhaustion from the wedding and the long flight meant that their first night together was clumsy. Though neither admitted it, it was rather disappointing. But the next morning, everything was different. They didn't emerge from the suite until midafternoon, when they decided to visit the Castillo de San Marcos, a stone fortress built by the Spanish between 1672 and 1765.

Perched on the edge of the Atlantic, Kate held Joe's hand as they walked along the fort's walls. The breeze picked up Kate's hair, brushing across Joe's freshly shaved face. She smelled of the ocean, Ivory soap, and sex, Joe thought to himself as he inhaled her scent.

"Think about all of the people before who stood on this spot or fought to claim it: Spanish soldiers, English pirates, Indians, and slaves," Kate said, her eyes searching the ocean's horizon.

Joe draped one arm around her shoulder. A sailboat passed, its white sails cupping the air. "We are all just a blip on history's screen. Shining for a moment, then gone."

Kate turned away from the water and faced her husband, circling her hands around his waist and resting her head on his chest. "I'm glad I get to spend my time with you. And even though we'll eventually exit this earth, at least we'll be able to leave the legacy of our own children behind. Thinking about creating something that is uniquely ours is very sexy, don't you think?"

Joe stroked her hair and kissed her head. "You hungry?"

"Famished!" Kate said with a sly smile. "I've worked up quite an appetite. Tonight, let's try to get to sleep a little early, okay? I've got a surprise for you tomorrow."

"What?" Joe asked.

"It's a surprise," Kate chided him. "Lights out early tonight, okay?"

Joe laughed. "The lights went out pretty early last night."

Kate slapped his shoulder playfully and blushed. "You know what I mean."

When the alarm went off the next morning at four, Joe groaned.

Kate reached over and smacked the clock, restoring quiet. "I told you last night we needed to go to sleep early," she reminded him, "but you wouldn't listen."

He pulled her warm, naked body close to him. "You can't blame me. My flesh is weak. Why don't you surprise me after lunch?"

"No, this is a very early morning surprise. Lunchtime will be too late," Kate cooed. "I figured you were going to need some convincing this morning, so I'm giving you a special wake-up call."

Kate's lips touched his chest, his stomach, his hip bones, then rested in a place they'd never ventured before.

She had Joe's attention. He groaned, his right hand slipping down to rest lightly on top of her head. "Whatever you say, dear," he whispered.

Kate insisted they stop by the check-in desk, where a picnic basket and a thermos of hot coffee waited. The bellhop handed Kate a map marked in red and they were on the road by five.

"What's this all about?" Joe asked, though he didn't much care. Happiness meant simply being with his beloved Kate.

"We're going to the beach to experience the sun rising over the ocean," Kate announced.

"Sunrise on the beach," Joe said. "What gave you the idea?"

"I was talking to the concierge yesterday, while you were grabbing a map to the Castillo de San Marcus. He's the one who mentioned it."

"Was he hitting on you?" Joe asked. He posed the question with a smile to mask the uneasy sensation in his gut.

"Oh, don't be silly," Kate said. "I'm on my honeymoon. C'mon, you drive, I'll read the map to you."

They headed north on Highway A1A. The road ran right along the highway, the ocean off to the right, a black space that contained rush of the morning tide. "It's as though we're driving on the edge of the world," Kate remarked.

Kate ran her fingers along the nape of Joe's neck as he guided the car in the dark. "Kate, if you keep doing that, I'm going to have to pull over the car," Joe warned.

"How about some coffee?" she suggested, pulling her hand away from her husband.

They shared a comfortable silence, savoring the scent of coffee mingling with the ocean breeze.

"Here's the turn-off!" Kate said enthusiastically.

Joe pulled into a little gravel lot. Already, a few fishermen were making their way to the beach.

Kate grabbed the beach blanket and picnic basket out of the back seat. "C'mon," she urged, giving her husband no time to dawdle.

The sky was shifting from black to smoky gray and continued to lighten, but the sun had not yet appeared.

Kate spread the turquoise blanket, trimmed in white, across the dark gray sand. She took off her shoes but left on her jacket. Her legs were bare, a pair of white shorts showing them off.

"We have muffins and orange juice," she announced.

"Does it have pulp?" Joe asked.

Kate poured a glass. "Yep."

"I hate pulp," Joe said grumpily.

"It is just bits of orange."

"I think pulp is disgusting. I can't stand the sensation of chunks sliding down my throat when I'm drinking liquid."

Kate shook her head. "Okay. No pulp. I'll remember that. Why don't you finish up the coffee instead?"

They sat in silence.

"Oh! Oh look, Joe!" Kate said, squeezing Joe's hand and pointing out to the horizon, the spot the earth ended.

A blazing reddish-orange ball emerged from the water; the crown of its head appeared, followed by the midsection, before the bottom wrestled free from the waves and the entire star climbed steadily up into the sky.

"It looked like the ocean just gave birth to the sun, don't you think?" Kate said, her arm wrapped around Joe's as they sat on the blanket.

"I've never seen a baby being born," Joe admitted, "but that sunrise was spectacular."

"One day, I'll be like the ocean, Joe, and I'll give you a son," Kate said confidently, her voice thick with emotion.

He pulled her close, pushed the hair away from the nape of her neck, and kissed it gently.

She wriggled away. "Not now, Joe. There are people around."

Kate jumped up and ran out to greet the low tide. Joe remained, lounging back on the blanket, watching his wife as she wormed her toes into the sand with foaming water swirling around her ankles.

He was content. He had the career he wanted and the woman he loved.

Would children come between them? he wondered as he watched her. They would be rivals for her attention, for her time, for her caresses, and for her breast. What if she were to die in childbirth? It could happen.

"Joe, Joe, come here!" Kate squealed. "Hurry up!"

In a few big strides he was at her side. About six inches in front of her was a crab, its pincers aimed at Kate as he scurried toward her. Half-screaming, half-laughing, Kate scrambled behind Joe and jumped on his back.

"It is probably more scared of you," Joe told her, yet even he took a few steps back as the crustacean marched toward him.

"Hey, you're a chicken, too!" Kate teased, still laughing.

"You're the one who climbed on my back," Joe said.

The crab must've been satisfied that they weren't going to eat him for lunch because it began burrowing its back legs into the sand and eventually disappeared under a blanket of gray.

Kate jumped off Joe's back and bent down to inspect the beach. "A sand dollar!" she announced triumphantly.

The shell was as big as the palm of her hand. She ran her fingers over the pattern etched into the beige disc. The giggling was gone. A more contemplative Kate stood on the beach.

"This is a sign, Joe," Kate said. "Finding a sand dollar is hard; finding one that is complete is even more difficult. Together, we're like a fully formed sand dollar, a rare find in this unforgiving world."

Joe circled his arms around Kate's waist and pulled her to him, pressing his mouth tenderly against hers.

"Kate, you are my ocean and my sun, my earth and my moon, my sunrise and my sunset. I loved you from the first moment I saw you. I love you even more now."

Kate's hair and skin glowed in the halo of the sunrise. "Take me back and make love to me," she demanded.

CHAPTER THIRTY-ONE

Joe watched as Kate picked through the organic apples in the produce section at the grocery store. Compared with the pesticide-laden variety, the organic ones were smaller, the red skin not quite so bright. When Kate grabbed an apple with a worm hole and put it in the plastic bag, Joe shuddered. She'd always been attentive to her diet but since the experiment began, she had been obsessed with organic fruits and vegetables.

"Don't you think going organic is a waste of money?" Joe asked.

"I don't want all of those chemicals inside my body," Kate said, "and we can afford them."

"The pesticides are safe," Joe said confidently. "They've been tested and retested. Besides, you're using chemicals on your face."

Kate sighed.

"Joe, let's not fight. I would prefer natural produce. Whatever is deemed safe today is declared dangerous tomorrow."

"Well, I don't want any of that crap," he said.

Tearing off a new produce bag, Kate said, "Fine, I'll get the usual stuff. Or better yet, why don't you select the apples yourself?"

"My job is to make the money to cover the cost of our provisions," Joe responded, "yours is to gather needed items from the grocery store and cook the meals."

Kate shoved waxy red apples in a bag. "You know, I earn a salary, too."

I make more," Joe reminded her.

He thought they'd settled this debate thirty years ago. A man had certain expectations from his wife and there were certain things a wife could expect from her husband. Kate's duties included grocery shopping, cooking, cleaning, and taking care of the laundry. Joe would make sure he was always employed, handle making repairs around the house, and make sure the cars were serviced by the mechanic.

But lately she seemed to be testing the rules, Joe thought, only they weren't subject to renegotiation this late in their married lives.

"We're out of orange juice," Joe reminded Kate.

As she pushed the cart past other shoppers, Joe couldn't help but notice men giving Kate a second glance, their double-takes reminding him of the reaction Stan and Huff had that morning in the lab.

"We're not doing anything this Saturday, are we?" Joe asked.

Kate shook her head. "No, I don't think so. Why?"

"Huff and Lauren want us to join them, something about going to a nightclub performance," Joe said. "What I really suspect is that Lauren wants to examine your face."

Kate shrugged. "It doesn't bother me. I would enjoy going out for a change. And this is a good opportunity for you to get a little face time with the boss." Kate smiled at her lame pun as she reached for the orange juice.

"What are you doing?" Joe asked. The edge in his voice caught the attention of the surrounding shoppers and they turned to look at him for a moment before resuming their duties. "You're picking juice with pulp in it. You know I hate pulp."

"Oh," Kate said. "I guess I was just distracted thinking about going out Saturday night. I don't have anything to wear."

CHAPTER THIRTY-TWO

APRIL 1971

The newlyweds lived in the apartment Joe had rented after graduation, only a few blocks from campus. The Holly apartment was on the third floor of a three-story brick building built in the 1920s. In the summer, the brick turned the space into an oven, and, with no air conditioning, they might possibly have to sleep outside on the balcony, the landlord had said. But that April, breezes flowed through the open window, cooling off the bedroom and forcing the couple to mute their lovemaking, which had dropped from two or three times a night to three times a week. While Kate was responsive in the bedroom, Joe thought she lagged in undertaking her other wifely duties.

"Kate, where's a clean shirt?" Joe asked one morning as he tried to get ready for work.

Kate, dark shadows ringing her eyes from staying up all night trying to master statistics, replied, "Shirt?"

"Yeah, you know, a clean shirt," Joe said as he started tossing clean clothes out of the closet.

"Joe, I've got a big test today. I haven't done any laundry for a few days."

"Kate, my job is to make money for us. Your job is to take care of the laundry, cook, go to the grocery store, and keep this place clean." Gesturing toward the stack of dishes piled high in the kitchen sink, Joe said, "You're failing miserably at all four parts of the job description."

Kate got up from the table. "C'mon, give me a break. This is the hardest class I've taken yet and I'm barely passing. I'll get the place cleaned up as soon as my test is over today."

"But that doesn't solve my laundry problem."

Kate culled through the dirty laundry basket, taking out Joe's dress shirts and sniffing them. "Here, wear this one today. There's no smell and no stains. Your lab coat is going to cover it up anyway."

"You expect me to wear a crumpled shirt?"

"I'll iron it right now," Kate said as she unfolded the ironing board.

Joe stomped out of the room. "I'm going to get some orange juice."

"Um, about the orange juice," Kate shouted as she waited for the iron to heat up, "all we have is the pulp orange juice."

"I gave you money yesterday with specific instructions to get the pulp-free juice," Joe said. The dirty dishes in the sink rattled when he slammed his empty glass down in the white Formica cabinet.

"Calm down, Joe, please," Kate said a she hastily pressed his shirt and handed it to him, still warm from the iron. "Let me help you with the buttons," she said as he slid his arms through the sleeves.

"Cut it out," Joe said, brushing her away. "I know that you're new to all this wife stuff, but you need to learn how to run a home. Perhaps I've been too lenient with you. I feel like I need to teach you a lesson."

He nudged her aside and picked up the statistics study guide. "I hate to do this," he said before he began ripping it into shreds.

"What are you doing? Stop! My formulas are written in the study guide. I need it for my test."

Joe walked into the bathroom, dumped the bits and pieces into the toilet, and flushed. "You need to start taking some responsibility," he declared.

"And another thing," he said, "you're still dressing like a single college girl. Don't you think that miniskirts and hot pants are inappropriate for a married woman?"

Kate said nothing.

"This week, I'd like you to get rid of all your go-go girl clothes and purchase something a little more suitable for the wife of a businessman."

The pictures on the wall shook as Joe slammed the door behind him. Through the open windows, he could hear her crying.

CHAPTER THIRTY-THREE

Kate was as giddy as a schoolgirl. Unfortunately, Joe thought, she was also dressed like one. "You're going to go meet Huff, Stan, and Lauren wearing that?" Joe said as Kate walked out of her closet.

Instead of her age-appropriate black slacks, tasteful-yet-conservative powder blue blouse, and a pair of black pumps, she had donned something Joe had never seen before: a pair of dark, slim-fitting jeans that hugged her hips and thighs and a clingy, ribbed sweater in black. Instead of a pair of diamond studs that seemed suitable for a woman of a certain age, large silver hoops dangled from her earlobes. On her feet, a pair of black leather boots with a high heel.

Kate stood in front of the mirror. "What's the matter?"

"Aren't you a little old for that getup?"

She furrowed her brow and examined her clothes. "The sales lady said it was perfect for what we had planned this evening and assured me I could pull off the look."

"Well, she must work on commission," Joe said, "because she lied."

"I'll go change," Kate volunteered, turning back toward the closet.

"No, you won't. We'll be late if you do. You're just going to have to live with the outfit for this evening—perhaps this will teach you a fashion lesson."

"Please, Joe," Kate pleaded.

"No, we've got to meet everyone in twenty minutes."

The club was in downtown Clayton, an inner suburb of St. Louis. A small, intimate venue, the tables were draped with white linens and surrounded the stage; a raised area for additional seating; wine, dinner, tapas.

"Oh my God, you look fantastic!" Lauren shouted when Kate and Joe appeared.

"Really?" Kate asked.

"Oh my gracious," Lauren said, "absolutely amazing. Huff told me I'd be surprised but didn't warn me to be stunned. You look so refreshed and alive. And your outfit! Who knew you had such a great figure? You really should show it off more often."

"You don't think I'm dressing outside my demographic?" Kate asked.

"Please forgive me for saying this," Lauren said, "you seemed a little worn out and, well, dowdy at our house party."

Lauren turned to Huff. "If your miracle gel can do this for Kate, you've got a blockbuster on your hands. When can I get my hands on this stuff? Every single one of my friends will be storming the cosmetic counter to buy your product. There is no question in my mind."

Huff smiled. "I must confess, one of the reasons I invited everyone here tonight was to gauge Lauren's opinion. She's our target market. She has a knack for knowing which products will sell and how strong the market demand will be. This is the most enthusiastic she's ever been."

Stan caught the last of the conversation. "So Lauren approves?"

"Wholeheartedly," Lauren said.

"Mrs. Holly, you are a vision," Stan said, taking Kate's hand in a grand fashion and kissing the top of it.

Heat radiated from Joe's earlobes. The fawning over Kate, Lauren's statement implying the anti-wrinkle gel was Huff's, infuriated him.

Goddammit, Joe thought to himself: This is my product. My experiment. My wife.

Fortunately, no one detected Joe's fury because they were too busy staring at Stan's companion, a woman in her mid-thirties with ample breasts. Clad in a short black leather skirt, it was impossible for anyone not to notice her long legs. Her hair was straight and hung halfway down her back, a trendy reddish color.

"This is Cece," Stan said. As Stan ticked off the names around the table, Cece gave a little wave and smoothed her straight brunette locks tinted with red highlights that flowed past her shoulders.

Stan sat down on one side of Kate, Joe on the other. Rather than speak to his date, Stan lavished his attention on Kate. Cece, unperturbed by the fact that Stan wasn't draped all over her, pulled a compact mirror out of her purse, fiddled with her bangs, and then smothered her lips in shiny gloss. At least she had the good sense to use one of Galatea's products, Joe thought.

The lights dimmed. A fit young man with dark hair, olive skin, and thin build picked up an acoustic guitar and began to tune it. The rest of his band appeared and took up their instruments.

"This guy is great," Huff said. "He's got a mellow sound that I think you'll like. His lyrics alternate between Spanish and English."

"Well, if he sings as good as he looks, I guess we're in for a treat," Kate said with a smile.

Joe nudged Kate with his foot, sure he'd noticed the singer stifle a smile after her remark. Didn't she realize they were close to the stage? She's making such a fool of herself," Joe thought to himself.

The music began. Joe watched as Kate's face warmed, a reaction to the wine and the romantic rhythms. He wasn't the only one who noticed. Stan could barely take his eyes off Kate.

CHAPTER THIRTY-FOUR

MARCH 1972

"What would you like for graduation?" Joe asked Kate as she placed a plate of spaghetti before him. Her cooking still wasn't great, but after fifteen months of marriage, she was improving.

"Oh, I don't need anything," Kate answered as she pulled up a chair to the tiny two-person card table.

"Any garlic bread?" Joe asked.

Kate motioned to the basket on the table covered by a white linen napkin, a wedding present. "Kate, you shouldn't use these linen napkins to cover greasy bread. The stains might not come out."

Kate shrugged, picked up her fork, and twirled the noodles with the tines. "I forgot. Sorry."

"Treat the stain before you throw the napkin into the washing machine," Joe advised. "Now, back to the question of an appropriate present. Don't you want to mark the occasion? It isn't every day you graduate from college with summa cum laude honors."

"There is something I'd like for graduation," Kate said. Setting her fork down, she reached across the table for Joe's hand. "Joe, why don't we start a family?"

He pulled his hand away. "A baby? Now? Honestly, do you think this is a good time? Look around. We're still living in a crummy, one-bedroom apartment with barely enough room for the two of us, let alone a baby with all of the baggage they bring with them."

Kate's shoulders drooped.

"Besides," Joe continued, "don't you want to work for a while? The money you make can help us set aside a down payment on a proper house faster than on my salary alone."

Kate pushed her plate away. "Joe, you know I've been applying for jobs. So far, the only positions with openings are secretarial. Once they find out that I'm married, they tell me I'll just end up getting pregnant and quitting. What's the use?"

"Tell them you can't have kids," Joe suggested.

"What, lie?" Kate asked.

"I wouldn't call it a lie. After all, there won't be any kids until there's a house," Joe reasoned.

"I'm uncomfortable with being dishonest," Kate admitted.

"Kate, do you want a family?"

She nodded.

"Do you want to be able to buy the house we need to start having a family? A home with a backyard, a white picket fence, and a nursery?"

Kate sighed. "Yes."

"Do you think it is fair that the men who are graduating with a business degree, whose grades are inferior to yours, already have jobs lined up?"

"No, I don't."

"Then why worry about lying to the same employers who aren't treating you like they're treating the men in your class? They don't deserve your honesty," Joe said. "Sometimes, the end justifies the means."

CHAPTER THIRTY-FIVE

Kate walked into the bedroom wearing a long silk nightgown. The neckline plunged down between her breasts and clung gently to her hips. She'd had a few glasses of wine at the nightclub, but it wasn't alcohol to blame for her boldness. The reaction she'd teased from Stan during the evening left her relishing her feminine power.

"Are you lonely?" Kate asked in sing-song voice. She lifted the covers on her side of the bed, crawled in, then laid her head on Joe's shoulder, sliding a hand between the buttons of his flannel pajama top.

"Need some attention?" she cooed, pressing her body against his.

"If there was an attention bank, you would have certainly emptied all accounts tonight," Joe said. "Frankly, Kate, I'm embarrassed. You acted like a five-year-old parading out in front of adults in a new dress looking for applause."

"You're exaggerating," Kate said, moving her hand down to his waist. She kissed his neck and began tugging on the buttons of his pajama trousers.

Joe grabbed her hand. "Don't."

"For God's sake, what's with you?" Kate asked, pulling away from him. "You have everything you ever wanted, Joe Holly. Why are you so insecure? Your invention is a success. You've proved your worth at Galatea. I didn't go through with plastic surgery.

"Why can't you be happy?" she asked before throwing aside the covers and stomping away to sleep in the guest bedroom.

CHAPTER THIRTY-SIX

MAY 1972

It was a week before graduation and Kate still hadn't landed a job. She'd scoured the classified ads every day, visited the campus career services office so often she was on a first-name basis with everyone who worked there, and she dutifully passed out her résumé at all the campus job fairs.

"This is hopeless," Kate said one evening after Joe returned home from work. She stretched out on the couch, the news blaring on the black-and-white television set. "What? Vietnam?" Joe asked as he set his briefcase down by the front door and loosened his tie.

"Well, that too," Kate said. "No, I'm talking about my job prospects. I can't seem to get past the first interview. As soon as they notice my wedding ring, the only questions I'm asked pertain to you, our marriage, and family plans."

"Are you telling them you can't have children?" Joe asked.

"Yes, I lie," Kate admitted. "Can you believe that one of the guys from my finance study group, someone I helped get through the class, was just offered a management position? Here I am, near the very top of my class, and I can't even get hired on as a secretary. My male classmates are being asked about their goals, their ambitions, their academic careers. Me? I field questions like, 'What's a pretty girl like you doing majoring in business?' A few of my interviewers told me flat out that I was too attractive. I'd be a distraction for the men in the office."

Joe sat down next to his wife and placed his hand on her knee. "I'm not going to let you give up. You're much too smart and talented to sit at home and do nothing all day but dust shelves. You just need a chance and you'll shine."

"But I can't even get my foot near the door," Kate said. "Equality is a myth. No matter how smart, how educated, or how hardworking we are, women, especially married women, won't be admitted into the business world."

"I have a surprise for you," Joe said. "I've been quietly asking around about openings on your behalf. Galatea won't hire you because you're my wife and they have a strict nepotism policy. But Stan Markowsky has a friend who runs the personnel department at King Industries. They're looking for temporary secretaries. I talked to Stan's friend on the phone today and he offered you one of the slots. He said that if you do well as a temp, they'll probably get an offer in something that isn't clerical. You just need to prove yourself."

"Without an interview or submitting a résumé, they're offering me a temp job?" Kate asked.

"Yep," Joe said. "It is temporary, so the interview process isn't quite as strenuous. Plus, as you'll find out once you shed the life of an academic, sometimes it is who you know, not what."

Kate leaned over and gave him an affectionate kiss on the cheek. "Thank you."

"Hey, I'll always be here for you," Joe answered.

CHAPTER THIRTY-SEVEN

Joe woke to the slamming of cabinets and the clanking of pots. Cleaning the kitchen was Kate's preferred method for releasing rage; wiping away streaks of grease and grimy fingerprints was a form of therapy for her. After Joe rejected her the night before, she made it clear she was upset—as if his night alone in their bed wasn't his first clue.

Joe slid his feet into the slippers near the bed.

"Good morning," he said, ignoring her tirade.

Three furious squirts of cleaning solution sprayed across onto the countertop. Kate's body blocked his access to the cabinet containing the breakfast dishes.

"Excuse me," Joe said, "I'd like to grab a bowl for my cereal."

She continued without speaking, but now she cut off his access to the cupboard with the glassware. Every morning he followed the same routine: a bowl for his Cheerios; a glass for his juice, a mug for his coffee, then a spoon from the silverware drawer.

"Excuse me, but I need to get my juice glass," Joe said.

Kate slammed the kitchen cleaner, along with the rag, down on the counter, the plastic container making a dull thud, before she stomped out of the room.

Even though it was the weekend, he'd eat his breakfast and go into the office. She's only making herself miserable, he thought as he reached inside the fridge for his orange juice.

"Kate!" he shouted. No answer. "Kate," he yelled again. No response.

Joe picked up the orange juice and went searching for his wife. He found her in the master bedroom making up the bed.

"Kate!" he yelled.

Her body spasmed, her arms jerked reflexively into the air, and her fingers—which had only a moment before been clutching a clean pillow case—straightened, sending the entire pillow into the air. "Good grief, you almost gave me a stroke," Kate said.

"What is this?" he asked, thrusting the sun-colored orange juice container in her face.

She folded her arms across her chest. "Looks to me like a carton of orange juice. Now, if you would please leave me alone, I'd like to finish cleaning, a chore you don't seem to do around here very often."

"Dear," he said in the most patronizing tone he could muster, "look closely. Don't you see any problem with this container?"

Her icy gaze remained fixed on his face. "The only problem I see is with the man holding the container."

Joe's mouth gaped. Kate never challenged him head on. Her preferred fighting method was passive aggressiveness.

"This orange juice has pulp! You know how much I hate pulp and you know how much I enjoy a glass of orange juice every morning. Is it too much to ask for a glass of orange juice without chunks of flesh floating in the glass? Did you do this just to spite me?" he asked, his voice rising in rage.

"Gee, I wish I could say I bought it for that very reason," Kate said, her voice full of sugary sarcasm. "The truth is I didn't think it was such a big deal. Pulp, no pulp, who cares?"

"I do!" Joe shouted.

"Hmmm, well, if you care so much, why don't you get off your lazy ass and go to the grocery store?" Kate said, brushing past her husband.

He followed her out of the room. "You've always done the grocery shopping. That's your job."

"Well, I don't like grocery shopping. You know what else I don't like doing? I don't like straightening up the house after you. I don't like washing your clothes. I don't like putting them away. I don't like making your food. And I certainly don't like supplying the constant massaging that your ego demands. Why I did these things for you in the past is beyond me, but some things are going to change around here," Kate said defiantly as she reached for her purse and car keys.

"Where are you going?" he asked.

"I'm going out. Alone."

"Oh no, no you are not. You aren't walking away from this fight and I'll be damned if I'm going to tolerate ultimatums."

Joe stood before the front door, attempting to block it.

"Joe, you better move away from that door," Kate said, her voice even and firm.

"No."

"I said you better move," Kate repeated. Her eyes were ice cold.
"Or what?"
"Move now, let me out, and I will come home. Block my way and once I do finally set foot outside this house, I vow I'm not coming back."

Kate nudged Joe aside. He didn't resist.

CHAPTER THIRTY-EIGHT

SEPTEMBER 1973

King Industries' personnel office realized almost at once that Kate's abilities exceeded those needed in the typing pool. When a single secretary got pregnant and the father turned out to be her married boss, a permanent secretarial position opened up. Management decided a married woman would be a better choice for the philandering executive. Kate was offered the job immediately after her predecessor was fired. But the executive, of course, kept his job. Kate wasn't thrilled about remaining secretarial, but it was one step up. She was determined to continue climbing.

Kate's salary and Joe's raises allowed the couple to move out of their apartment and into a proper house, a red-brick, two-story home in the inner suburb of Clayton built in the 1940s. The windows were drafty, and the wooden floors were little bit warped, but Kate loved the stained glass windows, the arched doorways, and the black-and-white ceramic tiles on the kitchen floor. The home's one bathroom was still in good shape; tiny little tan one-inch tiles that had been laid out on the floor gave the place in old-fashioned feel. A few of the ceramic tiles had popped out, but a little grout and glue would make things right.

The living room and dining room, separated by French glass doors, were on the first floor. A mud room off the kitchen led to a small backyard and beyond that, a detached garage.

The oak staircase leading to the second floor contained two square landings for right turns; three steps to the first landing, another eight steps to the second landing, then three more steps to the top. The master bedroom and two smaller rooms that could easily have been mistaken for large walk-in closets occupied the second floor. Kate suggested making one an office and the other, a nursery.

The house also had a limestone basement. It was a great place for their first washer and dryer. A new boiler had been put in for the radiator heat. One basement door led outside, a few steps up and into the backyard.

Joe and Kate agreed the house somehow suited them—a solid, warm structure ideal for building a family.

"Joe, I've done everything you asked, and I haven't complained—well, I haven't complained too much," Kate said one Saturday morning after they'd moved into their home. "I'm ready for a baby."

They were lounging in bed, Kate's head resting in the crook of Joe's arm, her hand holding his hand, their fingers laced together tightly.

Before Kate spoke, Joe had been floating in the drowsy space between slumber and wakefulness, relishing the cool sheets against his skin and the soft heat from Kate's body. Kate broke the spell the instant she broached the subject of babies.

"I would prefer we waited," Joe answered. "Our lives right now are perfect. If we had a child there would be no way we'd be lying in bed enjoying this moment. Instead, you'd be changing diapers and warming bottles. There would be no more Friday night movies or restaurant dinners. We would become hostages in our home—slaves to the whims of an infant tyrant."

"How can you say such things? This is our unborn child we're talking about, half of me, half of you. A baby isn't all drudgery and work. What could be more heavenly than a fat little bundle sitting here between us, smiling and giggling as we kissed her toes or nibbled his fingers? What about the joy of receiving big, sloppy, open-mouthed kisses from a toddler? What about going to Little League games or Christmas musicals?"

Joe sighed. "You're ignoring the stress and tension a baby brings to any relationship. It happens to everyone we know. All my coworkers talk about is how they're ignored by their wives after a baby is born. The baby hoards all a mother's love and drains the family of money. No wonder so many of those men were having affairs with their secretaries."

Kate sat up. "Was it a lie then? Was it all a lie?"

Joe lifted himself up onto the backs of his elbows, his body still outstretched across the bed. "What lie? I've never lied to you."

"That's how it seems to me," Kate answered angrily. "When we were dating, when we were students at Wash U, you told me you couldn't wait to have kids, you loved kids, and when you asked me to marry you, you promised one day we'd be a family."

"But we are a family," Joe argued.

"When you said we'd be a family, you were referring to children. Are you going to keep your promise?"

Joe knew he'd run out of excuses. He didn't have any more good reasons left for delaying a family.

"Geez, you're getting awfully worked up. I just wanted to make sure that you are ready for the responsibility of motherhood, the changes our lives will experience." Joe sat up on the bed and rubbed her arm. "Okay, if you're ready then so am I."

Tears welled up in Kate's eyes. "I knew you wouldn't let me down."

She leaned toward Joe, cupping his face with one of her hands, and pulled him to her for a passionate kiss.

CHAPTER THIRTY-NINE

One, two, three, then four hours passed after Kate stormed out of the house following the argument over orange juice. Tired of waiting for her to return home, Joe left for the lab, the one place where natural law still ruled.

To Joe, Kate seemed determined to rewrite the decades-old rules governing their relationship; the unwritten guidelines that spelled out the division of labor, their roles within the marriage. The rules even controlled how they fought. And now, it was as if they were reenacting the early days of their marriage, only this time without the benefit of a powerful sexual bond that smoothed over the rough spots.

It isn't just Kate's face that seems to be going back in time, Joe thought as he finished up paperwork in his office, her personality is also on rewind.

He tried calling Kate's cell phone in the afternoon, but he was sent straight to voicemail. She didn't answer at home either. He fought the urge to get in the car and go searching for her. The best approach to bring Kate back under control, Joe thought, was to feign indifference.

Joe remained in the lab until eight that evening before making his way home. As he pulled into the driveway, Joe was relieved to see Kate's car.

When he opened the front door, Joe was greeted by rows of boxes filled with their household items.

"Kate?" Joe called out.

She didn't answer. Joe wandered into the kitchen where he found Kate, her head stuck deep inside a kitchen cabinet.

"What in the world are you doing?" he asked.

Kate jumped, hitting her head. "How about a little warning?" she said, rubbing the crown of her skull as she emerged from inside the cabinet.

Joe ignored her. "What are you doing?"

"I'm purging junk," Kate said.

Although he was relieved to hear the items in the hallway weren't moving boxes, it bothered him to think she was already over their earlier fight. Usually, she fretted.

"How long have you been at this?" Joe asked.

"I don't know, since one?" Kate answered, resuming her work.

"I tried calling you. You didn't answer."

"I didn't want to talk to you," Kate responded.

Joe stammered. "How immature."

"I disagree," Kate replied. "You're the jerk, not me. I've got nothing to apologize for. Until you're ready to take some responsibility for your own actions, there's nothing to discuss."

Joe stared at Kate, searching for the right response. "What is the matter with you? You never talk to me like this."

Kate shrugged. "Joe Holly, I should have stood up for myself a long time ago."

She walked over to one of the empty boxes and began filling them with items she wanted to give away.

"Why are you getting rid of those?" Joe asked, his voice rising in pitch as Kate placed two wineglasses into the donation box.

"I told you. I'm getting rid of junk," Kate said.

"But that's not junk," Joe said, pointing to the wineglasses in the box.

"Sure it is. The glass is cheap. There's only two. Judging by all of the accumulated dust, they haven't been used in years."

Joe shook his head. "Don't you remember? We plan to use them on our fiftieth wedding anniversary."

"Why? We own several pieces of nice crystal."

"Don't you remember?" Joe asked.

Kate shrugged her shoulders. "Remember what?"

Joe shook his head. "Are you sure you're all right?"

"Never felt better."

"I think you need to see a doctor. I'm worried you might have had a silent stroke. Or perhaps you bumped your head harder than I realized."

"Oh, don't be silly. All this over a couple of old, cheap glasses?"

"Those aren't old cheap glasses. They're the ones we drank out of the day I proposed to you at Forest Park. Remember? The picnic basket lunch at the Grand Basin? You said yes. I opened the wine and we drank out of these glasses. I bought them at Famous-Barr for the occasion."

Kate shook her head. "I don't remember."

CHAPTER FORTY

APRIL 1974

After Joe agreed to start a family, the quest for a baby dominated Kate's life. Her efforts at seduction were creative, Joe had to admit. One evening, to spice things up, Kate came out of the bathroom wearing a racy black merry widow outfit. Another night, she wore a red teddy. The parade of sexy outfits also included a white silk dress-like evening gown that looked like something from a 1940s movie and, in a nod to Playboy and Hugh Hefner, she even tried bunny ears and a cotton tail.

Initially, Joe couldn't wait to get home from work, just to see what Kate had cooked up for the bedroom. But that soon changed. Four months of trying, without success, had cast a bit of a cloud over their procreation efforts. Each time her period arrived, it signaled failure. After six months, sex became a chore Joe resented. Kate was trying to conquer motherhood with sheer force of will. It was no longer an act of love with a partner. For Joe, it was just a physical act with a remote, distant, and sad wife.

Sex was no longer a way to connect. Instead, it was tearing their relationship apart.

After ten months of effort, if they didn't move beyond the pursuit of parenthood, Kate's spirit would break; their marriage nothing but a shell, Joe concluded.

One evening, as Kate washed the dinner dishes, Joe waded into the question of children.

"Maybe we should postpone our efforts to start a family," Joe suggested.

"Postpone?" Kate asked. "Joe, you agreed to try."

"We've been trying. Maybe we're trying too hard," Joe said.

"I'm not getting any younger," Kate replied. "The older I get, the harder it will be for us to start a family."

"I'm afraid this pursuit is taking a toll on you mentally," Joe said.

"Well, can't you understand why?" Kate asked. "I'm afraid that I can't have kids, that I'm defective."

"Don't say anything so ridiculous," Joe said. "You're the perfect woman, with or without children."

"You do think there's something wrong with me!" she snapped.

"No, of course not," Joe said. "Maybe I'm the one throwing a wrinkle into your plans."

Tears welled up in the corners of Kate's eyes.

"Listen to me," he said, wrapping his hands around her upper arms, barely able to tolerate her tears. "Listen to me," he repeated.

Kate looked at him with red-rimmed eyes, her lips pursed together to stifle a sob.

"Listen to me," he said again in a softer tone, still holding her close. "Where is the woman who doesn't give up? Where is the woman who always finds an answer? Why don't we see a doctor? I'm sure nothing is wrong. If the doctor does find something amiss, I'm sure he can correct the problem. Wouldn't you rather take the steps to find out?"

Joe felt the tense muscles in Kate's back relax. He pulled her even tighter. She didn't resist his embrace. Kate sighed then laid her head on his shoulder.

"You're right, Joe," she sniffed. "We need to visit the doctor and find out what is going on, why we can't have a family."

"There are lots of specialists out there we can consult," Joe volunteered.

"No, I want to start with Dr. Mitchell," she said resolutely.

Robert Mitchell was their family doctor. He was the last man Joe wanted for a fertility exam, but he didn't dare argue with Kate about the choice, now that he'd finally calmed her down.

"Okay," Joe said. "Let me handle setting up the appointment with Dr. Mitchell. Tonight, let's sleep."

CHAPTER FORTY-ONE

"Jesus, Joe, what the hell happened this weekend?" Rachel asked as soon as her boss walked into the lab Monday morning. She'd been lying in wait and launched a barrage of questions before Joe had time to set down his briefcase.

Unwilling to admit that the list of things that had gone wrong was extensive, he replied, "What you mean?"

"Huff called me this weekend and quizzed me about our miracle cream," Rachel said.

"Why?" Joe asked, wondering why Huff hadn't bothered to ask him. He had plenty of opportunities to do so on Saturday night.

"Kate made quite an impression on Lauren. Once she saw what our miracle gel had done for Kate, I guess Lauren couldn't shut up," Rachel said. "According to Huff, Lauren not only raved about the results all the way home, she's lobbying to be added to the trial."

Joe groaned. "Perfect. Just what we need, the CEO's wife involved in an experimental trial."

"Almost as bad as the chief researcher's wife volunteering to be the test subject, wouldn't you say?" Rachel retorted.

"We've been through this a million times," Joe said, "We chose Kate so she would stop pressing for plastic surgery. Lauren isn't threatening to go under the knife. Furthermore, Kate is a suitable candidate for testing because the aging process has impacted her to a greater degree. Lauren is what, in her late thirties, at most? She's also from a different generation than Kate. She's probably been careful with the sun and has reaped the benefits of Botox and chemical peels."

Joe continued, "With Lauren's preemptive intervention, she would not give us the same kind of unadulterated results as Kate."

"You can rationalize using Kate as a subject all day, but the news gets worse," Rachel said.

"What do you mean?" Joe asked.

"In her excited state, well, Lauren told several of her friends."

"Wait a minute. She blabbed about our top-secret project?"

Rachel nodded.

Joe clenched his jaw, the muscles of his chest tightening. "We haven't disclosed this to our shareholders or to the public. Does she realize she provided insider information? If friends go out and buy Galatea stock based upon what Lauren said, my god, she could face criminal charges."

Rachel said, "Lauren didn't think through the consequences. But Huff has."

"I guess he's already called in the lawyers to talk about making the research public," Joe guessed.

"If I were a betting woman—which I'm not because science says the odds are against me—but if I were, I'd say you're right."

Joe loosened his tie and unfastened his top button.

"Are you okay?"

"I'm roasting in here. Did someone turn up the heat?"

"The temperature is fine. Your face is ash white," Rachel remarked. "We can talk about the rest later."

"Go ahead—you may as well turn a bad day into a thoroughly rotten one," Joe said.

"Kate came by my place this weekend. She was an absolute wreck; mumbling something about a fight."

"It was nothing."

"I don't believe you, Joe. In all the years I've known you both, Kate has never ever, not once, showed up on my doorstep in tears."

Joe opened his briefcase, an attempt to create a diversion before answering Rachel's questions. "Come on, Joe, you can talk to me."

Joe exhaled, not realizing he'd been holding his breath. "I'm not sure what's going on, Rachel. Kate is doing things she hasn't done since we were newlyweds. It's like she wants to rewrite the relationship rules we established soon after we married.

"Is that such a bad thing, Joe? Perhaps the changes she's experienced physically triggered new emotional growth. Now she wants your relationship to do the same," Rachel said as she sat down next to him, leaning her elbows on the table.

"Insanity, not maturity, is how I label her behavior," Joe said.

"You're exaggerating," Rachel answered.

"Am I? When a child touches a hot stove and burns himself and then intentionally touches it again, we'd say there was something wrong with that child. If someone was to nearly die after eating a poisonous plant and then he goes out searching for the plant to eat it again, we'd conclude he was mentally ill."

Joe continued, "For Kate to resurrect old fights we resolved decades ago; wouldn't you say that was a similar form of foolishness or carelessness? Maybe even mental illness?"

Rachel frowned. "No. Your view of an ideal marital relationship is a dead one—or at least one that's been on life support for some time."

"You've never been married. You can't fully understand what I'm saying," Joe said. "In some ways, your life has been easier."

"Unbelievable," Rachel said, crossing her arms tightly across her chest. "For so long, you've lived for only three things—satisfying your needs, satisfying your wants, satisfying your desires. You have no empathy. You are incapable of suspending your own ego for just a moment; to slip into someone else's skin and get a look at life from their point of view."

"Rachel, are you going through some sort of bad menopause flashback?"

"Don't deflect the focus," Rachel remarked pointedly. "You said Kate is acting strangely. As a scientist, your duty is to explore the question of whether our miracle cream is causing a physical impairment, a defect that manifests itself through her personality."

"However, the issue creates a new host of problems neither one of us is prepared to handle," Joe argued. "Kate would need to submit to a battery of tests. And if everything comes back normal, we'll have delayed the project for nothing. The worst-case scenario is that the entire project gets derailed. If Huff goes public with the project, and it fails, Galatea's stock price will take a beating."

"This is Kate we're talking about, not a lab rat," Rachel answered. "You would never forgive yourself if something happened to her."

"But why shut down the most important research project of our collective careers if it turns out she's okay?" Joe asked.

Rachel said nothing. Joe picked up an empty test tube, studied it for a moment, then asked, "Assuming we take some sort of step, what should it be? Suspend the trial? Take Kate to a psychologist? Force her to undergo a physical examination to make sure she hasn't had a stroke? Any one of these steps will trigger the need to disclose them to Huff and Stan."

Rachel added, "You're forgetting the public disclosure wrinkle. If Galatea announces the Phoenix Project publicly, as part of a financial disclosure, if you keep something hidden that should have been revealed, something that could impact the stock price, more insider trading issues."

Joe had turned his back to Rachel and began pacing the room. How in the world had he gotten himself into such a fix? How in the world was he going to get himself out—with his marriage and career intact? A few days ago, Joe stood on the summit of success: the inventor of a revolutionary product, the beautiful woman he loved at his side. Now, the product, his miracle cream, possessed the power to end his career—and his marital stability.

"We're scientists," Joe said. "I suggest we do what scientists do best. Let's observe her for a week, watch for behaviors that are odd or unusual for Kate. At the end of one week, we'll compare notes. If one of us thinks there is a problem, then I'll make an appointment with the doctor. Is that fair?"

Rachel warned, "There's no way you're going to be able to keep a lid on this for a week."

CHAPTER FORTY-TWO

MAY 1974

Dr. Mitchell extended a hand across a desk piled high with manila folders, each one containing a patient's detailed medical history. "Mr. Holly, good to see you," he said as the young man entered the office.

Mitchell, a family practitioner approaching sixty, had inherited the practice from the physician he went to work for after serving his residency at Washington University.

"How's Kate?" Dr. Mitchell asked.

"She's good," Joe answered reflexively. Dr. Mitchell had been Joe's physician since childhood. Once Joe and Kate got engaged, Kate decided to switch to a St. Louis doctor. Joe referred her to Mitchell. "Actually, that isn't true. She's in a bad way. Kate is the reason I'm here today."

I'm sorry to hear that," Dr. Mitchell said as he folded his hands together and leaned forward on his desk. "What's the matter?"

Joe decided that being cryptic and evasive would just prolong the uncomfortable meeting, so he plunged right in. "Kate needs to come in for a fertility exam. She can't get pregnant."

Mitchell pursed his lips. "You didn't tell her?"

Joe ignored the question. "We'll be coming in together for testing. But I wanted to make sure—"

Mitchell interrupted. "You want to be certain I will honor physician-patient confidentiality."

Mitchell looked out the window for a moment before answering. "Joe, I took an oath a very long time ago. I intend to go to my grave keeping it. However, I've known you since you were in cloth diapers fastened together with pins. I feel compelled to repeat the advice I gave you a few years ago.

You and Kate have something very special. Hide the truth from her and you poison the relationship. It will catch up to you, maybe not now, but someday."

Joe rose from his chair. "Thank you for honoring your oath."

CHAPTER FORTY-THREE

The line at the fast-casual restaurant began at the cash register, extended past the paper ticket dispenser with preprinted numbers, and ended at the trash can situated by the front door. The lunchtime crowd, noisy and irritable, taxed even the most alert, patient brain. If there was a short in Kate's mental wiring, Rachel would be better able to detect it in the frenetic environment.

Rachel, a sensible woman who didn't rattle easily, was left unsettled after the morning's encounter with Joe. With the threat of public disclosure looming, the wait-and-see approach was not a great option. She arranged to meet Kate for lunch the same day, using the weekend drama as a pretext for the get-together.

"Gee, I don't think so," Kate said initially when Rachel called. "Mondays are hectic at King. My Monday lunches typically involve a cup of yogurt eaten in front of my computer."

"Kate, you showed up on my doorstep this weekend in tears. I want to make sure everything is okay," Rachel responded, manipulating Kate's overdeveloped sense of guilt to her advantage.

Kate sighed. "I guess I do owe you."

Rachel arrived twenty minutes before their scheduled meeting time, staking out a table next to a window and near the front door, giving her the best view to study Kate's behavior inside and outside the restaurant.

When Kate finally breezed past the clear glass, she was ten minutes late. Kate was never tardy, but even Rachel had to admit a personality change diagnosis based on six hundred seconds seemed a bit excessive. After all, the postage stamp parking lot was insufficient to accommodate the jumbo-sized demand. When Kate strode past a young man and his dog sitting at an outside table, he glanced up and then craned his head to follow her with his eyes as she walked away, so focused on Kate he didn't realize Rachel was studying his reactions.

Rachel had known Kate almost as long as Joe, and she had become an astute observer of the effect Kate had on men. Men would often leer and turned their heads around for the young Kate. But somewhere in time, that had changed.

"I am so sorry," Kate blurted out when she spotted Rachel. "I couldn't seem to get off the phone at work. And then the parking. Don't get me started."

"You would think that with all the money they're making, they could at least afford a bigger parking lot," Rachel said. "Of course, the same could be said for the space inside the restaurant. I'm afraid if I get up from my seat, we'll lose our table. Do you want to order for the both of us?"

Rachel dug into her purse and pulled out a twenty-dollar bill. "I'd like a roast beef on sourdough with everything except no mustard, chips, and a Diet Coke. Can you remember my fussy preferences, or would you prefer I write it down?"

"No, I can manage," Kate answered.

The order was a test. Rachel wondered if Kate would be able to remember the information and repeat the list when she ordered.

Kate staked out her spot at the end of the line. While she was fishing around for her wallet inside her purse, a man wearing a dark pinstriped suit, who stood just in front of her, struck up a conversation. Rachel only caught a few snippets, small talk about the congested eatery and the weather. Once Kate pulled her wedding-ring-adorned left hand out of her bag, the conversation ended.

Rachel strained to listen as Kate ordered lunch, a task she executed without stumbling. As Kate walked back to the table, a food tray in each hand, Rachel concluded Kate had the balance of a circus performer.

After Kate set Rachel's tray down in front of her, Rachel said, "You look absolutely radiant."

Kate blushed. "It's the cream. I must admit that I was skeptical when Joe first told me about the project. Like every other cosmetics company, Galatea has a countless number of products that tout empty promises about youthful rejuvenation. I figured this was just one more. You and Joe have outdone yourselves this time."

"Joe's the one who dreamed up the concept of the cream—even if it was meant for burn survivors. I'm simply the one who noticed the rejuvenating effect on cadaver skin. Joe deserves the kudos."

"Whether he deserves the praise or not, I'm sure he'll claim the success for himself," Kate said.

Kate never criticized her husband, Rachel thought to herself.

"I'm a new woman. Or maybe I'm the old Kate I miss—but better," Kate confessed.

"Better? How so?"

Kate put her fork down and her hands in her lap and then leaned forward. "Remember when we were young? We had the beauty, health, and energy of youth. Yet, we lacked confidence, wisdom, and a certain level of comfort or acceptance of who we are as human beings, the sort of self-awareness and self-actualization earned through aging. I understand how the world works; life's joys, sorrows, and disappointments have mellowed and matured me. I wouldn't trade those lessons for anything.

"So, when I say better, I mean healthy and energetic in addition to feeling more comfortable—and confident—with who I am. I am able to have the best of both Kates."

"Then why so much upheaval at home, if you feel so good now?" Rachel asked.

Kate shrugged. "Maybe it is Joe's fault. I think he feels threatened with all the changes. And whenever he is threatened or scared, he becomes overcontrolling. But for now, I think there's a truce between us."

Rachel nodded and waited. Remaining silent was the best way for Rachel to get more information from Kate.

To compensate for the lull in the conversation, Kate talked. "Buying the wrong orange juice is no reason to start a screaming and bullying tirade fit for a cable news commentator. Now he's alarmed because I was going to give away some old wineglasses we haven't used in decades. Yes, we drank out of them when he proposed to me, but they've been buried back behind a mound of other dishes we never use; gathering dust in a cabinet that's never opened."

"Maybe he's sentimental," Rachel volunteered.

"Not really," Kate said. "I'm the one who clings to trinkets, bits and pieces of our old lives; saving mementos as if they possessed the power to conjure up a happy day from the past—or even an emotion from that day. Joe never seemed to care about that stuff."

Rachel tilted her head slightly. "But everything else is okay? You haven't had any headaches, nausea, appetite interruptions?" Rachel asked.

Kate laughed. "As you can see by the way I polished off my salad, my appetite is quite healthy."

Kate piled her fork, napkin, and empty plate on the tray next to her. "I hate to run but I've got to get back to work. By the way, when you tell Joe your assessment of my health, tell him I've never been better."

CHAPTER FORTY-FOUR

JUNE 1974

Waiting for the doctor to enter the room was never easy, Kate thought to herself after she had disrobed in the cold, sterile space and donned a faded, scratchy gown with an open back. But Joe's pacing and nervous chatter put her on edge.

"Why don't I wait with you?" Joe said, not waiting for her to answer as he sat down in the chair next to the exam table.

Kate fumbled with the back of her gown, pulling each side together even though it would gape open once she let go. "It is awfully nice of you, but I think you'd probably be more comfortable in the waiting room."

"Nonsense," Joe said. "I'll keep you company and distract you, so you won't be so nervous."

"It's embarrassing. Dr. Mitchell is going to ask me all sorts of intimate questions and then he's going to give me a dreadful exam you won't want to witness."

"Kate, I already know you were a virgin when we married so your answers can't be too shocking. Everything the doctor is going to exam, well, I've already seen, touched, or—"

A tap at the door cut Joe off at mid-sentence, much to Kate's relief.

"Come in," Kate said.

Dr. Mitchell, looking down at his file, said, "Hello, Mrs. Holly." His eyes widened upon seeing Joe.

"And Mr. Holly," Dr. Mitchell said, "what a surprise to see you here."

Joe stood up and shook the doctor's hand. "I thought my wife might like some extra moral support today."

Mitchell turned his gaze toward Kate, catching a slight grimace pass across her face. "How thoughtful of you," Mitchell said. "Unfortunately, since Kate is over the age of eighteen, you'll need to wait in the reception room."

Joe shook his head. "Kate needs me. Kate, you want me to stay, don't you?"

The white-haired doctor rested a firm hand on the young husband's shoulder and said, "I'm sure Kate would love to have you in here. I think the fact that you're so insistent proves you're a devoted husband. However, the bond between doctor and patient cannot be broken. To preserve that trust between me and Kate, you must leave. After all, you wouldn't want me to violate my oath with either of you, right?"

Joe shifted his weight from one foot to the other, then shoved his hands into the pockets in his pants. "Kate, I'll be outside."

CHAPTER FORTY-FIVE

The elevator came to a smooth stop when it reached Galatea's highest level. The offices on this floor were occupied by the ambitious few who had made a career out of stepping on, walking over, or undercutting their coworkers to move up the corporate food chain. The bell sounded. The doors parted. *This could have all been mine*, Joe thought as he got out of the elevator. Stan once tried to coax Joe out of the lab and into the executive suite. Joe declined. Science had been his passion—even before Kate.

But science wasn't the only reason Joe didn't leapfrog from the lab into the corporate office suite. Deep down, Joe knew he didn't speak the language of business. He didn't fully embrace the principals of shareholder return, maximizing profits and cutting budgets. Inevitably, Stan would realize Joe was not suited for the business side of Galatea. Better to play it safe because in the lab, Joe was king.

And despite Huff's campaign to recruit fresh, young talent armed with superior and more advanced technological and scientific skills, Joe remained on top. He might not have an office on the executive floor but still Joe understood office politics. As a result, the new hires had not been able to unseat him in the lab.

But today might bring an end to his reign, Joe admitted to himself. He'd been summoned to the top floor's executive conference room for a hastily organized meeting. Through the conference room's wall of interior windows, Joe spotted Stan, seated at the head of the gray marble table. Huff was immediately to his right. On the left side of Stan sat Galatea's general counsel, Blake Tate, a middle-aged humorless lawyer who favored navy pinstriped suits, shoe shines, running marathons on the weekend, and vetoing most all corporate or research requests. As Joe neared the conference room door, Blake stopped speaking and frowned.

"Am I late? I just received the message you wanted to see me," Joe said as he walked into the room. To Joe, every seat in the room was the hot one.

There were no good choices, only the least bad. Rather than sit across from Blake, who looked as though he might throw one of the fat, three-ring regulatory books in Joe's face, Joe opted to sit right beside him, counting on the discomfort of craning one's neck to prevent long, icy stares.

Stan cleared his throat. "No, you're fine, Joe. We called you up here because we need to discuss the Phoenix Project."

Joe leaned forward and hunched his shoulders, adopting a ready position much the same way a second baseman might just before a pitch is thrown to a batter. "What would you like to know?"

"Can we go ahead and announce the project publicly to our shareholders?" Stan asked.

"I think it is still too early," Joe said.

"Is there a problem?" Huff asked. "I mean, Kate looks great; don't you think it is time to let our customers know that we've got this miracle anti-wrinkle gel in the works?"

"No, no," Joe said emphatically, "no problems. I'd like a little bit more time to follow the results before the marketing department gets carried away with a big announcement and publicity rollout."

Like a coiled snake unleashing with a poisonous lightning strike, Blake spoke. "We don't have the luxury of time and because of you and Huff, we have big problems. Why in the hell would you ever run a scientific trial on your own wife? I still don't understand why no one talked to me. If the FDA decides this test amounts to a drug trial, Galatea's going to be on the receiving end of some very uncomfortable regulatory heat."

The lawyer continued, "As for Lauren's big mouth, well, because she leaked insider information, an investigation from the Securities and Exchange Commission is a danger we must consider. If the SEC launches one, the plaintiffs' lawyers will follow by filing big fat securities class action lawsuits. Do you really want to spend all our company's profits on legal fees?"

Joe's neck tightened. The collar on his shirt seemed to be closing in on his airway. "Why did Lauren disclose the project?"

"Why did you decide to experiment on your wife?" Huff shot back.

"Gentlemen, why don't we stay focused," Stan said from the head of the table. "What do we do next? That is the question on the table. Joe, with this new information, is there any reason at all you can think of that would prevent us from circulating a press release announcing that Galatea has an anti-aging gel that is in the research and development stage? Any reason at all?"

An invisible vise wrapped itself around Joe's head and began squeezing at the temples. "No reason," he said loud enough to overcome the ringing in his ears.

"Good," Blake said, slamming his fist down on the table. "I hope the press release will be sufficient to solve our insider information issues. As for using Kate as a test subject, someone please tell me we at least got a liability release from her."

Joe nodded.

"That's a relief. But we need to start designing a bigger trial and perhaps we can hide Kate's participation inside a big group," Blake said, thinking aloud. "Joe, you should start working toward that aim. Huff: Tell your wife to shut up."

CHAPTER FORTY-SIX

JUNE 1974

Joe opened the door for Kate as she climbed out of the tomato red Triumph TR6, relishing the ritual. She had no idea the rush he felt every time he caught a man staring at his car and the dazzling blonde in the passenger seat. Even today, with all of Kate's tension, he still enjoyed the jealousy of others.

"Come on, it won't be so bad," Joe said, taking his wife's hand in his. "We're not going to a funeral."

"Might as well be," Kate said. "If Dr. Mitchell says I can't have children, what's left?"

Joe stopped Kate. "Listen to me."

Kate stared straight ahead, trying to control her tears.

"Kate, please," he said, this time more gently as he turned her body toward him. "Everything is going to work out just fine. No matter what Dr. Mitchell says today, I love you. I'll always love you. Nothing changes."

Kate sniffed. Before her tears had time to streak her face and ruin her carefully applied Galatea makeup, Kate wiped them away from the corners of her eyes.

When the couple entered Dr. Mitchell's office, Kate had calmed herself. Joe, on the other hand, paced the room as they waited for the doctor to finish a patient's exam.

"Kate, you should take a look at these books," Joe said as he inspected the medical tomes perched in stacks on the doctor's shelves. "They're ancient. They were published in the 1940s."

"Ssshhh," Kate said as the door opened.

Dr. Mitchell glanced sideways at Joe as he strode into the room. "Mr. Holly, someday I guarantee a young scientist will mock the books in your office."

"Sorry about that, Doc," Joe said as he took a seat next to Kate.

Mitchell eased himself into the chair behind his desk, opened Kate's patient file, and pulled his glasses slightly down his nose. Without meeting Joe's eyes, he added, "Everything comes full circle in the end.

"Well, Mrs. Holly, here's the good news," Dr. Mitchell said, changing the subject. "Everything is in good working order for you. You are fertile and you're able to bear children."

A smile spread across Kate's face. "Really? Oh my! I could kiss you, Dr. Mitchell." She smiled at the old doctor and noticed he wasn't beaming. "So why haven't I been able to get pregnant?"

Dr. Mitchell glanced at Joe. Joe winced but didn't speak up.

"I'm afraid the reason you haven't been able to conceive is because your husband is sterile."

Joe didn't move.

Kate's back stiffened. She folded her hands in her lap, swallowed hard, and then sighed. "Joe, I'm so sorry," she said, breaking the silence in the room. She reached out and laid her hand on his.

Kate asked, "What are our options, Dr. Mitchell?"

"Well, of course, there's adoption. Couples are also increasingly turning to artificial insemination to conceive. I had my receptionist type up a list of adoption agencies. Because I'm an old doctor, I haven't delved into the emerging area of artificial insemination, but I also had my receptionist compile a list of reputable specialists who are working in the field."

"But Doctor," Kate said, "isn't there anything that can be done for Joe? I've been his wife for quite a while now and there's never been any problem," she blushed, "you know."

Dr. Mitchell nodded. "A man who is sterile can still have intercourse and still ejaculates. He just does not have any sperm to impregnate a woman."

Joe cleared his throat. "Okay, thank you, Dr. Mitchell." He pulled his hand away from Kate. "Can we go now?"

CHAPTER FORTY-SEVEN

"You told them what?" Rachel asked as if she hadn't heard Joe the first time.

"Shut the door," Joe commanded.

Rachel slammed it.

"How can you, in good conscience, allow Galatea to send out a press release about the Phoenix Project and gear up for a bigger trial?" Rachel asked. "The questions surrounding Kate's condition are still unanswered. It would be unethical to proceed. You realize this announcement not only risks destroying your reputation as a scientist, but you also risk prison by knowingly putting out false information."

"Back up, Rachel," Joe said, holding up his hands up in the air. "We don't know if there's anything wrong with Kate. Maybe I am subconsciously reacting to her transformation. In a matter of weeks about twenty years have melted away from her face. A changed or altered relationship is foreseeable even for a longtime married couple."

Rachel shook her head. "You would risk everything to avoid admitting a problem exists? You would risk Kate's health, the health of many other women, the survival of Galatea, and even prison to avoid a little pain now?"

Joe shook his head. "You're the one who is letting emotions run wild, Rachel. You're not thinking rationally. If you weigh the probabilities, your outlook is much too pessimistic."

"Well, I have to say something to Stan and Huff," Rachel said.

"Please, Rachel," Joe said, "don't. The press release is minor. An announcement to inform the public and shareholders we're working on the product. That prick lawyer upstairs made it clear that he was not going to hint at any results yet. As for expanding the trial, I bought us a couple of weeks."

Rachel frowned. "I don't know."

"Let's study Kate for a few more days. If there's even a hint of a problem, I'll let you know and we'll decide what to do. Together."

Rachel sighed.

CHAPTER FORTY-EIGHT

JUNE 1974

It had been a week since Dr. Mitchell had delivered the news. Kate walked around their home clutching the piece of paper with the names of adoption agencies and physicians who specialized in artificial insemination as tightly as a lover clings to a letter from a soldier stationed overseas. The note was the last thread left connecting her deep-seated desire—a desire that Joe didn't understand nor appreciate.

Kate wanted to discuss their options, but Joe, by his early departure in the morning and late nights at work, signaled his wish to avoid the conversation altogether.

When he pulled into their driveway near midnight on Friday, he was relieved. The house was dark, save for the one lamp in the hallway right inside the front door; the light left on until everyone was safe inside.

Joe pushed open the door to his sports car and climbed out. He should have been out with friends—or with Kate. Instead, he'd spent another long evening lost in his lab work. Work usually brought with peace and solace but ever since the meeting with Dr. Mitchell, a numbing sensation had settled into his chest dulling pleasure and pain.

If only Kate wouldn't mope so much, he thought to himself as he trudged toward the front door.

He slid the key into the lock; the bolt clicked, giving way. He crept inside, placed his briefcase in the hallway, and only then did he loosen his tie. Perhaps, Joe thought, he would sleep on the couch.

"Joe, is that you?" Kate's voice called out from black void of the living room.

"Kate? What are you still doing up? Why are you sitting in the dark?" Joe asked as he reached over to turn on the light.

"Please, don't," Kate asked.

Ignoring Kate's request, Joe flipped on the light, revealing Kate's red-rimmed eyes and the crumpled tissue clutched in her right hand.

"You're crying," he said.

"Joe, we need to talk," Kate pleaded.

"Not now, I'm tired," Joe said. "Let's go to bed. We'll talk in the morning."

Kate jumped up from her chair. "No! Tonight you say tomorrow morning. When I wake up, you'll be gone. You'll get up early and go to work on Saturday. You are avoiding me."

"That's not true," Joe said. "I'm trying to give you space. Dr. Mitchell's news, the fact I can't have children..." Joe's voice trailed off. "I don't know what to say."

"You need to talk to me," Kate begged. "We have options. We can still have a family. Please, Joe, talk to me."

"What? Adoption?" Joe said. "I don't want to adopt. Adopting a baby is a long, arduous, heartbreaking process. If you are ultimately successful, you never know who the child's real parents are. Perhaps the father is a serial rapist, or the mother is a barely literate girl with little intelligence. I don't want to be a parent to a child like that."

"How can you say such cruel things?" Kate asked. "We have so many gifts. Don't you think it would be wonderful to share them with a human being in need?"

"I know, I'm a terrible person for saying it. It is how I feel," Joe said. "Don't you want me to be honest?"

"Well, what about artificial insemination?" Kate asked. "The child would be half me and we could review the life history of the father?"

"I find the proposition repugnant," Joe said through clenched teeth. "The thought of another man's semen inside you makes me sick. Aren't we happy? At least, weren't we happy before all this baby stuff started? Why can't we go back in time?"

Tears began rolling down Kate's face. "You can't freeze a relationship, Joe. Time passes. Relationships evolve."

Joe slumped onto the couch and put his head in his hands. For several moments, he was silent. When he finally spoke, his voice cracked with emotion. "Kate, you're young and healthy. I'm defective. You deserve so much more out of life than I can give you. I don't deserve you."

He stopped for a moment, his eyes glistening from moisture. "I can't believe I'm going to say this, but I love you too much to make you suffer. A family is important to you. But children brought into our marriage through adoption or artificial insemination will remind me how I failed you; a reminder that will turn to resentment and, like a slow-moving poison, will doom our marriage. So, if you want to end our marriage now, you can find a man who can give you what you want. I want you to be happy, Kate."

Kate paced the room, trying to absorb Joe's offer to give her a divorce, when her eyes settled on the sand dollar she'd picked up on their honeymoon. She'd had it encased in glass and framed, then displayed on the fireplace mantel. Kate picked it up, tracing the outlines of the sea creature with her fingertip.

She spoke. "Joe, you are my ocean and my sun, my earth and my moon, my sunrise and my sunset. I love you. Don't you get it? I would never leave you."

CHAPTER FORTY-NINE

Kate studied the sand dollar encased in glass. The frame and glass had aged almost forty years. The sand dollar had been around even longer.

"The case has held up pretty well, wouldn't you agree?" Joe asked as he walked into the living room. The sand dollar had been given a prominent location in all three of their homes: their first apartment, their first house in Clayton, and now their custom-built mini-mansion in the outer St. Louis suburb of Chesterfield. Joe had designed the master bathroom. Kate had a say in how the first floor was laid out. This house duplicated the first home they owned, with a living room and fireplace off the main hallway. But the luxury home featured a formal living room; the fireplace, a grand stone structure with openings on two sides, one facing the formal gathering place and the other for the more casual family room.

Joe watched Kate as she studied the fragile shell. The day she'd plucked it off the beach during their honeymoon, the marine animal's skeleton was a rich tan. Now, the sand dollar was ash gray.

Kate seemed lost in thought, tracing the outline of the sand dollar with her forefinger, ignoring Joe's entrance.

Joe realized her hands had changed. Blue veins no longer bulged from the back of them. Like waves at low tide, they seemed to be retreating into the recesses of her body. The creases and lines on her fingers, the ruts around her knuckles, were gone.

The anti-wrinkle cream had only been applied to her face. Perhaps, he thought, when she applied the gel with her fingertip on her right hand, the ingredients went to work on her hand. But her left hand also appeared as though it belonged to a younger woman. She never used her left hand to smooth the marula mixture on her face.

Does the anti-wrinkle gel enter the bloodstream and go to work on the entire body? he wondered.

Joe stepped next to Kate to peer at her lower arms, trying to determine whether the brown sun spots that appeared on her forearms about fifteen years earlier were still noticeable. The sun spots were still present, but to Joe, the marks appeared smaller.

"Kate, has your body experienced any new changes?" Joe asked.

"What do you mean?" she replied, still holding the sand dollar in her hands.

"Other than your face, has your body experienced any other age-related developments?" Joe asked.

"Hmmm," Kate said with a laugh. "I guess I've been focusing so much on the area above my neck I haven't paid much attention to anything else."

"Look at the back of your hands," Joe said.

They'd once been one of her more admired features; movie ticket takers, waiters, and grocery checkout clerks often mentioned her elegant hands. It had been years since anyone had admired them. Kate also ignored her hands—it was easier than acknowledging the aging process.

Kate raised them up to her face. Surprised, she dropped the sand dollar case she'd been holding. The glass shattered. The sand dollar busted into three pieces.

"Oh my goodness," Kate said. "I can't believe I did that."

Joe knelt to pick up the pieces, bracing himself for the tears that were surely to come. She treasured this piece of their past.

"Oh, Kate, I'm so sorry," Joe said. "Maybe superglue will fix it."

Kate shook her head and furrowed her brow. "Don't go to the trouble. I can't remember why we kept it anyway."

CHAPTER FIFTY

Twenty years had elapsed since Dr. Mitchell retired and passed his practice down to a young physician, James Forrester. Dr. Forrester picked up where Dr. Mitchell left off, treating the same patients in the same space.

Joe, who insisted Kate get a physical after she couldn't recall the link between the sand dollar and their lives, noticed that some changes had been made. The burnt orange plastic chairs with the aluminum legs, the brown shag carpet, and the dingy white blinds were gone. Now, the room was lined with olive green sofas and chairs covered with suede fabric and stuffed with semi-firm filling; soft enough to be comfortable but firm enough to avoid trapping older patients in a pit of pillows. The walls were painted warm beige. Large potted plants sprouting healthy green fronds brightened the room. Cream carpet with green and tan flecks unified the space.

A gold plaque with Dr. Mitchell's profile hung on the wall next to the check-in counter, a touch Dr. Forrester added when the old doctor died ten years ago.

Joe sauntered up to the receptionist's desk to sign his wife in for her exam. "This place sure looks nothing like what I remember."

The young receptionist smiled. "I've worked here for three years. The waiting room hasn't changed."

To Joe, it seemed like yesterday he'd fled the office after Dr. Mitchell announced the results of the fertility tests. Joe switched physicians soon after and had never returned.

Even though the space had changed dramatically, the agitation and hammering heartbeat that Joe experienced long ago returned.

Joe's face whitened.

"Are you okay?" Kate asked.

"Yeah, yeah, I'm okay," he said, trying to quiet his growing anxiety.

The waiting room door opened. A nurse, her purple scrubs stretched taut across her middle-aged stomach, appeared. She scanned the name typed across the top and called out: "Kate Holly."

"Jane, I'm over here," Kate called out.

A wave of relief washed over Joe. If Kate could remember a detail as trivial as the nurse's name, she must be okay.

The nurse's eyes searched the room for Kate—then widened with surprise. "My goodness, Kate, you look fabulous! New diet? New exercise regime?"

"Sort of," Kate said, blushing from Jane's reaction, aware the other patients were staring at her.

Kate headed for the door with Joe closely behind. As he passed a sour-faced old woman sitting next to her trembling husband, Joe heard her whisper loudly with disdain, "Plastic surgery."

Joe smiled and silently congratulated himself on his genius.

Jane led them to a small examination room. Kate's weight and blood pressure were recorded; blood was drawn. Before the nurse disappeared, she instructed Kate to get out of her clothes and into a medical gown.

Moments later, knuckles rapped on the door.

"Come in," Kate called from her perch on the examining table.

She was wrapped in a checkered blue and white smock, faded from repeated washings in bleach. Her underwear was visible from the back of the frock. Her feet were bare, but for the bright pink nail polish on her toes.

Dr. Forrester shut the door and studied Kate carefully from afar.

"The nurses are buzzing about your appearance, Kate. They're saying you appear twenty years younger. They wanted me to discover your secret—either you found the fountain of youth or an incredibly talented cosmetic surgeon. I didn't believe them, but I was wrong. They were right."

Dr. Forrester stepped over to his chair, a black stool on rollers, sat down, and scooted over to the examining table. "So, Kate, what is your secret?"

Kate beamed with a mixture of pride and embarrassment. She put her hands down on the table, twisting her legs so that one foot wrapped around the other at the ankle. "Ask Joe."

Dr. Forrester swiveled his seat to face the spot that her husband had staked out in the corner and held out his hand. "I don't believe we've ever met. Jim Forrester."

Joe shook the younger man's hand. "Miracle cream," Joe said. "You might have heard about it in the news. My company, Galatea, circulated a press release about the project. I tried to invent a cream for burn survivors—to reverse the damage done by heat and flames. I wanted to remove the mask of burn trauma, give them back their former face. I used some rare ingredients from Africa. I tried everything, but nothing worked. One day in the lab we discovered the gel seemed to be having an impact on normal, aged skin. The skin was rejuvenated somehow. Kate has been using the prototype of the product."

"I'd say you have a blockbuster on your hands," Dr. Forrester said as he opened his folder. "Now, Kate is in here because of some memory lapses, right?"

"Yes," Joe answered for his wife. "Even though her face glows with vitality, the gel does nothing for Kate internally. She's still a woman in her late fifties. I'm worried she may have suffered a small stroke."

"Hmmm," Dr. Forrester said as he jotted notes down into the manila folder. He set the chart aside, turned to Kate, and asked, "So how are you feeling?"

Kate shrugged her shoulders and shook her head. She didn't share Joe's concerns. "Fine, never better. I'm now a firm believer in the link between the mind and body. Once I started using the anti-wrinkle gel and began looking like my old self, I started feeling like my old self. I'm happy. I'm excited for each new day."

"Before you started using the cream, did you experience a sense of dread about the future?" Dr. Forrester asked.

"I don't know if dread is the right word, numb or defeated might be a better choice. I floated through my days, an invisible ghost. I could see and hear everything, yet no one seemed to see or hear me. That's changed. Getting my face back meant getting my voice back, getting my power back," Kate admitted.

"Your experience—at least in terms of the invisibility and numbness—isn't unique. Many women your age come into my office complaining of something similar. It is a normal, sane reaction to a culture that celebrates teen stars and is fixated with the pursuit of youth. The experience is particularly intense for women. The ideal woman is now a cartoonish figure with giant breasts and a pre-pubescent pelvis. Normal, older women are indeed invisible. Some seek pills and others ask for the name of a good plastic surgeon. I wish I had a magic pill—not for my patients but for society—to cure this unhealthy obsession," Dr. Forrester said. "Tell me more about your memory lapses."

Kate sighed. "Joe's the best person to ask."

"Doctor, she seems to have forgotten important events from earlier in our marriage," Joe told him, explaining the sand dollar incident and the now-silly-sounding fight over orange juice.

"Let's take a look," he said.

He checked her blood pressure again, peeled back her eyelids as far as possible, and examined her eyes. He probed her ears and made Kate breathe in and out deeply several times to listen to her heart with a stethoscope. He popped her knees with a small hammer to check her reflexes, had her balance on each leg, then had her recline on the table so he could press her abdomen.

Once he was done, the doctor sat back down in his chair. "Everything appears normal. Your heart, eyes, ears, throat; everything is as it should be. But I am concerned about the memory loss. I should get the blood test results back in a few days. In the meantime, I want Kate to get a CAT scan. I'm sure that everything will turn out normal, but I'd like to be certain. If the CAT scan reveals something, then she'll need to see a neurologist. In the meantime, I want her to stop using the anti-wrinkle cream."

"Do you think the cream has anything to do with it?" Joe asked the doctor.

"Probably not. It is likely just a coincidence. However, let's discontinue the experiment as a precautionary measure," he answered.

"What do you think it is?" Joe asked.

"I hate to speculate. The CAT scan and blood work should be able to tell us that. I don't detect an irregular heartbeat. Perhaps Kate suffered a bump on the head that caused some bruising or swelling, a condition that can be watched and will hopefully resolve itself. Then there are the other dangers, Alzheimer's, dementia. I think that is a worry of last resort, though. Kate doesn't have any family history of those diseases in her family. My suggestion is to keep track of her symptoms but go about your normal daily lives while we look into it."

Dementia and Alzheimer's were not conditions to mention and then suggest acting as though there was nothing to worry about, Joe thought, but said nothing.

Joe asked, "Doctor, since Kate has been using the prototype of my cream, part of our monitoring includes watching her physical health. It is standard operating procedure at Galatea for volunteers to submit to periodic physical testing. Is it possible for me to get a copy of her records?"

Dr. Forrester frowned slightly. "Mr. Holly, I can't give you Kate's medical records due to the privacy regulations in force today. Kate, however, can sign a medical authorization and order the records. If she chooses to give them to you, it is no business of mine."

The doctor turned to Kate. "If you want your records, stop by my office manager's desk on the way out. She'll have the form ready for you to sign as well as your CAT scan appointment time. I'm going to push for her to get you in today."

CHAPTER FIFTY-ONE

Joe understood why the old folks in Dr. Forrester's waiting room were so cranky. Shuffling from doctor's appointments to testing facilities all day long truly qualified as the first circle of hell.

Dr. Forrester's office manager scheduled an appointment for the CAT scan, but the earliest time slot available wasn't for another two hours. Kate had suggested grabbing a cup of coffee in the hospital cafeteria adjacent to the medical building.

The walls of the cafeteria had been drenched in cheery yellows; a bright nature mural was painted along one wall. Yet the faux happy atmosphere seemed to do little to lift the spirits of the grim-faced customers: young parents holding squirming toddlers; middle-aged children who kept vigil by an elderly parent; bald teens pushing around IV poles.

"This is depressing," Joe said. "Thank goodness we're healthy and don't live this sort of life every day."

"Where's your compassion?" Kate asked. "Honestly, Joe, you're as whiny as some of the kids we saw at doctor's office. How many times did I say you didn't need to come?"

"Well, I'm here now. I can't leave because we rode together," Joe said matter-of-factly.

"My test is only a few floors away. Leave. I'll call you when I'm done," Kate urged.

Joe glanced at his watch. "No good. Not enough time. We should go ahead and get upstairs."

Kate shook her head. "Admit it. You're nosy and you can't stand not being present for every little test. You can't resist hearing every single question and volunteering your own responses."

"We need to go upstairs, otherwise we'll be late," Joe said.

As soon as they arrived for the next round of tests, Kate's name was called almost immediately. Joe got up and followed his wife.

"I'm sorry, sir, only the patient is allowed past this point," the nurse said, blocking his entry into the testing area.

"Joe, why don't you wait for me?" Kate said. "This won't take long; not much in my head to examine anyway," she tried to joke.

"Give me one good reason why I can't come back," Joe asked the nurse who stood in his way.

"Radiation," she answered.

"What do you do when you have an infant or small child who needs a CT scan? Do you let mom come along to calm the child down? I bet you have some adult-sized lead aprons for just that purpose."

The nurse crossed her arms. "Your wife isn't a child."

"We're here because she's having memory problems. I need to be present in case she forgets something important that is said. If you don't believe me, call Dr. Forrester."

Neither the nurse nor Joe budged. Kate shifted her weight from one foot to the other, arms crossed, and lips pursed.

"Look," Kate said. "Just let him come back so that we can all get on with our lives, okay?"

The nurse scowled and led Kate into a gray, institutional room. On the walls were gadgets with red lights, green lights, and red LED numbers. Unlike Dr. Forrester's examination room, there were no cheap, friendly posters of mountains, beaches, or the food pyramid. This was utilitarian, a place where a brain was shot with radioactive rays so that a three-dimensional image could be splayed onto a black film and held up to a white light by a radiologist who was looking for tumors and defects.

The nurse grabbed a lead apron and whispered something to the technician. He frowned and pointed to a corner far from the monstrous machine in the middle of the room. "The husband needs to sit in the corner," he said.

"You heard him," the nurse said, heaving the heavy lead armor into Joe's arms.

In an only slightly less gruff manner, the technician ordered Kate to lie down on a table. At the end of the table was a donut-shaped device, a radiation portal that would map Kate's brain.

"You need to lie still," the technician said, "very, very still. If you remain motionless, this will take about an hour. If you move, we'll have to start over," he warned.

"Gotcha," Kate said.

The technician put a rigid pillow under her head and slid a U-shaped contraption around it, each end of the device resting on her shoulders while the bridge fit snugly over the top of her head.

"This prevents your head from moving or wiggling from side to side," the technician said to Kate. "Put your arms down along your body."

The machine hummed and whirred for forty-five minutes. When the ordeal was done, the nurse grabbed the apron and the technician shooed the couple from the room. "A radiologist will review the results and call your doctor."

The door had barely closed on the elevator just down the hall from the lab when Kate turned to Joe. "I can't believe you."

"What?" Joe asked.

"What? Unbelievable!" she said. "You treat me like a child. I'm a grown woman. Hell, I'm old enough to be a grandmother. The last thing I wanted for you to do was to hover like a goddamn hen."

"What is with you and the sailor's mouth?" Joe asked.

"That's not the point," she answered.

"Yeah, it is the point. You never used to act this way. You would never have started cussing at me."

"You know what, Joe, swearing is the only way I can forcefully express my anger. Speaking in a calm manner doesn't get your attention. Calling you an asshole, however, really drives the point home—in a most satisfactory way."

"This has been a really long day," Joe said, trying to defuse Kate's rage. "I'm sure you're feeling anxious about these tests and to get repeatedly poked, prodded, and examined is wearing thin. I should be more patient with you."

The elevator door had barely opened when Kate stormed out. Joe raced to keep up.

As they reached the parking lot, Joe grabbed his wife by her upper arm. "Slow down!"

Kate whirled around and jerked her arm out of his hand. "Let go of me," she hissed.

"You're overwrought," Joe said, regaining his composure. "Why don't I call Dr. Forrester and ask if he can prescribe something for your nerves, something to take the edge off."

"I'm not the one who needs to be drugged, Joe. It's you! You didn't listen to a word I said to you. Instead of understanding that I'm angry at the way you acted for the CT scan; instead of owning your own behavior; you twist everything around so that I'm the problem."

"C'mon, get in the car," Joe said. "Let me get you home."

Kate crossed her arms across her chest defiantly. "No. I'm not getting in the car with you."

Joe took a deep breath. "Kate, I've been out of the office all day. I've got to get back to the lab. I don't know why you're throwing such a temper tantrum. I haven't seen you like this since we were first married. But if this is how you want it, then it's up to you. So, for the last time, do you want a ride home, or do you want me to leave without you?"

"I'd rather walk home than ride with you," Kate said.

CHAPTER FIFTY-TWO

"Where have you been?" Rachel asked when Joe walked into the lab. "I've been calling your cell phone all day. You don't answer. You don't call back. What's wrong?"

"I had to take care of some personal business," Joe said.

"Please don't tell me your absence is related to Kate," Rachel asked, her voice rising in panic.

Joe pursed his lips and shook his head vigorously. "No. I had to take care of personal business."

"Well, thank God you're here. The reception area outside the lab is filled with people who want to participate in the Phoenix Project," Rachel said.

"What?" Joe shouted. "The press release, the meeting with Huff and Stan, that all happened yesterday. How can we have a group of subjects already? Who in the hell is the idiot responsible for rushing this project?"

"That would be me." Joe didn't need to turn around to around to figure out who was speaking.

"Huff, why wasn't I consulted?" Joe asked.

Huff slapped Joe on the back a little sharper than usual. "Joe, last time I checked, I was the CEO of Galatea. Now that the project has been revealed publicly, I see no need for restraint. Besides, the longer we dally on getting this product to market, the more time our competitors have to steal our formula. By the end of the day, I anticipate you'll have the subjects subdivided into two groups—one that gets the miracle gel and the other that receives a placebo—and their first dose should be applied."

Huff walked to the door and abruptly halted. "Joe, Rachel, one more thing. Lauren is one of the participants. Make sure she gets the real thing."

As soon as Huff was safely out of the lab, Joe hissed, "Why didn't you tell me this was going on?"

Rachel put her hand on her forehead and shut her eyes briefly as if to calm herself before answering. "I tried to tell you. I've been trying to reach you all day. Before you take an even nastier tone with me, you should know Stan and Huff were looking for you all day, too. Every time they called the lab, I made up some excuse as to why you couldn't come to the phone."

Joe slumped down onto a lab stool. "I'm sorry, Rachel. Thank you for covering for me."

Rachel looked at Joe carefully. In all the years they had worked together, she had never heard him say thanks for anything. With the bombast sucked from his manner, he sounded like a defeated old man. "Are you okay?" Rachel asked.

"Yeah, I'm fine," Joe said wearily. "Why don't you go ahead and start dividing up the group."

Joe's cell phone rang. He jumped.

"Hello," Joe said. "Oh, Doctor, it's you. Could you please hold on a second?"

Rachel mouthed silently, "What doctor?"

"One moment, Doctor, let me go to my office," he said, ignoring Rachel's question.

Once the door was shut to his office, Joe continued the conversation.

"Yes, Dr. Forrester, any news?"

"I tried to call Kate, but I haven't been able to reach her," Forrester said. "I thought I'd contact you instead."

"Is anything wrong?" Joe asked. They had been told it would be a couple of weeks before the results of the CT scan would be available.

"I was able to pull some strings and get Kate's scan read today," Forrester said. "Fortunately, it is normal."

"Wonderful!" Joe exclaimed. "So she's healthy?"

Dr. Forrester paused. "I'm not sure. The CT scan results are normal but I'm still concerned. I want Kate to be examined by a neurologist. I took the liberty of making an appointment for her tomorrow morning. Can I give you the information?"

"Sure," Joe said.

"One more thing," Forrester said. "The neurologist wants you to bring along a sample of your anti-wrinkle cream to analyze at the lab."

"That won't be necessary," Joe said. "We've got a lab here. I know exactly what is in the gel."

"There's no harm in double checking the ingredients," Forrester said. "Perhaps you missed something."

"I can't turn over the cream," Joe said. "Instead, I'll analyze it again and bring a list of the ingredients tomorrow."

A few seconds after Joe hung up the phone, Rachel knocked on his door.

"We've got the groups divided. Can we go ahead and give them their samples and show them how to apply the gel?"

"What are you using for the fake, substitute gel?" Joe asked.

"So that both samples would look identical," Rachel said impatiently, "I had our lab techs mix up the emulsifier we've been mixing with the marula and added a benign light green tint to match. Basically, it is our youth gel without the synthetic ingredients added."

"Hmmm," Joe nodded, "good thinking."

"You still haven't answered my question," Rachel said. "Can I go ahead and have our subjects, including Huff's wife, Lauren, proceed with the first application?"

It was already past five. "Don't you think it would be better to send everyone home and bring them back later, maybe next week?" Joe asked.

"Joe, these women will wait all night if they have to. If you send Lauren home empty-handed you're going to have Huff gunning for your head."

"Stan will protect me," Joe said.

Rachel waved her hand in front of his eyes and laughed. "Helloooooo. Are you blind?"

"What are you talking about?"

"If you think Stan is going to continue to be your guardian angel, you've got two big problems. First, Stan is as eager as Huff to get the youth gel to market. The only reason he's not hounding you more is because he stepped back and let Huff be the bad cop. Huff would not have been able to push us so hard without Stan's blessing."

Joe rubbed the back of his neck. What Rachel said made sense. Even though Stan had stepped down as Galatea's chief executive, he kept a tight hold of the reins. The gel's potential wasn't limited to transforming appearances. It had the potential to transform Galatea from a cosmetics company into an international corporate powerhouse.

"That's one problem," Joe said finally. "What's the second?"

"Have you noticed the way Stan stares at Kate?"

Joe clenched his fists and his jaw tightened. His eyes blazed with anger. "What?"

Rachel took two steps back and put her hands up in the air as if to surrender. "Hey, don't shoot the messenger. I'm just calling it like I see it."

"And," Joe said slowly, "what do you see?"

"Ever since Kate started using our youth gel and returning to her old self, Stan seems to make up any excuse possible to be in the lab when she comes by," Rachel said. "And when Stan sees her, his face lights up like a school boy with a bad crush."

"That's impossible," Joe said.

"Is it? A lonely, wealthy, powerful widower falling for a beautiful woman doesn't seem impossible to me," Rachel answered.

"Stan could have a million beautiful women thirty years younger than Kate," Joe argued.

"Sure. But Stan isn't Huff. Huff is a man only interested in a trophy. For Stan, Kate is the best of both worlds. She's beautiful, and, because they're from the same generation, they have a lot in common. Kate offers the wisdom gained from a lifetime of experiences. And," Rachel added, "since you've known Stan for so long, Kate is a direct link to his first wife."

Joe crossed his arms, not willing to embrace the observations Rachel had to offer.

"Face it," Rachel said matter-of-factly, "right now I'm the only one looking out for you."

Joe looked at his longtime assistant, her aging hands thrust firmly in the pockets of her lab coat, standing her ground.

"Can I have five minutes?" Joe asked.

"Five minutes, then I need an answer on the project," Rachel said. She turned around silently in her sensible shoes and firmly closed the door on her way out.

Joe grabbed his cell phone and dialed home.

"Hello?"

"Kate, you made it home?" Joe said.

"Of course I did, no thanks to you," Kate said in a hushed tone.

"How?"

"You know, I am a grown-up. I can figure it out."

"Okay," Joe said, "so what did you do?"

I called an Uber, of course," Kate whispered.

"Why are you whispering?" Joe asked.

"Do you want Stan to hear that you drove off without me today?"

"What the hell is Stan doing there?" Joe asked.

"He said he needed to talk to you about the gel project," Kate answered. "I told him you were still at the office."

Joe's chest tightened with jealousy. "Then what's he still doing there?"

"I know you've got a lot riding on this project. I didn't want to be rude and slam the door in his face," Kate said. "I invited him in for a drink and to wait for you."

"I'm sure he was very happy to receive the invitation to spend some time alone with you," Joe said, the words leaving a bitter taste in his mouth.

"C'mon, Joe," Kate said softly. "This is Stan you're talking about. He's one of our oldest and dearest friends."

"That's what he wants you to think so that you'll let your guard down," Joe said. It was the way he had chosen to woo Kate and now it appeared Stan was adopting the same approach.

"Don't be silly," Kate said. "Look, I've got to go. What should I tell

Stan?"

What a clever move, Joe thought to himself. Stan knew that the lab was busy with the newest phase of the study. If Joe left now, it would look like he was shirking his duties as head of R&D. "I won't be home for a while. We've entered a new phase in the Phoenix Project and I have to be here." Joe felt a stabbing pain in his heart. "I won't be home until late tonight."

"I'll tell him," Kate said cheerily.

Joe felt a wave of panic. "You didn't tell him about the medical appointments, did you?"

"No," Kate said. "It is none of his business."

Joe exhaled. "One more thing before you hang up: What do you think about taking a week off and flying down to St. Augustine for a vacation?"

"Sure, that would be nice," Kate said before hanging up. "I don't think I've ever been there."

Joe closed his cell phone and then opened his office door, where he found Rachel waiting just on the other side. Joe dropped the cell phone in his pocket and brushed past his assistant. "Let's get started with the first application."

It took just about every ounce of energy left in Joe to subdue the jealousy that had been gnawing at him. When he pulled into the driveway, Joe thought he had regained his much-prized composure. Stan's car was nowhere to be seen. Judging from the single light left on in the hallway, Kate had gone to bed.

Rachel was just trying to get him riled up, Joe told himself as he dropped his briefcase in the hallway and walked to the kitchen for a glass of orange juice. He opened the door and, much to his relief, Kate had stocked it with the pulp-free variety. He set the cardboard container on the granite countertop and reached for a glass. Two wineglasses in the sink caught his eye.

Joe reached into the sink for one wineglass, gripped the stem in his right hand, the cup in his left, and snapped it in two.

The nearly-empty wine bottle that his wife and boss had shared earlier that evening sat in the center of the kitchen table. Joe poured the remaining bit down the drain and dropped the bottle in the trash can, the loud thud filling up the otherwise quiet kitchen.

When Kate slipped down to the kitchen the next morning to make coffee, she discovered the orange juice had been left out all night and her husband asleep on the couch.

She pushed her husband's shoulder to roust him. "Joe, what are you doing on the couch?"

Joe opened his eyes. He recognized Kate, but it took a few seconds before he realized where he was. He struggled to sit up. "I didn't want to wake you," he lied.

"Nothing happened last night," Kate said.

"I don't know what you mean," Joe muttered.

"It really isn't fair to take your jealous rage out on a defenseless goblet," Kate teased.

"Are you making fun of me?" Joe said testily.

Kate laughed. "Actually, I find your jealousy a bit of a turn-on. It has been a long time since you've been worried about the intentions of another man. My appointment isn't for another two hours. You could take me upstairs and show me you really loved me."

Joe's brow furrowed. His calm, predictable life had seemingly turned upside down overnight. Kate's moods were mercurial, his closest friend had turned on him, his boss had stepped up his campaign to oust him, and Rachel was his only ally.

But how could he turn down the chance to take Kate upstairs? Another man was lurking in the wings, and it offered an opportunity to claim her as his own in the most intimate way imaginable.

"Let's go," Joe said as he started for the stairs. "You may be a little late for your appointment."

CHAPTER FIFTY-THREE

Kate's face was still flushed with passion when she walked into the neurologist's office. The doubt and fear that threatened to overwhelm Joe hours earlier had dissipated. He had forgotten how giving a woman pleasure could boost a man's confidence.

"Mr. and Mrs. Holly, I'm Dr. Inhope," the specialist said as he entered the examination room.

"Nice to meet you," Kate said warmly.

Joe thrust out his hand and Inhope gave it a brief, tepid handshake.

"We're here today because it seems as though Kate is having a problem with her memory," Joe began.

"Yes, yes," Inhope interrupted. "Forrester filled me in on all of the particulars. Kate has developed holes in her memory. Would you characterize these missing memories as ones of recent events or much further in the past?"

Kate looked to Joe. "I guess my husband can better answer that than me."

"She seems to be able to remember what happened this morning," he said with a smile as Kate blushed, "yesterday, and even last week. But events thirty to forty years ago are more troublesome."

Inhope clasped his hands together. "Can you give me some examples?"

"Yesterday, I suggested we go take a short vacation to St. Augustine," Joe said. "My wife doesn't recall ever visiting St. Augustine."

"Kate's probably visited many places in her lifetime," Inhope said dismissively. "Forgetting a brief visit to a place several decades ago doesn't alarm me too much."

"But that's where we went for our honeymoon," Joe protested.

Inhope frowned. "Dr. Forrester tells me that the symptoms started after

Kate began using some sort of experimental youth gel? Did you bring a sample for our lab to examine?"

"That won't be necessary," Joe said. "I'm a scientist and head of the lab at Galatea. I made the gel and therefore know all of the ingredients." Joe handed over an envelope marked confidential. "You'll find them listed in here. Naturally, I've left off the exact concentrations because this is a top-secret project. I could get fired just for giving you this envelope."

Inhope peeled open the envelope and read over the list of ingredients. "Mr. Holly, did you test Kate's personal sample or is this the generic list of ingredients?"

"Kate's personal sample was made from the so-called generic list of ingredients that you have in your hands. They're one and the same," Joe said.

"Well—don't take this as a personal insult—but perhaps there were some quality control issues with Kate's gel. I'd like to do my own testing," Inhope said.

"I'm afraid we can't do that," Joe said. "How do I know you're not going to share the information? After all, you don't even have any idea if there's anything wrong with Kate."

"That's where you're mistaken, Mr. Holly," Inhope said. "I've got a strong suspicion as to her diagnosis. I just don't know what triggered it."

Kate interrupted the two men in the room who were talking over her as if she wasn't present. "You do think there's something wrong? Have I had a stroke?" she asked fearfully.

"I don't think you've had a stroke," Inhope said. "No, the symptoms you describe lead me to suspect retrograde amnesia."

"Doctor," Joe said, "what do you mean by amnesia? Kate's forgotten little details, select scenes from our past, but it isn't like she's wandering the streets with no memory of who she is, where she lives. She still makes it to work on time in the morning and back home at night."

"That's why I suspect she's suffering from retrograde amnesia. It is a form of amnesia characterized by an inability to recall events in the past; old, long-term memories disappear. Most often, I see it in people who have been in some sort of accident with a head injury. With retrograde amnesia, as opposed to other types of amnesia, the accident victim remembers things after the accident but can't remember details of their life before the accident," Inhope explained.

"But Kate wasn't in an accident," Joe argued.

"Yes, I know. While accidents are the most common cause of amnesia, there are other causes—drugs and alcohol, for instance."

"If you're asking whether Kate is an alcoholic or a drug addict, I can assure you she is most certainly not," Joe said, outraged that the topic was even broached.

"But she is using this anti-wrinkle cream with some pretty powerful properties," Inhope shot back. "It could be the problem. Is anyone else using it?"

Joe switched the subject. "I still think your diagnosis is half-baked. She hasn't forgotten everything."

Inhope ignored the jab. "I realize that. Some people have absolutely no memory of their past. For others, bits and pieces disappear. That could be the case with your wife."

Kate finally spoke up. "Is it permanent?"

"I don't know. And again, this is just a hypothesis right now," Inhope answered.

She reached into her purse and took out the anti-wrinkle gel. "I don't care what my husband says, I want you to go ahead and test it."

Inhope grasped the gel from Kate's soft, smooth hand. "I'll put a rush on it."

CHAPTER FIFTY-FOUR

"Let me guess," Rachel said, her words outlined by contempt, "personal business."

"I'm only an hour late," Joe said as he brushed past his assistant, "and I was the one who stayed late and locked up."

"Good story," Rachel said. "I'd stick with that one for your meeting with Stan."

"What meeting?"

"The one that is happening in your office as soon as you walk through your door," Rachel said.

"Did that SOB say what he wanted?"

"Sshhhhh, watch your language!" Rachel hissed, alarmed at the sudden anger Joe unleashed. "What's gotten into you? In the past, you never let rivals upset you. And this isn't just any rival—this is Stan."

Joe closed his eyes and took a deep breath. "I know. It's just…" His voice trailed off. "It's just that Kate's physical transformation has been so rapid, I haven't had time to adjust. Plus, we've been working so hard. It is just a lot to absorb."

Rachel searched his face. "There's something you're not telling me. Has Kate's condition worsened? Is that the personal business you've been attending to?"

Joe paused a little too long to answer the question.

Rachel's eyes widened. "Joe, answer me. Is there something about Kate's medical condition that you're not telling me?"

Joe shook his head emphatically. "No, everything is fine."

"I don't believe you," she said, the color draining from her face. "If there's a problem with the gel, oh my god, all of the subjects we've got using it. Lauren. I've got to tell Stan."

Joe grabbed Rachel's forearm firmly. "Rachel, calm down! I told you, everything is fine. Now you're the one who is acting out of character." His voice had lost the uncertainty and fear from moments earlier. It had turned hard and resolute. "Get back to work."

It took Rachel's mini-meltdown to bring Joe back to his senses. His anxiety was making him careless and clouding his logical mind. It was logic that would help him figure a way out of his predicament. But if he lost his head, he wouldn't recognize the answer when it presented itself.

"Stan, to what do I owe the honor?" Joe said when he entered his office.

Stan was sitting behind Joe's desk; in Joe's chair. "You really do have a nice view," Stan said. Although Stan's hand gestured at the window, Joe could have sworn that Stan's eyes darted to the framed picture of Kate resting on the windowsill.

"I'm sorry I missed you last night," Joe said, shutting the door behind him but remaining standing, waiting for Stan to get out of his chair. "I was working late."

"Yes, I apologized to Kate for making you work such long hours," Stan said with a smile. Showing no signs of budging, Stan said, "Sit down. You look tired."

With a grin pasted on his face, Joe sat in one of the guest chairs across the executive desk from Stan. "What did you need to see me about?"

"As you know, I'm excited about Galatea's youth gel. It is going to be a mega blockbuster," Stan said. "Since the project has your personal attention, I know the research and development side is well taken care of, so I've been mulling over the rollout from the marketing end."

Joe nodded politely. "I see."

"At first, I thought that we should sign on a celebrity spokeswoman, someone with a platform who will give our product a boost. But then I had a better idea, a brilliant idea."

Joe could feel his cell phone vibrate in his pocket. He ignored it. "Go on."

"I was thinking that, for the average woman, it can be hard to relate to a celebrity. After all, they've already had access to all the best nonsurgical and surgical treatments that money can buy. Most of our customers are savvy. They'll just chalk up the ad campaign to puffing," Stan said.

"You have a point," Joe said, trying to ignore the cell phone that was vibrating again against his hip.

"What we need is a spokeswoman who is inspiring, beautiful enough to win our customers' admiration but still accessible," Stan said. He got up out of Joe's chair, walked over to the window and picked up Kate's picture. "I think Kate should be the face of the Galatea campaign."

"Kate!" Joe said, jumping out of his chair. He snatched the picture out of Stan's hand. "No! The last thing I need is for Kate to turn into a celebrity."

"Why? She's polished, well spoken, attractive, and friendly," Stan argued.

"I just don't want the intrusion. We'd have no privacy. She'd be traveling a lot. Besides, she already has a job and a career," Joe stammered. "Did you mention your plan to Kate?"

Stan headed for the door. Joe's phone vibrated again.

"No, I wanted to talk to you first," Stan said. "I was hoping, for the good of Galatea, that you'd be on board with the marketing idea and then we could present it to Kate together. Since you're opposed, I guess I'll have to ask her myself."

"Don't waste your time, she only listens to me," Joe said.

"We'll see," Stan said, smiling politely as he shut the door.

Anger radiated from Joe's center, making his hands tremble with rage as he reached into his pocket. His shaking fingers flipped open the phone and he scrolled through the numbers. Two of the calls were from phone numbers he didn't recognize. One was from Kate. Although he'd received three calls, only two messages had been left.

Joe dialed his voice mail.

"Mr. Holly, this is Dr. Forrester," the first message began. "I just got off the phone with the neurologist. He has some extremely urgent information for you. Please call him right away. If you don't reach him, please dial me and tell my office I said it was okay to interrupt me."

The message ended.

"Mr. Holly," the next message began. "Dr. Inhope. I need to talk to you right away. It is most urgent matter. I had the lab fast-track the testing of your gel. There's a problem."

Kate didn't leave a message.

Joe hit the redial button for Inhope. The phone rang, rang, and rang. There was no answer. Joe snapped his phone shut when he heard a knock on his office door.

"What?" he barked.

The door opened cautiously. "Is it okay for me to stick my head in here or will it get bitten off?" Rachel asked.

"Not now," Joe said. "Your timing is terrible. And if you're coming in here to deliver more bad news, you better turn around and leave."

"No bad news. I just wanted to go over the Phoenix Project timetable," Rachel said.

"Not now. Please shut the door on your way out."

Joe redialed Inhope's number. This time, his office picked up on the third ring. "Dr. Inhope," Joe said, his voice cracking.

"I'm sorry, he's with a patient right now," the indifferent voice replied.

"Get him," Joe snarled. "Now! This is Mr. Holly. I'm sure he's expecting my call."

"One moment," the bored receptionist responded.

The phone went silent. Joe looked at the picture of Kate beneath his windowsill. She must have already spoken with the doctors, he thought.

"Mr. Holly?" Inhope asked.

"Yes," Joe replied.

"I got the lab tests back this morning. I'm afraid your gel is contaminated. The lab found one compound that wasn't on your list," Inhope said.

"What?" Joe asked, his chest tightening with anxiety.

"Mescaline," Inhope answered, "or at least a synthetic version of mescaline."

"Mescaline? You mean the stuff in peyote? The psychedelic drug used by Native Americans?" Joe said incredulously. "Your lab must've made some mistake. Mescaline is a banned substance. I don't have access to it, didn't use it in the wrinkle cream, and while Kate might be forgetful, she certainly hasn't acted like she's high."

"I had them run a second test just to be certain. Both came back with mescaline," Inhope insisted. "It is a variant of the drug; an unusual one. The researchers say they've never come across anything like it. Like the marula you used in the cream, the mescaline is synthetic. The chemical makeup has been altered to suppress the mind-bending properties."

"So, what does this mean for Kate?" Joe asked.

"While the mood-altering properties are minimized, mescaline can also trigger retrograde amnesia. The version seems to enhance that property," Inhope answered.

"Have you told Kate all of this?"

"Yes," Inhope replied. "I called her first."

Bile rose up in Joe's throat. He fought the urge to vomit in his trash can.

"Mr. Holly, are you still there?" Inhope asked.

"I've got to go find my wife," Joe said, abruptly hanging up the phone. Taking nothing but his phone and keys, he dashed out of the office.

"Where are you going?" Rachel asked as Joe rushed past. "More personal business?"

"You've got to stop the trial," Joe ordered.

"What do you mean, stop the trial?" Rachel asked.

"I mean you have to stop the Phoenix Project testing," Joe said. "And you need to get back all of the testing samples. Now!"

"What's this about? I can't just stop the project. I need some answers."

"I don't have time to explain," Joe said. "Trust me. The trial must stop. Now!"

CHAPTER FIFTY-FIVE

Joe raced down the highway, one hand clutching the steering wheel and the other one gripping the cell phone he held to his ear, waiting for Kate to answer on the other end.

"Hello, I can't take your call right now," the voicemail message began.

Joe punched the disconnect button with his thumb and then dialed the direct line at work.

"This is Kate Holly, I'm on the phone or away from my desk," Kate's recorded voice explained. "Please leave me a message. If you need immediate assistance, please dial one and speak to my assistant."

Joe punched one.

"King Industries."

"This is Joe Holly. Where's my wife?"

"She left about an hour ago," her assistant replied.

"Did she say where she was going?"

"She said she had an appointment."

"What sort of appointment?"

"I don't know. It wasn't on our calendar, so it must be something personal," she said matter-of-factly.

"Was she acting strange?" Joe probed.

"Strange?" the perplexed assistant replied. "Not any different than she's been acting since she started her vitamin, exercise, and diet regime."

"Her what?" Joe asked.

"C'mon, you know what I mean. The one that has her looking like a new woman. I've been bugging her for the details. She keeps promising me she'll reveal all the particulars, but so far, nothing."

"Look, if she returns and calls in, will you please ask her to call me?" Joe said. "It is urgent."

"Sure."

As soon as Joe hung up, his cell phone rang. It wasn't Kate. It was Rachel. Joe picked up his phone and hit the ignore button.

As Joe neared home, he exhaled loudly. Kate's car was parked in their driveway. Expecting to find Kate distraught, worried, and upset, he braced himself before he walked through the front door.

But nothing could have prepared him for what waited on the other side.

CHAPTER FIFTY-SIX

"Kate, are you okay?" Joe yelled from the entryway. "Kate?"

There was no answer.

Joe walked into the living room. No Kate.

"Kate, where are you?" he shouted.

Joe searched the den, then the kitchen. Her purse was on the countertop, yet she was nowhere to be found. It wasn't like her not to answer. Surely, she hadn't done something drastic, Joe told himself.

He could feel his chest tighten with panic as he scrambled up the stairs.

"Kate!" he screamed.

The door to their bedroom was shut. He turned the knob but discovered it had been locked.

Joe pounded on the door. "Kate, are you in there?"

There was no answer. Joe could see light coming from underneath the door.

"Kate, please, unlock this door and let me in," he said, trying to disguise the dread in his voice. "Kate, Dr. Inhope called me and gave me the diagnosis. But don't worry, we'll fight this together. I love you so much."

Joe pressed his ear against the door. "Kate, you're scaring me. Please, let me in."

He thought he heard a sob.

"If you don't open this door, I'm going to break it down," Joe vowed.

He took three steps back and flung his aging body against the barrier. The door barely budged. Joe took four steps back and heaved his full weight against the door. He heard a crack, but it did not give.

Joe stooped over, put his hands on his knees, and struggled to catch his breath.

"Kate," he gasped, "I swear, if you don't open the door, I'm either going to call the police or go get my axe."

"Go away!" Kate shouted.

"Goddammit Kate, open this door," Joe commanded.

Her voice stoked his anger. She'd heard him and was intentionally shutting him out. His rage sent him hurtling toward the door one last time.

The sound of wood crashing against the drywall filled the room.

Kate's head snapped toward the direction of the sound, her red-rimmed eyes wide with surprise as she looked at Joe, who had fallen to the floor when the door gave way.

"Get out!" she screamed.

Joe picked himself up off the carpet. It was then that he noticed an open, half-packed suitcase on the bed.

"What in the hell is this?" he said.

"Exactly what it looks like, Joe," Kate said as she continued throwing clothes into the luggage. "I'm leaving."

"Oh no you're not," Joe said as he reached into the bag and pulled out her belongings.

"Get away from me," she said through a clenched jaw while taking one step back.

"Kate, I had no idea that the gel contained mescaline. You have to believe me," Joe said.

"Ha!" Kate replied. "I'm never going to believe a word you say ever again."

"What are you talking about?"

Kate walked over to the nightstand and picked up a thick, large envelope. She reached inside and pulled out a stack of papers.

"What's that?" Joe asked warily.

"My medical records," Kate said. "I came home after Dr. Inhope called. The mail had already been delivered. I want you to read this page."

She thrust a piece of paper filled with dense black ink. "Read it out loud," she growled.

"The patient is a healthy female in her mid-twenties, a married woman who has been unable to get pregnant. The results of her fertility testing came back normal and she should be able to conceive. The patient's husband had a vasectomy." Joe stopped and slumped down on the bed.

"Keep reading!"

Joe cleared his throat. "The patient's husband had a vasectomy because he does not want children. He has concealed this fact from the patient. Because the husband is also a patient and because he has forbidden the physician from revealing the information, the physician is unable to tell the reason why the husband cannot have children."

Joe let the paper drop from his hand and muttered, "That bastard betrayed me."

Kate let out the laugh of a woman losing her grip on reality. "I'm the one who has been betrayed!"

"Look Kate," Joe began, "you're making a much bigger deal out of this than it really is. Having children is a drain. They would have driven a wedge between the two of us. I know you. You would have sacrificed your career to wipe noses. For what? Little humans who drain you of money and then resent you once they've grown?"

"That was not your decision to make unilaterally. I desperately wanted children and you know it."

"You're not remembering things accurately," Joe said, trying to blame the amnesia. "You didn't want kids that badly. You should be thanking me for saving you from a lifetime of drudgery, misery, and heartache."

"The amnesia affected my brain—not my heart," Kate said. "From the very depths of my heart I knew that I wanted to have a family with you. You didn't save me from heartache. You caused it."

Kate shut her suitcase. When she tried to grab the handle, Joe ripped the luggage from her hands. Incensed, Kate said, "Clothes can always be replaced."

She stormed out of the bedroom and down the stairs. By the time Joe reached her, she'd retrieved her purse from the kitchen and was headed for the front door. Joe barricaded her exit with his body.

"I'm not letting you leave."

"Joe, you can't keep me a prisoner here forever no matter how hard you try. Move."

Joe shook his head.

"Then you might be interested in knowing that I called Stan before you got home," Kate said defiantly.

Joe clenched his jaw. "Why?"

"I thought he might be interested in knowing about the mystery ingredient in the gel."

"You didn't!"

"I certainly did," Kate said without a trace of emotion. "Now, get out of my way."

CHAPTER FIFTY-SEVEN

"Mr. Holly, I've been asked to escort you up to the executive conference room," the Galatea security guard said when Joe walked into the building.

After Kate had walked out on him there was nothing left for Joe to do but to go to work and try to repair the damage she'd done.

"Let me go to my office first," Joe said but as he started toward the lab the grim-faced security guard stepped in his way.

"I'm sorry, Mr. Holly, but I was told you were not allowed to go to the lab. I was told to escort you to the executive conference room and nowhere else."

Joe's shoulders sagged. "All right," he said with a sigh.

All his life, Joe had been able to use his quick wits to battle his way out of any corner. But he was weary. The will to fight was gone. Like a man underwater who can no longer hold his breath, he had resigned himself to giving up and exhaling; steeling himself for the painful, silent suffocation that was about to come.

The security guard opened the conference room door and ushered Joe inside. Huff, Stan, Rachel, and Galatea's lawyer sat around the table, grim-faced and tight-lipped. When Joe looked at Stan and Rachel, neither one would meet his gaze.

"Joe," Huff began, "I don't even know where to start."

"Look, let me explain," Joe stuttered.

"No," Huff growled. "Let me explain. Because of you, one person who has received the anti-wrinkle cream has suffered brain damage. Because of you, several other subjects—including my wife—may develop retrograde amnesia. Because of you, Galatea may be facing multimillion-dollar lawsuits over the use of this product; and once word of this scandal leaks out our stock is going to plummet. You know what happens when stocks nosedive?"

Joe didn't answer.

"Investor lawsuits, that's what happens," Huff said.

Joe put his hand to his forehead and massaged his temples, trying to ease the pressure building in his skull.

"You're exaggerating," Joe stammered. "You're acting like this is the apocalypse when the fact of the matter is the project has just hit a little snag."

Stan, who had been sitting quietly, jumped abruptly to his feet. "I do not call single-handedly ruining my company a little snag. Forget Galatea for a moment," Stan said as he began pacing the room. "How could you let this experiment continue when you suspected that there was something wrong with Kate? I could never live with myself if it had been Barbara instead of Kate. Never! Not only that, but then, knowing there was potentially a very serious problem, you deliberately put other people at risk. I don't know if it was hubris, selfishness, or stupidity that caused you to do such a thing. What I do know is that you've hurt a great many people."

The lawyer cleared his throat and pushed a document and pen toward Joe. "Joe, we've got a separation agreement we want you to sign."

"You mean I'm fired?" Joe asked weakly.

The lawyer nodded. "Yes, and we want you to state in writing that you hid the problems with the Phoenix Project from the company."

Joe smiled. "That way if Galatea gets sued, I'm the scapegoat. Right?"

"That's the plan," Huff said.

"Joe, I think you better sign it," Rachel said, breaking her silence.

"Even you, Rachel?" Joe asked, a pained look spreading across his face.

Joe reached for his final papers, the ones that would end his once-promising career, with his left hand. When the tips of his fingers connected with the documents, it felt as though he had touched a live electric socket. A jolt traveled from his fingers, to his hand, through his arm, to his heart, and up to his head.

Then the floor came rushing toward his face.

CHAPTER FIFTY-EIGHT

It was the sound of Kate's muffled crying that woke Joe up. He had been moved out of the ICU and into a regular room. It was dark. The door was open. Kate's forehead was resting on a man's chest; Stan's chest. His hands circled her lightly in a comforting embrace. To a casual observer, Stan was offering friendly comfort to the wife of a sick friend. But Joe knew that was not the case. Stan had other plans.

Joe moaned. Stan let Kate go.

"I'll be in the waiting room," Joe heard Stan say, "in case you need me."

Joe groaned a second time.

"Everything is going to be okay," Kate said as she hustled into the room. There was no makeup on her face. The skin under her eyes was dark. Sure, she looked worn down, Joe thought, but she also looked vulnerable. And a vulnerable Kate had always awakened a protective instinct in Joe. He felt it when Kate showed up in their economics class, devastated after being assaulted by Harry. And he felt it now.

"I had a dream. We were on our honeymoon. At the beach. You were wearing that black-and-white polka-dot bikini. Remember?" Joe asked.

Kate shook her head. "No, Joe. I don't remember."

He reached up to stroke her cheek with his left hand, only it wouldn't move. Joe grimaced. "My hand."

"Shhhh," Kate said. "You're still weak."

"What is Stan doing here?" Joe asked.

Kate looked surprised. "You saw him?"

"Yes," Joe said. "Did he fire me—or was that a dream, too?"

"He wants to make sure you're okay," Kate said.

"That's not what it looked like to me," Joe said.

"What do you mean?" Kate asked.

"I saw him just now, his arms around you. He isn't here for me. He's here to get you."

"You're delirious, all the medicine pumping through your veins. You had a stroke. You were in a drug-induced coma. The doctors said that as you came out of it, you could be confused. You were probably just hallucinating. The doctors said coma patients can have trouble separating fiction from fact," Kate said. "You've been through a lot and you've got a long road ahead of you, Joe." She patted Joe on the chest, smoothed the hair away from his forehead, and whispered into his ear, "Go back to sleep."

"Stop telling me to go back to sleep and stop treating me like a child," Joe demanded angrily. "I have no idea what day it is. While I have been trapped in this hospital, the world has continued spinning along without me."

A nurse walked into the room. "Is everything okay?"

"Yes, everything's fine," Kate said.

"Does the patient need more medication," the nurse asked, "for his nerves?"

Joe vigorously shook his head no. "I don't need any more drugs."

"I think we're fine," Kate reassured her.

"Okay then," the nurse said before walking out of the room. "Just call me if you change your mind."

Joe continued, "Kate, I need some answers."

Kate paced the room and began twisting her fingers together. That wasn't a good sign.

"Listen, Kate, I need to know what I'm up against," Joe said wearily. "Our relationship, my career, and my body have all let me down. I'd rather have all the bad news right now, in one fell swoop. It would be worse to get it in drips and drabs, several arrows shot into my heart over time rather than all at once."

Kate was quiet. What Joe said made some sense.

As Joe watched her struggle with what she should keep secret and what she should reveal, he realized that, to a stranger, they must seem like an odd pair. Kate was luminous. Had he dreamed it—or had he overheard nurses on the floor discussing Kate's beauty, a slight hint of envy in their voices? He could have sworn he heard snippets of a debate among the nurses about whether Kate had plastic surgery. But if she did go under the knife, they agreed, none of them could spot the scalpel scars or the unnatural tightness left after the procedures. They speculated she had stayed out of the sun, used moisturizer, and never smoked. Perhaps she was simply one of the very few blessed with great genes from her ancestors. Maybe it was all of the above.

But as Joe scrutinized his pacing wife, he noticed there was something else about her that hadn't been there before: a slight flush in her cheeks, a becoming shade of pink, the exact shade he struggled for decades to conjure up in the lab as a blush. He'd come close a few times, but never quite attained the precise hue. *Why was it so important for so long?* he wondered. When the answer came to him, he could feel his heart pound against the wall of his chest. *That's the shade of romance,* he realized even if Kate didn't quite know it yet.

"Maybe we should talk later," Kate said, hoping to avoid a confrontation.

"For cris'sake, Kate, I'm a man, treat me like one!"

Kate sighed. "I think you're right, Joe, it is better to get it all over at once."

"I'd rather not take the news in bed," Joe answered. "Having my wife stand over me while I'm in bed makes me feel like a child. I'd rather sit in the chair."

"You can't get out of bed yet," Kate said. "Maybe this can wait."

"No," Joe growled, feeling lightheaded as he tried to lift his body out of the bed, only to fail without barely rustling the covers.

"I wish you'd let me call the nurse," Kate said anxiously. "Why don't you let me just raise your head a little using the bed?"

Kate leaned over Joe and pressed a button long the rail. As she moved over him, Joe breathed in his wife's scent, the faint and familiar combination of citrus and summer. He closed his eyes and he tried to memorize how his body felt—even heavily sedated—when Kate was near.

"Dr. Roberts said that once you emerged from your coma, there would be tests to determine how much damage was done to your body," Kate said. "Then you've got a long road of physical therapy ahead of you."

Kate continued, "I have been interviewing home nurses. I found one that I like. She would live at the house. She'll be responsible for making sure you receive all of the medications the doctor is going to put you on to control your blood pressure, she'll take you to your physical therapy appointments, and she's responsible for assisting you around the house and making you the meals that a dietician will be recommending."

Joe shook his head no. "I don't want a nurse. I don't want a stranger living with us, either."

"Living with you," Kate said quietly. "I've already moved my things out of the house. I won't be coming back."

"How could you move out? I mean where can you go? You haven't even had time to look for a place," Joe said as he searched Kate's face, looking for some hesitation or wavering on her part, an opening that he could exploit to get her to change her mind.

Kate looked out the window before meeting his eyes again. "Stan offered me the guest house that sits on the edge of his property. It is a little place, quite lovely and very peaceful."

In his brain, Joe clenched the fists of both hands. But physically, only the fingers in his right hand tightened into the fighter's position. The fingers on his left hand were frozen into a meek claw.

"That bastard! He wants you. Don't you see? He's trying to steal you from me."

"Joe, you have it all wrong. He's been very kind, supportive, and understanding. He's been nothing but a friend to me," Kate said.

"You're so naive. It is all an act to turn you into the next Mrs. Markowsky," Joe said.

Kate pursed her lips tightly and folded her arms across her chest before speaking again. "I'm not going to argue with you. I understand that you're upset but you're not going to change my mind by being mean and crass."

"We've been married for over thirty years, Kate. What kind of wife leaves her husband after a stroke?"

"I'll tell you what kind of wife," Kate said angrily, "the kind of wife who was betrayed by her husband, the kind of wife who believed her husband's lies. Any obligation or debt that I might have owed you was repaid long ago."

Joe's forehead dropped into his right hand. He shielded his tears from her, but he could not disguise the involuntary sobs caused by the pain that started in his heart and racked his chest with convulsions.

Kate, her beautiful face frozen by bitterness and betrayal, said nothing. After several minutes passed, she finally spoke. "Shall I continue?" she asked.

"Do you enjoy this?" Joe asked without looking at her. "How could you come to the hospital, hold my hand, stroke my hair, and whisper words of encouragement?"

"I'm not cold-hearted, Joe. I do have compassion. I don't like seeing anyone in pain, especially my husband. But that doesn't mean I have forgiven you. I wasted most of my life on a marriage that was a lie. I don't intend to squander the little time I have left with you."

Joe struggled to regain his composure. "What about my job?"

"Nothing had gone through human resources yet at Galatea. Stan agreed to table the firing for now. I don't think they're going to welcome you back in the lab, but for now, you have health and disability insurance. You'll also continue receiving your paycheck. There will be plenty of money to cover the medical expenses and keep you comfortable in our home. I thought that was very kind."

"I'm sure that's what Stan wanted you to think. I wonder if you would've been so quick to move out if you knew that I didn't have any money coming in."

Before Kate could answer, the nurse entered the room.

"Joe is very tired. I think we should give him some time alone," Kate said.

He didn't have the strength to protest as the nurse lowered his bed and covered his broken body with a sheet.

CHAPTER FIFTY-NINE

The day after Kate confessed she had moved out—and announced that she didn't intend to return—she brought the home nurse to the hospital. In her early thirties, Maggie Henry had the athletic build of a disciplined marathon runner. Her lean body moved with purpose and precision. Joe's patient chart, not the patient himself, was the first thing she wanted to see upon being introduced. It was only after she flipped through the pages quickly that she finally spoke.

"Mr. Holly, I've met with your wife, your doctor, and the nurses. They've fully briefed me on your medical condition as well as your prognosis. It sounds like you had quite a scare but with hard work you should be able to regain much of the movement that you lost because of the stroke."

Joe looked at Kate before addressing the nurse. "Well, Miss Henry—it is miss, I presume?"

Maggie nodded yes.

"Well, Miss Henry, I don't want or need a nurse. I'm perfectly able to take care of myself."

Joe thought he detected a condescending smile pass briefly across Maggie's lips before she regained her matter-of-fact composure.

"I understand your hesitation, Mr. Holly. I really do. Most of my clients feel that way at first. But soon after they walk through the front door of their home, they come to realize the wisdom of having a home health nurse."

"I'm not most patients," Joe said stubbornly. "I don't need or want a nurse."

"Could you give us just a minute alone to speak privately?" Kate interrupted.

Maggie nodded and slipped out of the room.

"Listen up, Joe. I know what you're trying to do," Kate said sternly.

"I'm not trying to do anything except fire a person whose services I don't need," Joe retorted.

"You know damn good and well that you're trying to get me to change my mind and move back in with you," Kate said.

"First of all, I didn't say anything of the sort," Joe replied. "And second, it is our home."

"It is not my home. It is a house I shared with you, a house built on a foundation of lies," Kate said through clenched teeth. She inhaled deeply. "Your doctors and your nurses agree that you cannot live on your own. You will need some help. If you won't go along with the home nurse, then I'll be forced to place you in a nursing home."

Horrified, Joe shouted, "You can't do that!"

"Oh no? Don't push me or I will. I'm your wife. I'll push for a guardianship. Your doctors will support my position, and instead of going home, I'll check you in to an assisted living facility. It would be ideal for me. Instead of living in Stan's guest house, I'd just move back into the house, but the place would be mine."

"You wouldn't dare," Joe said, his eyes wide.

"I don't want to put you into a nursing home. But if you force me to choose between a nursing home for you or a sentence of servitude for me as your nurse, I'll choose the former. I'm finally putting myself first," she declared.

Joe eyes burned with rage. But his body remained weak and the will to argue had drained from his body.

"Good, you understand my position," Kate said before opening the door and inviting Maggie back into the room.

"Everything settled?" Maggie asked, looking to Kate.

"Yes," Kate answered.

"Great," Maggie said as she opened a notebook. With pen in hand, she said, "Now, why don't you begin by telling me what you prefer to eat for breakfast, lunch, and dinner?"

From that point forward, Maggie made it a point to stop by the hospital each day to check in on her patient. To her, Joe was another challenge, a set of issues to be managed, a project with a goal and a job. Joe realized that she treated him the way he used to treat test subjects in the lab, not a whole person, but pieces of an experiment he controlled.

And once the neurological tests came back showing he had not suffered any brain damage, Dr. Roberts pronounced it was time for Joe to go home. But home to what? Joe wondered.

And when the day came for Joe to be discharged, Kate was at the

Erasing the Past

hospital to oversee the task. She watched as Joe signed the release forms that set him off to a new life.

Maggie followed the hospital nurse out of the room to obtain last-minute instructions and fetch the wheelchair.

"Joe," Kate said, "I'll see you to the car, but I won't be going back to the house with you."

Joe was silent. His life was being twisted into something he no longer recognized. Something that he did not have a hand in creating.

"Okay," Joe said.

Kate eyes widened. She had been prepared for a flood of objections. But instead, he was but a shadow of his former combative self.

Joe looked down at his hands for several seconds before speaking. "Ever since I first laid eyes on you, Kate, I feared this moment; the moment you would walk away. The irony is that if I had only surrendered, let go of my need to control, we could have had a wonderful life."

He peered into Kate's eyes. "Kate, I'm so sorry for hurting you so deeply. Perhaps it is just as well that you don't remember our past. Unfortunately, that's all I have left."

CHAPTER SIXTY

On his first morning home from the hospital, Joe's body woke up, ready to go to work. After decades of showing up on time at Galatea, he didn't need an alarm clock to rouse him. Only now, he had nowhere to go. And now, he only had the ghost of Kate next to him in bed.

Joe quietly made his way down to the kitchen. Perhaps he'd find some comfort in a cup of coffee.

The stroke was as much of a marker in Joe's life as the time he first spotted Kate, their first date, the day they married. Before he'd had his stroke, Kate would have made the coffee the night before and set it on an automatic timer. A stiff brew would already have been waiting for him by the time he got to the kitchen. But this morning, the first morning home after the stroke, the carafe was empty. It was not even smudged by old coffee stains. It had been rinsed clean in the dishwasher.

Joe reached into the top cupboard for a filter. The box was on the top shelf. Two hands would have made the task of pulling it down much easier. But since he now only had one, Joe quietly pushed a chair over to the cabinet and climbed up. If Maggie walked in, he knew there'd be hell to pay.

After successfully getting out one of the filters, Joe was confident the rest would be easy. But getting the lid off the tub of coffee presented another hurdle. To hold it steady, he wedged the tub between his body and the end of the cabinet. With his right hand, he yanked on the lid. It came off—but in the process of pulling, Joe stepped back. The leverage he had against the tub was gone. It dropped to the floor, spewing fresh coffee grounds throughout the room.

Joe looked at the mess he'd made. He tried to scoop coffee off the floor with his good hand, but the more he tried to fix it, the worse it got. He tried sweeping up the mess with a broom, but he couldn't operate the dust pan. Finally, he sank down on the ground, amid the mess, and gave up.

"Mr. Holly?" Maggie called from the hallway. "Are you okay?"

Maggie entered the kitchen, paused for about two seconds then answered her own question. "You could be better." If she was alarmed by his physical state or pitied him, he couldn't tell.

"First, let me help you into a chair," Maggie said. Without waiting for her patient to answer, she locked her arms underneath his armpits and yanked him to his feet.

"Now, let me have that broom."

Joe could hear the bristles of the broom slide across the tile floor, but he did not watch. Instead, he sat at the kitchen table and stared into the dark dining room.

"How about I make you a cup of coffee?" Maggie volunteered.

Joe nodded.

"You shouldn't even be drinking this stuff. It has caffeine. I bought some decaf for you."

"I like my coffee full strength, not decaffeinated," Joe said angrily.

"Decaf is much better for you and you want to get better, don't you?" Maggie asked.

"I want regular coffee!" Joe insisted.

"Well, Mr. Holly," Maggie said firmly, "I'm afraid that isn't going to be possible this morning. You just spilled all the regular coffee. You have no choice."

Joe pretended to ignore her. Maggie went about doing exactly what she said she was going to do.

"Here you go, Mr. Holly," Maggie said, sliding a cup of coffee in front of Joe. "If my memory is right, you like it black. Would you like some company, or would you prefer to be alone?" Maggie asked.

"Alone," he answered.

She slipped quietly out of the room. After she was gone, Joe raised the mug to his lips and took a sip. Kate always made the coffee strong, added a nice bite to it. This was coffee-flavored water with no kick. He put the cup back down on the table and went back up to his room.

Joe sat down on the bed and dialed Kate's cell phone. "I'm sorry, that number is no longer in service," was the message Joe received.

Defeated, Joe lay back down on the bed and willed himself to sleep. At least slumber was an escape.

The sound of running water in the master bathroom startled Joe. The clock on his nightstand said 10 a.m. Kate! he thought as he headed for the bathroom. But when he opened the door, it wasn't Kate.

"What are you doing in here?" Joe asked his fully clothed nurse.

"Just drawing you a bath," she said.

"I didn't ask for a bath," Joe muttered.

"But you need one," Maggie said cheerily.

"I'm perfectly capable of drawing my own bath," Joe said. "And could you stop talking down to me? I feel like I'm in preschool."

Maggie pursed her lips. "Mr. Holly, the bathroom is one of the most dangerous places in the home, especially for someone like you."

"Like me?" Joe said testily.

"Like you—a stroke patient. You're still much too frail to take care of yourself."

"I can take care of myself just fine," Joe snapped.

"After cleaning coffee up off the floor, I beg to differ," Maggie reminded him. "Now, are you going to get out of your pajamas and let me help you into the bath or am I going to have to remove them?"

Joe shook his head in disbelief. How did his life get to this point? he wondered.

"If I let you help me in the bath, will you give me an hour or so to read alone, in my room?" Joe asked.

"Sure," Maggie said as she began unbuttoning his pajama top, her aloof expression telling Joe he might as well have been a doll—or a cadaver.

"King Industries," the receptionist answered when Joe dialed Kate's office.

He'd finished his humiliating bath ordeal with Maggie. Other than his mother and Kate, no woman had seen him bathe at home. Kate and his mother were women bound to him by the bonds of love and affection. Maggie was simply their paid surrogate, but no amount of money could buy tenderness.

After the bath, Maggie brought him the daily newspaper. "Now, let me read in peace," Joe said. "And close the door."

Joe waited five minutes before taking the cordless phone off the cradle. He dialed Kate's direct line, but it was rerouted to the general receptionist.

"I'm sorry, I was trying to reach Kate Holly," Joe said.

"May I ask who is calling?"

"This is her husband. I need to talk to her."

"I'm sorry. Ms. Holly isn't accepting phone calls. May I take a message?"

"Do you know when she will be taking phone calls?" Joe asked.

"No sir, I don't. Do you have a message?"

"No. I'll try later," Joe said before hanging up.

Instead of putting the phone down to rest, Joe dialed Rachel. She would have some answers. But when he called, Joe was subjected to the same treatment. Rachel's direct line had been forwarded to the general receptionist. Rachel was not taking calls, he was told. When Joe received the same treatment from Stan and Huff, he knew they had coordinated their response. He had become invisible.

"Mr. Holly," Maggie said before opening the door. "You have a doctor's appointment in just a bit. We should get you ready to go."

"A few more minutes," Joe begged.

"Mr. Holly, we need to get ready now," Maggie said. Then putting her hands on her hips she added, "They're not going to talk to you."

"What are you talking about?" Joe asked.

"Your wife. Your former coworkers. They aren't going to talk to you," she said again. "It is useless to try to reach them. It would be better if you concentrated on getting better."

"Are you spying on me?" Joe asked.

"Of course not," Maggie said. "I've been hired to make sure you're safe."

Joe laughed. "That's a good one. You've been hired by them to keep an eye on me."

"Mr. Holly, we need to go," Maggie said firmly.

CHAPTER SIXTY-ONE

The only threads that tied Joe to his former life were the paychecks that were directly deposited into the bank account he shared with Kate. Every day, he logged in to check his financial status. With his job in limbo, he worried about money; everything he had worked years to attain could be drained overnight by health care costs.

But that wasn't the only reason he kept close tabs on the account. Joe also hoped that the daily reports would give him some clues about Kate. Where and how she spent her money would give him an idea of what she was up to.

Yet the more he checked, the more the picture grew hazy. Although Kate was still listed as a joint owner of the account, her paychecks were no longer going into their mutual pot of money. She wasn't withdrawing money from their account, either through debit card purchases or checks. She hadn't taken a dime of the sizable sum they had in their savings. With his paychecks, the account continued to grow. And the cost of employing Maggie was not reflected anywhere. Even though Galatea's health insurance was unusual in that it was a generous plan, it didn't cover home health. Maggie was buying the groceries and picking up the medicine. But the costs weren't deducted from the account. Joe decided he needed answers.

"Maggie, who is paying you?" Joe asked bluntly after another day of looking at his accounts. He'd emerged from the relative privacy of his bedroom. He had a physical therapy appointment in an hour and it was almost time to leave.

Maggie shrugged. "I assumed you were."

Joe didn't believe it. "How are you paying for the groceries and the medicine?"

"Mrs. Holly gave me a credit card to use for those expenses," Maggie answered.

"Did she tell you how she's paying off the credit card?" Joe probed.

"No, Mr. Holly, she didn't. It isn't my concern," she replied before switching the subject. "By the way, your physical therapy session was canceled. I got a call about fifteen minutes ago. It has been changed to tomorrow."

Joe nodded and headed back up the stairs to the privacy of his room.

"If you aren't going to need anything for a while, I think I'll go for a run. Do you mind?" Maggie asked. "I'll take my cell phone with me."

Joe waved his hand. "Go."

It was the soft sound of footsteps in the bedroom closet that woke Joe from his nap. He sat upright in the bed. "Maggie, what are you doing in here?" he asked angrily.

But it wasn't Maggie who emerged with an armful of clothes.

"Kate?" Joe asked, not sure if he was awake or dreaming.

"I didn't mean to wake you," Kate said. "I didn't think you'd be here. I thought you had a doctor's appointment."

"No, it was rescheduled," Joe answered. Perhaps it was because he hadn't seen her in two months, but to Joe, his wife seemed even more youthful and vital than he'd remembered. She shifted from left foot to right, just as she always had when she was nervous.

"How did you know I had an appointment?" Joe asked. "Are you talking to Maggie?"

"Yes, I do talk to her," Kate admitted. "I receive updates on how you're doing. I am your wife. I feel some responsibility."

"Still lurking in the shadows of my life," Joe said.

"I came to get some more of my things from the closet. I also wanted to check the kitchen, make sure Maggie was stocking the fridge properly and just check on the condition of the house in general. You can never be too careful when it comes to these home health people."

"Would you like to sit down?" Joe asked.

"No, I don't think so," Kate said. "I hear you're regaining some movement in your arm."

"Some. I can move the arm, I can just barely make my fingers into the shape of a cup, but in terms of gripping or moving each finger on its own, I don't know if I'll ever regain those motions. That's not good. Hard to conduct experiments when you can't grip a test tube, hold a petri dish without fear of dropping it, or handle tiny instruments designed for microscopic intervention," Joe said, his voice trailing off as the realization of all the things he might not ever be able to do again sunk in.

But it wasn't just the loss of his hand he mourned. Looking at Kate, her arms loaded down with clothes, he realized he'd also lost her. A part of him hoped that if she had her space, she'd ultimately return.

"How are you feeling? Is the amnesia still a problem?" Joe asked.

Kate shrugged. "I'm not sure. I don't have you around to remind me what I've forgotten so if I'm missing anything, I don't know it."

She stepped forward as if to leave. Joe had to keep her at home if only a few minutes more.

"The cream must still be working," he said. "You look, you look," his voice faltered, "you look like an angel."

Kate twisted her fingers together. "I'm using the cream again. Rachel figured out what went wrong. They tested it on lab animals. Now they are running trials. I'm not part of the trials—because of my, um, condition." Then she smiled. "But Stan is slipping me some on the side. I've got to go now, Joe. Take care," she said before walking out of the room, her arms tightly folded together.

Joe heard Kate shut the front door behind her. He listened as she started her car and pulled out of the driveway.

Joe got out of bed and went to the closet. His briefcase was in there somewhere. Maggie had taken away the keys to the car. She said he wasn't fit to drive. One more way they'd all been able to control him.

But in his briefcase was a spare set of car keys tucked into a hidden pocket—in case of an emergency. Maggie assumed she'd seized his ticket to freedom, but she was wrong. The keys were exactly where he'd left them. Using his right hand, he slipped the key into a pocket in his pants.

As he walked down the stairs, Joe listened for Maggie. He hoped she was gone on one of her two-hour runs. There was no sound coming from the guest room. He checked the kitchen, still no sign of his warden. He slipped into the garage where his car had been parked since the day of his stroke.

It feels good to take control, Joe thought to himself as opened the car door with his right hand. He slid into the tan leather driver's seat then reached across his chest with his right arm to shut the door. He clumsily fished around his pocket until he felt the cool metal of the keys. His hands were sweating. He was nervous about driving—and about the prospect of getting caught. And he wondered how he became a prisoner of his own life.

He slid the key into the ignition and the car came to life. The engine purred softly, happy to finally be useful. All that was left was to get out of the driveway.

Joe pushed the button on his garage door opener. He moistened his dry lips with his tongue, put his foot on the brake, and, with his right hand, moved the gearshift from park into reverse. With a one-handed grip on the steering wheel, he lifted his foot off the brake gently and the car jerked backward.

He eased out of the driveway and down the road. For so long, he'd taken driving for granted. But today, he experienced the same exhilaration he felt the first time his dad gave him the keys to the old Buick and let him take it for a spin.

When he was fifteen, it felt as though he were driving toward his future. He had no future now, only the past.

Joe knew the route to Rachel's house by heart. She had lived in the same place since the early 1980s. He parked his car five houses down, turned off the engine, and waited. It was five o'clock. She'd be coming home from work soon. If Joe couldn't get through to her at the office, he would confront her at her home.

He didn't have to wait long.

Rachel pulled into her drive without noticing his car; it is easy to look past the unexpected. To Rachel, her boss was a broken man who answered to a nurse. He was the last person she expected to see.

As Rachel got out of her car and unlocked her front door, a fierce rage took hold of Joe. He started his car, then stepped on the accelerator. He whipped the auto into the driveway, pinning Rachel's car between his and the house.

Wide-eyed, Rachel watched Joe as he climbed out of the car.

"Are you even supposed to be driving?" was all she could think to ask.

"The real question, Rachel, is 'Are you supposed to be running another trial with my wrinkle cream?'"

Her mouth dropped. "How did you know the project is back on?" she asked.

"Kate dropped by to see me today and she let it slip," Joe answered.

"Kate dropped by to see you? Was Stan with her?" Rachel asked as her verbal combat skills returned. "I suppose you know they're quite the item."

"I'm here to talk about the cream, not Kate and Stan, so don't try to change the subject," Joe lied.

"Look, if you want to know about the cream, come inside. I've got all the time in the world to fill you in. In fact, I'm going to enjoy it."

Rachel opened her front door and gestured toward a chair in her living room. Everything was tidy and clean. It was the home of a woman who had only to clean up her own messes, not the messes of others.

"Can I get you something to drink, water, tea, a glass of wine perhaps?" she asked.

"No, I don't want anything. I want to talk about the cream," Joe insisted.

"Suit yourself, but I want some tea. I'm not going to talk about anything until I have a hot cup in my hand. So, I'll repeat my question: Would you like something to drink?"

"I'll repeat my answer: No."

Rachel retreated to the kitchen and turned on the water. Then a kettle clanked down on the stove. She could have stuck a mug of water in the microwave for a minute but instead, she drew it out as long as possible.

"That's much better," Rachel said when she finally reappeared, sipping a cup of hot tea. "I find that after a long day of running the lab nothing relaxes me more than chamomile."

"Have they hired someone to replace me?" Joe asked.

"Why yes," Rachel said with a smile.

"Who?"

"They finally came to their senses and hired the person who should have been running the lab a long time ago," Rachel said. "Me."

"You're head of research and development?" Joe sputtered.

"Didn't anyone tell you? I was given your old job," Rachel said in between sips.

"I haven't even been fired. How could you get my old job?" Joe asked.

"Well, you haven't technically been fired. Stan's just keeping you on the payroll while he figures out his next move. If you don't have a steady paycheck, he's afraid that Kate will feel guilty. If Kate feels guilty, she might leave that cozy little guest house she's occupying rent free and come back to take care of you. From what I can tell, he's doing everything to make sure that doesn't happen," Rachel said smugly.

Joe stared at his former assistant and wondered how he had missed her cold, calculating nature for so long.

"Does he love her?" Joe asked.

Rachel shrugged. "Do men ever really love Kate or do they love the way she makes them feel? Is she a person or an object to be owned? I suspect you know the answer to that one much better than I."

"Of course she's a person, not an object," Joe said angrily. "And she should know better than to fall for someone like Stan."

Rachel laughed. "Oh please, Joe. If she was a person, she wouldn't have been so caught up in having plastic surgery. I think her value is as an object. But, once an object becomes scuffed, worn, and broken down, it isn't worth very much, is it? A patina might be good for some sort of antique gas pump, but it doesn't boost the value of a woman."

"Kate is irreplaceable no matter what she looks like. You can't put value on a human life, especially one as kind, pure, and trusting as Kate's," Joe argued. "You of all people should know that. How can you simply stand aside and let Stan continue to give her that cream, one that robs her of a lifetime of memories?"

"It didn't seem to bother your conscience when you were doing it," Rachel shot back. "Besides, that's not a problem anymore. You see, I figured out what went wrong and fixed it."

"How did you do that?"

"Well, it wasn't that hard. You see, I created the problem in the first place."

Joe fell back against the back of the chair and stared in disbelief as Rachel continued sipping her tea.

"You created the problem? You hurt Kate on purpose? How could you?"

Rachel smiled. "I didn't hurt Kate. I hurt you. And you deserved it. You've been climbing up the corporate ladder by stepping on my back ever since you arrived. I've always propped you up and kept you out of trouble. I bolstered your career and Kate boosted your ego. I decided I had had quite enough."

"That's not true. You know it isn't true," Joe stammered but Rachel ignored him.

"You remember in college when I won that coveted fellowship?" she asked.

Joe nodded.

"Well, what you didn't know is that the project I was working on involved biological warfare agents. My employer had a contract with the Army's chemical research and development laboratories. My job was to work with incapacitating chemicals that caused retrograde amnesia. Mescaline was one of the chemicals I handled. As you know, I'm very good at my work. I was also very proud of it. Even though the work was classified, I kept copies. Little did I know it would come in handy decades later, the moment you chose bad, reckless science; bypassing proper clinical trials and trying the cream out on your own wife without testing it on animals, I decided to mix some of the synthetic mescaline in with the synthetic marula. The result was better than I could have ever dreamed: You got a beautiful wife who couldn't remember why she married you in the first place."

Joe jumped up out of his chair. He had never wanted so badly to hit a woman. As far as he was concerned, her evil heart had made her into a monster.

Rachel put her tea down, stood up, and got right in front of his face and laughed. "You think you're going to hurt me? Maybe you think you can run to Stan and he'll make everything better? Fat chance. He cares about two things right now. The first and most important is making money. I fixed the miracle cream and he doesn't give a damn why it was broken in the first place. It is going to make the company zillions of dollars. Second, he wants Kate. He had a personal interest in making sure that you're to blame for her problems."

Rachel walked to the front door. "I have to say, this has been a most completely satisfying day. To make it a perfect day, there's only one thing left to do—throw you out of my house."

CHAPTER SIXTY-TWO

The car had not even pulled into the driveway before Maggie flew out of the house. "Stop right there!" she screamed, pointing to the side of the road. "Where have you been?"

Joe intended to ignore his keeper's orders—until he noticed Stan's car.

"What do you think you're doing? You haven't been given clearance to drive," Maggie said angrily.

Joe turned toward Maggie, his face inches from hers. "Don't you dare scold me," he growled. "I don't know who you think you are. You aren't my wife or my mother. You wore out your welcome long ago. I think it is time you packed your bags."

"You're trying to fire me?" she asked, the words cloaked with disbelief.

"I'm not trying to fire you," Joe said, "I am firing you."

"Ha," Maggie said. "You can't fire me. The only one who can get rid of me is him," she said, pointing at Stan.

Stan was standing on Joe's front porch, looking as if he owned the place.

"I'll deal with you later," Joe promised Maggie before walking up his front yard to meet Stan.

"You take my wife, you take my life, are you here for my house too?" Joe said angrily.

Stan refused to take the bait. "Joe, old friend, come inside. You should sit down. We need to talk business."

Joe looked at the man he once considered one of his closest friends, a contemporary with whom he shared a lifetime with; a man Joe had made extremely rich.

Joe brushed past him and stepped into the living room.

"I hear the miracle cream is back in production," Joe said. "I've heard that you've given Rachel my old job. And I've also been told that you plan to marry my wife."

"You have good information," Stan said calmly. "I'm just surprised it took you so long to figure it all out. You were always a clever man, I expected you to uncover the truth much sooner."

"If you haven't noticed, I've been a hostage in my own home," Joe responded.

"You may think of it as being imprisoned, to everyone else, you're well taken care of," Stan said. "Maggie has done an excellent job."

"Maggie and Rachel, do you intentionally surround yourself with monsters?" Joe asked.

"What do you mean?" Stan said with a smile.

"Rachel sabotaged the wrinkle cream. She added a mind-altering ingredient that causes retrograde amnesia."

Stan cleared his throat. "Rachel told me you might come in claiming that was the case. She said your feeble physical condition as well as the mental stress and anguish you're going through led you to concoct the accusation at her house. She said you'd probably bring the same charge to me."

"Well, what are you going to do about it?"

"What am I going to do about it?" Stan said, shaking his head. "Absolutely nothing. It is your word against hers. Why would I believe you? You're a desperate man who will stop at nothing to get his old life back. And if you're thinking about telling Kate, she's not going to believe you either. After all, you're the man who deceived her for most of your marriage."

"You're going to let a psychopath run my lab?" Joe said, his voice trembling with anger.

"It's my lab, Joe, not yours. And it is my anti-wrinkle cream, not yours. Perhaps Rachel did do something that she shouldn't have; maybe her ambition did get the better of her. I've known for years that she's jealous of you. In fact, I always thought that the rivalry and resentment she's harbored for you benefited Galatea tremendously. I always knew that by harnessing her competitive spirit, always keeping her just out of reach of her goal, I'd get a better product. Now, I've hit the jackpot."

"You would allow someone who meant to hurt Kate, who made a deliberate and conscious choice to cause brain damage, to be in charge of Galatea's research and development?" Joe seethed.

"Look, even if I believed you, whatever happened to Kate all worked out for the best, at least for me," Stan admitted. "I've got a beautiful, intelligent woman living at my estate; someone who is less like a daughter or granddaughter, more of a peer. My children aren't threatened by her. In fact, they're rather smitten with Kate. And because she's too old to have children, their fortune is secure."

Stan continued, "I'm a patient man, Joe. I have no doubt I'll be able to woo her into my home, into my bed, and convince her to become a permanent part of my life."

"I wouldn't be so sure about that," Joe said fiercely. "I'm also a patient man. I won her hand once, I can do it again."

"I don't think so," Stan said matter-of-factly. "What you did, what you robbed her of, is to Kate, unforgiveable. Plus, I can give her something you can't. I can give her a family and grandchildren. They may not be hers by blood, but she'll make do. It is all she has."

"You are despicable," Joe said. "I can't believe you and Rachel and probably Huff too won't tell her the truth about what happened with the youth gel; how she was purposefully poisoned. How can you love her and lie to her at the same time?"

Stan laughed. "Easy. I've watched you do it to her for thirty years."

Joe slumped down onto the sofa. "You're here to rub all of this into my face?"

"Not exactly," Stan said as he paced the room. "I really wasn't sure what I was going to do with you, or about you. I've been trying to decipher Kate's feelings for you. It hasn't been easy. What I've decided is that you still have a slight hold on her. My suspicions were confirmed today. The fact that she told you that the Phoenix Project is back on, that she talks to Maggie daily to find out how you're doing, and that she comes by to check up on Maggie, it all tells me she somehow feels responsible for you. If she is racked with guilt over leaving you at the lowest point in your life, I'll never possess her completely. She may not remember why she loved you in the first place, but she has a stout heart and believes in quaint notions like responsibility. Today, when Maggie called and said you had disappeared, I could see the distress on her face."

Stan continued, "As long as you're weak and vulnerable, you'll still have a hold on her. I've decided to give you ten percent of the net revenue generated from Galateal. You'll be a very rich man."

"What is Galateal?" Joe asked.

"That's the name of the miracle cream you invented. It's going to be a blockbuster. You will be a multimillionaire, if not even richer than that."

"But I'm fired," Joe said, still not following Stan's absurd logic.

"I've decided you aren't going to be fired, you're going to be retired. It will be explained that your illness has forced you to step down at Galatea, but you'll be exiting the company a very rich man."

"I don't want your money," Joe spat.

"Consider it a dowry, the price I'm willing to pay for Kate."

"You disgust me. You can't have her."

Stan pulled a neatly folded packet of papers out of his breast pocket. "I have your divorce papers right here. All you need to do is sign on the dotted line."

"Divorce?"

Stan handed him the legal pleadings. "Yes, these are your divorce papers. Kate went to a lawyer, who drew everything up. Just sign the waiver of service and sign on the dotted line, everything will be over with. You won't even need to appear in court."

Joe placed the agreement on the coffee table and flipped it with his right hand. "Let me guess, the lawyer is someone you recommended."

Stan nodded.

"She's giving me the house?" Joe asked.

"She won't really need it once she marries me, will she?"

"But Kate gets half of everything else," Joe noted. "And half of the Galateal royalties?"

"Even with a five percent share, you'll be a rich man," Stan noted. "Kate's half will flow back to me. Eventually."

Joe pushed the papers off the coffee table and onto the floor. "I'm not signing it."

Stan patiently picked up the documents and placed them back on the table. He reached into his breast pocket and pulled out a pen. "As your friend, I have to tell you that it is in your best interest to sign."

"Friend?" Joe repeated incredulously.

"Yes, friend," Stan answered. "Even if Kate doesn't wind up with me, she's never coming back to you. She needs someone to look after her, just in case the amnesia worsens. You can't do it. Besides, now that you've run off today and scared her half to death, Maggie is going to tell Kate you're uncontrollable. To punish you, my guess is that Maggie will recommend that Kate place you in an assisted living facility or up your medicine, which will turn you into a drug zombie."

Joe looked at the papers and then at Stan.

"If I sign them, will you get rid of Maggie and leave me be?" Joe asked.

"I'll do my best," Stan replied.

"I'm afraid that's not good enough," Joe said defiantly.

Stan walked out of the living room and returned with Maggie.

"Maggie, I'm afraid it is time to let you go," Stan said.

"But," Maggie stammered, "Mr. Holly needs someone to care for him."

"I think he'll be just fine on his own," Stan said. "But before you go, I need you to witness his signature."

Stan picked up the pen and placed it in Joe's right hand.

"Once you sign this, I can't double-cross you," Stan explained. "If Kate tries to claim you're feeble and send you to a nursing home, it would call into question whether you had the legal capacity needed to sign this document. The divorce could be voided. I'm going to say you're competent and you're going release Kate."

Joe stared at the pen he held in his hand.

Love and fear. When was it that he let one of those emotions smother the other? He loved Kate the instant he saw her. The power love held over him gave him the strength to be patient and wait while her relationship with her high school sweetheart self-destructed. Love gave him the strength to reach out and be her friend even though he wanted so much more. Love was what Kate saw when she gazed into his eyes, a love so powerful that all she could do was surrender to it. His love had wrapped itself around her, enveloped her with warmth and security, and pulled her into him.

But fear choked it. Fear is sneaky. It kills love like carbon monoxide, slowly poisoning the air until it reaches the point that love simply falls asleep, never to wake again. His fear had slowly choked the love out of Kate's body. His fear had killed their marriage long before she applied the first dab of youth gel to her face.

Joe continued to study the pen. His wife was gone. His career had ended. He was a broken old man with nothing to live for, nothing to look forward to. His life was over and yet he still loved Kate. Loving her meant giving her one more chance at happiness.

With a stroke of his pen, he ended their marriage.

Stan smiled. "You've done the right thing. I'll take good care of her, don't you worry." He started walking toward the door then stopped. He reached into his pocket and pulled out one final item for Joe.

"You might want this," he said as he handed Joe one of his business cards. "Flip it over. Remember the woman I took with me as a date to the nightclub? That's her number on the back."

CHAPTER SIXTY-THREE

Maggie was gone before dusk. Stan had given the order. One week later, a copy of the divorce papers Joe had signed arrived in the mail. According to the letter from Kate's attorney that accompanied the mailing, the divorce would be final in two months.

Joe took the documents to his own lawyer. "Could we contest the divorce based on her brain damage, the amnesia?" he asked.

Although his lawyer was sympathetic, she was also a realist. "The legal threshold for showing incapacity is very high. From what you told me, she hasn't had any problems at work. The problem hasn't impacted her day-to-day life, only her ability to recall distant memories."

"But if they were going to have me put in a nursing home based on a similar argument, I don't see why I can't make it," Joe argued.

"You can make the argument. They can make the argument. But I'm telling you, based on my legal experience it is very hard to convince a judge to take away someone's freedom. If you had come to see me before signing this, I'd have said the same thing about their claims concerning you."

The middle-aged lawyer calmly folded her hands together and leaned forward. "Mr. Holly, what do you hope to gain by trying to contest this?"

"Kate," Joe whispered.

Her eyes softened. "Mr. Holly, I can see you really do love your wife. But I can assure you that you won't win her back by waging a protracted battle in court. If anything, you'll only drive her further away from you. My advice to you is to let it go."

She continued, "You two were married for a very long time, she's entitled to half. She's giving you the house which is all paid for. She's leaving you with your entire retirement and pension fund. She's claiming her retirement and pension fund, but yours is significantly higher. She's giving you the title to your car and the contents of the house. She's laying claim to half of your savings and stock accounts, one of your two certificates of deposit, and one-half of your ten percent of the Galateal net revenues.

"Mr. Holly, Kate is no longer your wife. The life you shared is just a memory. For Kate, it isn't even that. The only thing you can do now is wait; see if she'll return to you."

The day the divorce was final, Galateal was rolled out to the public. The offering was accompanied by a huge media blitz. It was impossible to escape the buzz. Business news programs charted the meteoric rise in Galatea's stocks. The science media interviewed Rachel about the research and development end of the product. Stan and Huff appeared on the cover of *Fortune* magazine. Even celebrities were getting into the act, touting Galateal as the must-have cosmetic in *People* magazine. The gel that he had initially conceived to help burn survivors ultimately only helped the vain and moneyed who least needed it.

But Joe was able to measure the real success of Galateal after the first business quarter. That's when he checked his bank account and saw it had been fattened by more than a million dollars.

Joe was a rich—but empty—man. To fill up some of the void in his life, he landed a part-time job as a chemistry instructor at Washington University. A strategically announced bequest from Joe to the chemistry department secured the position.

Joe returned to his attorney and asked to set up a trust for Kate.

"I'll do it for you," she said, "but why would you do such a thing? She's already getting half of the proceeds from Galateal."

Joe looked wistfully out her window. "I know for a fact that the man who wants to marry her plans to fold the money into his own fortune. I'm also certain he'll take the rest of her assets under the guise of 'managing' them. At some point, Kate will figure out Stan has deceived her, too. I don't want her to stay with him because she's afraid she has no money. Promise me that when I die, you will personally and privately inform her that this trust exists."

The lawyer studied her client's face. "I promise."

"I also want to set up trusts that will benefit the St. Louis Art Museum, Powell Symphony Hall, and the general maintenance fund for Forest Park," Joe said.

"I'll make sure it is written into the document," his lawyer said. "By the way, how do you like condo life?"

Shortly after the divorce was finalized, Joe had sold the home he shared with Kate and moved into the Central West End, a neighborhood of mansions, luxury high rises, and hospitals adjacent to Forest Park.

"It is convenient. Getting to physical therapy is much easier. I take Metrolink light rail to work. I can walk to the park. It is ideal—except that it doesn't include Kate. I'm headed to the park as soon as we're done here."

Joe had initially meant to go to the art museum; to lose himself in the rich tapestry of colors left behind by the medieval masters. The oversized masterpieces, with God, angels, and luminous women, had a way of reaching out and pulling him in so that he forgot his increasingly lonely existence. He needed to forget.

But something pushed him away from the art and toward the Grand Basin—to the fountains and reflecting pools.

It was an early summer evening, so Forest Park was filled with joggers, college students from Washington University zooming past on roller blades, and helmeted cyclists in black, tight shorts. There were young families in paddleboats churning up white froth in the ponds, middle-aged men and women walking together, being led by dogs sniffing the grass and tugging gently on leather leashes. All around him life swirled about in the warm breeze, surging forward—yet also frozen and suspended in time.

His legs were tired, and his head clouded. Joe found a bench that looked up Art Hill and at the front entrance of the museum and King Louis astride a giant sculptured steed. Even more immediate in his line of sight was a geyser of water pushing high out of the pond then tumbling down with a loud crash. The water seemed to be enjoying the descent; his heart had also soared to those same great heights, yet the fall down was crushing him.

He carried the *St. Louis Post-Dispatch* in the crook of his right arm. It was the first time that day he had a chance to read it.

The gossip column caught his eye.

Glitterati celebrate nups of cosmetic king and his beauty queen— *The Lou's very own Stan Markowsky, topper and founder of Galatea Cosmetics wed comely Kate Holly this weekend in a star-studded service. Serving as ring bearer and flower girl were the Markowsky grandkids. Stan and Kate Markowsky will honeymoon in Europe and Asia at the same time the company rolls out its blockbuster cream, Galateal, in those markets.*

The newspaper showed a picture of a beaming Kate and gloating Stan, his arm circling Kate's waist possessively. Joe let out a wounded cry.

"Are you okay?" a gentle young voice asked.

Joe looked up and into the freshly scrubbed face of a girl in her mid-twenties. His trained eyes noted that the glow of youth was the only makeup she wore.

"Is there someone I can call to help you?" the distressed young woman asked.

Joe, his eyes clouded by tears and time, knew that there was no one who could help him. It was too late. He was too tired. He grabbed the young woman's hand as he slipped down to the ground, closed his eyes, and mumbled:

"I am alone. Alone in my regret. Alone in my grief. Alone with my pain. It wasn't always this way. Once upon a time, I was happy. Once upon a time, we were happy. But that's all changed. My future has vanished and the present laid waste; all because the past was erased."

"Help!" the young woman shouted. Joe felt his shoulders shake. And a distant voice begging: "Please, please, Dad, open your eyes."

There was something about the desperation in the woman's voice. He looked at the woman, her cheeks streaked with tears.

"Dad!" she screamed as people began to crowd Joe.

CHAPTER SIXTY-FOUR

"What is going on?" Joe asked, his voice barely above a whisper. "Who are you? Where am—"

A middle-aged woman next to the bed spoke. "Mr. Holly, my name is Maggie, I'm your nurse."

"No," Joe whispered. "No. This isn't real."

"Mr. Holly," the nurse interrupted. "Please, save your strength. You had a stroke. You're coming out of a medically induced coma. You're bound to feel disoriented and confused."

An older man in a white jacket rushed into the room. "How's our patient? He's awake?"

Nurse Maggie nodded.

"Mr. Holly, my name is Dr. Inhope. I'm your surgeon."

"No," Joe said softly. "No, you're my wife's doctor. You're the doctor who ruined my marriage."

Dr. Inhope's brow furrowed.

Joe looked again at the nurse. "I got rid of you. Or Stan got rid of you. You're not supposed to be here."

"Mr. Holly, please save your strength. Please don't upset yourself," Dr. Inhope said as he looked into Joe's eyes then studied the machines spitting out data. "You had a stroke. We had to perform surgery to stop the bleeding in your brain. We put you in a coma to try to minimize brain damage from the event."

"When?" Joe asked angrily. "I already had a stroke. Why didn't you let me die? I can't live with the loss of Kate."

Dr. Inhope looked at his watch and said, "Mr. Holly, please. Your wife has been by your side for several days. She just went away for a short break. We were worried about her."

The doctor turned to the nurse. "Let's give Mr. Holly a sedative. Just to calm him down a bit."

The nurse grabbed a syringe and injected something into the IV that was connected to Joe.

A young man rushed into the room. "Dad!"

"Who are you?" Joe tried to shout, only his throat was raspy and hoarse from a breathing tube that had only recently been removed.

"I'm Andrew," the young man said. "Your son." Andrew gestured to the young woman Joe had seen at Forest Park. "There's Michelle, my sister."

"I don't have kids. I don't know you," Joe said.

Maggie, the nurse, who was still checking the machines that were hooked into Joe, spoke. "Mr. Holly, you've been in a medically induced coma. You had a stroke and surgery. Your brain has been through a shock. You may have some memory loss. Vivid hallucinations are normal. Sometimes this make-believe world can seem more real than the one that actually exists."

Michelle reached for her father's hand as he felt himself slipping from consciousness. "Mom has been here every day. And most of every night. By your side. She's been talking to you. Every day she told stories from when you met. When you were dating."

Maggie added. "The nurses on the floor have been captivated by your love story. You were right to get your wife the summer internship. That Harry. He sounds awful. In fact, we were taking bets on whatever became of him."

"Where's Kate?" Joe whispered.

Andrew spoke up. "She was looking pretty run-down. We were all worried about her."

"We?" Joe said, his voice slurring.

"Me, Andrew, Stan, Rachel, and Huff," Michelle explained. "Stan bought her an afternoon at a very fancy and expensive spa to get a massage, facial, you know, some pampering. For a little mental health break."

Andrew chimed in, "We couldn't have you two sick at the same time. And the way Mom was starting to forget things, because of the stress, I think. We all talked about it."

"Who is we?"

"Me, Michelle, Rachel, Stan, Huff, the doc, and Nurse Maggie," Andrew explained. "We decided she had to get out of here for a while. It was what was best for you both."

CHAPTER SIXTY-FIVE

It was the sound of Stan's voice that woke Joe up.

"Yes, yes, the kids say he came out of the coma," Stan said. "Kate doesn't know yet."

There was a pause as Stan listened to the person on the line. "She was supposed to be taking a break. I didn't want to interrupt her in case this was a temporary thing."

Stan was gazing out the window while talking on his phone. His back was turned away from Joe.

"I've got to go," Stan said. "Thanks for taking over in the lab, Rachel. You're doing a great job under difficult circumstances." He hung up and shoved his cell phone into his pants pocket, then turned around.

"Joe!" Stan said, realizing that the man in the bed was awake.

"Stan? What are you doing here? You and Kate…" Joe said as his voice trailed off, the memory of the wedding announcement searing in his head. He wanted to get up out of the bed and punch his old friend. Only his arms and legs barely budged.

"It is so good to see you," Stan said, a smile spreading across his face. "So, it is true, you did wake up. We were worried for a while that you might not."

"I don't understand," Joe mumbled.

"From what I've been told by the doctors, it is common to experience confusion after what you've been through."

"Remind me again, what have I been through?" Joe asked, even though he was afraid of the answer.

"A stroke, old friend. A stroke."

"But how? When?" Joe stammered.

"I wasn't there, but from what Kate said, you two had an argument. Something about plastic surgery? And by the way, I agree with you. Kate is lovely. She doesn't need plastic surgery. Why mess with nature? I mean, of course she's not twenty. But she doesn't have to be. She shouldn't be. That would be freakish. You're a lucky man."

"An argument?"

Stan nodded. "Poor thing. Kate is broken up over it. She blames herself. She tries to be strong in front of your kids. But when everyone is gone, she's cries on my shoulder. I'm just glad she feels comfortable enough with me to be vulnerable."

Joe started to cough.

"I'll get the nurse. You could probably use some ice chips. Just a guess. After spending so much time in the hospital with Barbara, I know how dry your throat can get. And they don't let you gulp down water."

Stan left the room for a few moments. Joe pondered the latest bit of information, trying to construct a timeline.

"Maggie, the head nurse, she's sending someone in with ice," Stan announced as he returned.

"When?" Joe asked.

"The ice should be here in just a minute," Stan replied.

"No," Joe said shaking his head. "When was the argument? I mean, which argument?"

Stan chuckled. "From Kate's stories, I can see why you'd ask that question. You two have certainly had a lot of fights over the years, haven't you? But did you have to be such a jerk about the orange juice? I would have left you at that point."

Stan ran his fingers through his hair. "At least you were smart enough to give in on adopting. I think she really would have left you if you hadn't agreed to that."

A nurse entered the room with a Styrofoam cup in one hand and a small plastic spoon in the other. "Here we go," she said in a cheery voice that was in sharp contrast to Stan's sober tone.

"Do you want to give him the ice?" the nurse asked Stan.

"No, I should let him rest. I'll let you do it," Stan said as he headed toward the door.

"Wait," Joe whispered. "When did I have my stroke?"

Stan turned around. "You were coming into work. You had gotten in your car at home. You were in the garage. You pushed your foot on the accelerator, your hand was on the gearshift, you were about to put it into reverse when you slumped over the steering wheel. Thank God the car was still in park. You would have shot out of the garage and probably crashed—maybe into some poor unsuspecting soul on the way to work as well."

CHAPTER SIXTY-SIX

The cling of a bell roused Joe from his slumber. He opened his eyes. A game show flickered on a small television screen, letters were being turned, and an unseen audience was clapping.

A white cup with a plastic spoon sat on a tray near his bedside, although Joe couldn't see inside because he was stretched out flat on his back.

There had to be a call button somewhere nearby, he thought to himself. His neck seemed stronger, he was able to get a better look around. On the railing, he spotted the control. Focusing his attention on his right arm, he willed it to reach the button. It was as though he'd been asked to lift the lifetime of regrets that had seemed to surround him in the room—rather than simply raising his arm.

He pressed the button, dropped his hand, and waited while enduring the TV chatter of a happy quiz announcer detailing possible prizes.

Nurse Maggie's face appeared over his. "You were able to push the call button, Mr. Holly?"

"Yes," Joe answered softly. "It wasn't easy."

"That's very good news. Dr. Inhope will be delighted when I tell him. Now, what can I do for you?"

"Please, help me raise my head a bit. And turn off the TV. Put me out of my misery."

Maggie reached for a control that lifted Joe's upper body so that he could see.

"How's that?" she asked.

"Much better," Joe said. "Can I also get some ice?"

Maggie grabbed the cup. "You're in luck. It hasn't all melted," she said as she scooped out the chips.

"Where's my wife?" Joe asked as the cold chunks melted quickly in his mouth.

"Your kids went to go get her. Kate doesn't know you're awake yet.

They wanted to make sure that they were around when she arrived," Maggie answered. "They seemed to be worried about both of you."

"Is Stan still here?" Joe asked.

"Hmph," Maggie huffed reflexively. She looked around the empty room and back at the doorway—where no one stood.

"I probably shouldn't say this, but," she began, "well, let's just say that I don't think we'll see as much of him as we saw when you were in a coma."

"What do you mean?" Joe asked.

Maggie shrugged. "I see a lot of lonely men in my job. And I see sad women. A sad, beautiful woman can be quite a temptation for a lonely man. But who am I to say? After all, he seemed to do everything he could to make sure you were properly taken care of."

A new voice chimed in, a woman's voice. "Who made sure Joe was properly taken care of?"

It was Rachel.

The nurse stiffened and forced her lips to smile. "I was just telling Mr. Holly that his friend Stan Markowsky was a real help around here. And a support for Mrs. Holly."

"Yes, Stan's been a tremendous help," Rachel agreed. "Joe, it is so good to see you awake. How are you feeling?"

"I don't know," Joe answered. "I don't know how I feel. I don't know if this conversation is real. I don't know if you're my friend or…well…not my friend."

Rachel smiled. "We've been friends forever, Joe. And this is real. But it is normal to be confused."

"So, you're in charge of the lab?" Joe asked tentatively.

Rachel shifted her weight from one foot to another. "Just keeping your seat warm for you."

Joe nodded. "I appreciate that. How's the Phoenix Project coming?"

Rachel frowned. "How'd you know about that?"

"We've been working on it, right?"

"Sort of," Rachel said. "I guess in a sense you've been working on it. How'd you know about it?"

"It was my idea," Joe said.

"No, it was your doctor's idea. And Kate decided to go ahead. The treatment was risky. Really risky. But you were in such bad shape. Joe," Rachel paused, "we weren't sure if you'd make it."

"What? Isn't the Phoenix Project a beauty cream?"

Rachel shook her head and frowned. "A beauty cream? Heavens no. You are the Phoenix Project. A new treatment that has showed some promise for stroke victims. But it is new—and untested. Part of it involved putting you in a medical coma to try to preserve your brain function."

"Why would Kate agree to such a thing?" Joe asked.

"It was a tough call. But she knew that you would be unhappy if you lost the one thing that you've always counted on—your intellect, your brain. She gambled."

"And did she gamble wisely?" Joe asked.

"Well, you're here. You're talking. I guess only time will tell if she made the right decision."

Joe tried using his arms to push his torso up into a more seated position. He was weak. The effort to adjust a few inches left his arms shaking. "I'm getting stronger. I think I'm getting better. I'll be back to the lab in no time."

Rachel cleared her throat. "Listen, I am saving your seat. I really am. But I'd be careful about Huff."

"What do you mean?" Joe asked, starting to feel a wave of nausea. He didn't know if it was Rachel's tension or the powerful drugs that had taken over his body.

"I overheard Huff talking to Stan. Huff had come up to the hospital to check on you. They were in the waiting area. They didn't see me."

Rachel paused. Joe waited—only the sound of medical machines filled the space between them.

Rachel continued. "Stan was saying that you might not make it. And if you did make it, that you might not be in any shape to come back."

"What did Huff say?"

"Well, after the polite statements that you're strong, you have a good family support, and you should be fine, Huff did say that it might not be bad to bring new blood, young blood into the lab. Might be time to try some new things."

Joe could hear the beeping of the monitors get faster.

"Deep breaths, Joe," Rachel said. "Nothing is a done deal. I'm sure everything will be fine. That's nothing for you to worry about now. Really."

Rachel's phone started to ring. "Damn. Sorry. I thought I turned this off."

She pulled it out. "Look, I've got to go. I'll check in on you later."

She patted Joe on the shoulder and waited until she was out of the room before answering. But she didn't get so far away that Joe couldn't hear her.

"Huff," Rachel said. "Good to hear from you. He's awake. But awfully confused. I don't think he'll be ready to return to work anytime soon."

CHAPTER SIXTY-SEVEN

It was the smell of a man's cologne and the sound of a woman giggling that brought Joe back. He recognized Huff's trademark scent. And no doubt he was showing off a fancy watch and flirting with a nurse fresh out of school.

"How's he doing?" Joe overheard Huff ask.

"Still too soon to tell," a young voice said. "Sometimes he's with us. And sometimes he isn't. He could still go either way."

Joe frowned. It was hard to listen to people speak about you as if you were not there. And where was Kate? If there was no guarantee, perhaps he wouldn't get to see her before he was gone again. That seemed to be an act too cruel for even the most vengeful version of God that man could muster.

"Joe!" Huff exclaimed as he walked into the private room. "Good to see you awake, old man! We were worried. But I knew you were stronger than your age suggests. How are you feeling?"

Joe inhaled, trying to catch a breath that didn't seem to fully fill his longs. "I've been better. But I think I'm getting stronger by the minute."

"Take your time. There's no rush. Our medical insurance is top notch," Huff said. "And I already had human resources process Kate's request for the disability insurance. That will ensure you two still have an income stream."

"Money. Yes, I guess Kate needed money. How is she doing?" Joe asked.

"I think she is okay. I'm sure she asked for family leave from her employer. And Stan has graciously offered a bridge loan if she needs it," Huff volunteered. "Stan has made sure Kate has nothing to worry about—except you, of course. Although if I were you, I'd worry about Stan," Huff said with a laugh. "He and your wife seem to get along pretty well."

"He's a good friend," Joe said, half-heartedly, wondering if there was some truth to Huff's teasing. "How are things in the lab?"

"Nothing to worry about there," Huff said. "Rachel has been a tremendous help. It is almost like she's used to running the place. But, of course, we miss you. We can't wait to have you back, when you're ready."

"I trained Rachel well," Joe said, feeling as though he was fighting for his job even from a hospital bed. "I always believed it was important to have someone who could step in if something happened. That's a key tenant of good management, isn't it?"

"It certainly is," Huff said with an easy smile. "In fact, it makes me think we really dodged a bullet—thanks to your foresight. Perhaps we need to do a better job of cross training everyone else in the lab so that if one person is out, we don't lose valuable institutional knowledge. After all, your lab is what helps power our innovation. And the more I am here, the more I think we should start pushing a dermatological line in our company. If a customer had to get a prescription for our product—imagine how much we could sell it for."

Maggie walked into the room. "I'm sorry, but I'm going to have to ask that we end the visit. We have some medical tests to perform. I'm sure you two can talk about work later."

Huff nodded. "Absolutely. I just wanted to see how Joe was doing. I'll be sure to check in later."

As he walked out the door, Joe watched Maggie shake her head subtly in disapproval.

"What?" he asked the nurse.

Maggie busied herself with bandages and dry clothes.

"You're thinking something," Joe said.

"It's none of my business," Maggie said. "I'm not your guardian angel, your conscience, or a tattletale."

"C'mon. Tell me what you're thinking."

Maggie cleared her throat. "Look, all I'm sayin' is that he's sneaky aggressive. Tries to pretend he's giving you a compliment, but really, it's a criticism."

"That's what I thought," Joe said.

"I don't know what you did to make that lady mad at you but seems to me that the guy who just left and that lady have found some common cause by ganging up on you."

"What lady? Kate?" Joe asked.

"No. That lady you work with," she answered.

"Rachel?"

"Yeah, I think that's her name," Maggie said. "You'd be amazed what people say when they don't think anyone is listening. And for some reason, when people are visiting in a hospital, they don't think nurses or doctors or janitors—or even patients—are listening."

CHAPTER SIXTY-EIGHT

It was a soft touch. A gentle circle was being traced on the back of Joe's hand. As each loop was closed, it generated a feeling of well-being. One that traveled up Joe's arm and released a small deposit of endorphins. There was only one explanation.

Joe opened his eyes slowly, afraid that his unreliable brain was tricking him again.

He made out a familiar smile. His gaze connected with a gaze that was both familiar and somehow had been away too long.

"Hey," Kate said softly.

"Hey," Joe whispered. "Where have you been?"

"I could ask the same question of you," Kate answered. "I've been waiting for you. I've been by your side day and night. It seems that only once I was persuaded to leave that you finally arrived."

"Stan sent you away," Joe said, unable to hide the irritation in his weak voice.

"Shhh," Kate said. "You should have seen everyone. Just because I was forgetting some things, they started worrying. They thought I was losing my marbles. Well, I sort of was. But that's normal when you're afraid the love of your life is leaving you."

Kate smiled, the wrinkles at the corners of her mouth dimpled in a way that Joe had grown used to. There were lines around her eyes and a few folds in her lips. The brown spots that had been on her cheeks were gone.

"You're old," Joe said.

"Gee thanks," Kate replied. "It has been a bit rough lately. But I thought that my beauty treatment and makeup were giving me a refreshed look."

Joe smiled. "I'm sorry, Kate. You look beautiful. In fact, never more beautiful."

He continued, "My dearest Kate. I'm so sorry for all I've put you through."

"Joe, I'm sorry. I'm sorry we fought," Kate said.

"I was being a jerk," Joe said. "In fact, I've been a jerk to you for a long time. I mean, I'm sorry for yelling at you about orange juice. I'm sorry I dumped your notes before a big exam. I'm sorry for being controlling. You've been nothing but a good partner to me. And I guess I always feared losing you." Tears welled in his eyes. "Kate. God, Kate. I don't know what is real and what is a dream. But I am so afraid that I have lost you. That you left me. And yet, I can't lie to you. I think I did something very bad early in our marriage."

Kate put her hands to Joe's lips. "No, Joe, we both made mistakes. We were young. Young people do stupid things. I did, too."

"No, I think I did something unforgiveable. I love you so much. Almost too much to tell you about something I've done. But I need to tell you."

Kate rubbed Joe's hair. "It's okay. You just need to rest."

The beeping on the monitors sped up enough to get the attention of Maggie, who entered the room and stood near the door, trying to decide whether to stay or leave.

"I need to tell you," Joe insisted.

"If it will calm you down, tell me," Kate said.

"When we couldn't have kids," Joe said.

"Yes, when we couldn't have kids. We still adopted. And now we have a boy and a girl. And even a grandchild."

"But," Joe stammered, looking away, "we couldn't have kids because I got a vasectomy without telling you. And then I think I was so scared I'd lose you that I eventually agreed to adoption."

Kate laughed. "Oh, Joe, the doctor said that you'd have dreams that felt very real. That had to be one of them."

"No, I really think I did," Joe insisted.

Maggie spoke up. "Look, if it was a long time ago, they had to use a method that left some incision scars. I can check."

Kate held her hand up. "No, that isn't necessary, nurse. I know my Joe. And I know he just couldn't have children. It took a while to convince him to adopt. But first we got Andrew, and then Michelle. He loves those two. And they love him. And I love our life together. That is all we need to know."

Maggie nodded and slipped out of the room.

Kate kissed her husband's lips. Softly, then more passionately.

Joe raised his hand, cupping Kate's face. "But what if this isn't real? What if I had a stroke in Forest Park while reading about your wedding to Stan? What if you really did marry Stan? What if I did invent an amazing gel that erased wrinkles, got rich, and lost you?"

Kate smiled. "I have no idea what you are talking about. But Joe, what if this is real?"

"What if this isn't, Kate?"

Kate kissed Joe again.

"Then I guess you must choose the world you want to live in. Do you want to be here, with me? Or do you want to be in the other place?"

Joe studied her carefully.

"This is where I belong. This is where I'll stay. If inventing a youth gel, betraying your trust, and losing you is fact, then I'm choosing a fiction."

He looked into her blue-gray eyes that sparkled as brightly as they had done on the first day he spotted her on campus, when her laughter grabbed his attention. "I have no present or future without you. And I don't want to erase our past. This is the world I choose."

THE END

ABOUT THE AUTHOR

The idea for this novel came to me in a dream. I turned that dream into a short story and entered it into the Writer's Digest Popular Fiction Awards in 2006. It went on to win an Honorable Mention in the Sci-Fi/Fantasy category.

I started writing the novel soon thereafter. At that time my children were in middle school. (They are now in their twenties.) I would write at 4 a.m. or while sitting in the car, waiting for baseball or soccer practices to end. Four years later, I finally had a rough draft. Really rough. But due to a series of unfortunate life events, my attention turned to more pressing matters.

Over the years, I've done some editing. I was tempted to take it offline; however, my husband encouraged me to give my novel another chance. I'm glad I did. I decided it didn't need to be erased, but rather, revised.

This is a work of fiction. The novel's story and characters are fictitious. However, certain institutions and landmarks, such as Forest Park, the St. Louis Art Museum, and the St. Louis Symphony, are real. They're also lovely places. If you happen to be in St. Louis, I hope you get a chance to visit them.

The marula tree is real. However, when I first started writing this over a decade ago, the proliferation of products using marula oil did not exist. The anti-wrinkle cream described in this book is a figment of my imagination. It has no relationship to any actual product being sold on the market.

I would like to thank my husband, Enrique Serrano Valle, for his love, support, and encouragement. I also want to thank you, the reader, for giving me the opportunity to tell you my story. If you have a moment, please let me know what you thought of the book in either a review or a message on my Facebook page: Musings of Geri Dreiling.

Made in the USA
Monee, IL
25 March 2021